PALE
QUEEN
RISING

PALE QUEEN RISING

A. R. KAHLER

Published by 47North, Seattle

www.apub.com

Amazon, the Amazon logo, and 47North are trademarks of Amazon.com, Inc., or its affiliates.

ISBN-13: 9781503946934

ISBN-10: 1503946932

Cover photo by Kindra Nikole Photography

Cover design by Jason Blackburn

Printed in the United States of America

For the Dreamers
who knew the show must go on

One

Most people think my job as a royal assassin sucks. I don't blame them. There aren't too many perks when you kill for a living: the hours blow, retirement is a joke, and—excuse the pun—it's bloody thankless work. But when you factor in the small detail that I'm not killing for just any queen, I'm working for *the* Faerie Queen, things suddenly get a little more interesting. For one, my arsenal puts the world powers to shame. And the hits? Much, much more exciting than killing your usual middle-aged diplomat.

Take this guy. An hour ago, he was turning tricks in a seedy basement parlor in Queens. And no, not *those* kinds of tricks. I'm talking magic tricks. *Real* magic tricks. "Summon the dead" or "make that stranger fall in love with me" tricks. He's the real deal.

And I think, if he could speak, he'd appreciate that the cast-iron headpiece he's currently wearing is the real deal, too. Spanish Inquisition. They knew what they were doing when it came to witches.

I circle his chair slowly, tapping the flat of my dagger against my open palm and watching his frantic, bloodshot eyes watch me. The poor guy looks like shit—a fact I can only take partial credit for—with his shirt mostly undone and his jeans scuffed to hell. He definitely doesn't look like a guy you'd pay a hundred bucks to for a spell. He looks like a deranged barista coming down from an espresso high.

Which is partly true; he works in a café a few blocks down.

"You know why I'm doing this, don't you?" I ask when his back is to me.

He doesn't shake or nod his head or even grunt. The poor guy can't answer, of course. That's the whole point of the headpiece—a thick bar wrapped in old leather is firmly lodged between his teeth, theoretically to prevent him from casting spells.

"It's not because you let my espresso sit too long," I say, "though that's part of it. Seriously, that Americano was four bucks."

He moans. Okay, when I said the Inquisition knew what they were doing when it came to witches, I was kind of lying. This guy could still cast a spell on me without words—chanting has *very* little to do with real magic. Not that words don't have power. They have more power than most people ever give them credit for. In this case, though, the headpiece is just for show, for that shock factor. Most witches cave the moment I have their head in a bind. This guy is a little too stoic for my liking.

I finish my circle and crouch down in front of him, using the tip of my dagger to nudge his name tag. It reads "I'm Frank" and has a pencil drawing of an owl beside it. Damn hipsters and their damn owls. I inhale deeply, and it's not just the scent of espresso and cheap cologne that washes over my taste buds, but secrets. My next words unroll over my tongue like a scroll.

"I am here, Ludwig Fennhaven," I say, watching his eyes go wide with recognition, "because you've not been paying your taxes."

Every time I deliver that line, a part of me hopes for a laugh. I mean, c'mon, it's funny: here I am, this gorgeous six-foot bombshell with platinum hair and a penchant for leather, demanding he pay his taxes? *I* would have laughed, even if I were bound and gagged and about to be tortured—gotta enjoy life when you can. Especially when it's about to be cut short.

Ludwig just looks stunned.

True names do that to a person. Everyone has them, though most people don't know it and go through their lives thinking that whatever their parents called them is true to their nature, or whatever. It's not. A true name is bound to your soul, is an aspect of your full being. A true name is true power. It's probably for the best that most people don't know about true names, though—if you know someone's true name, you can control them. And mortals are horrible when they have the slightest bit of control over their fellow man. Not that I'm any better in moments like this.

I drop my grin and slide the dagger up to his throat, resting the tip in that pretty little indent between his clavicles, where a lone strand of chest hair lingers.

"You know who I am," I say. "And you know who I serve. There are two ways out of this encounter. In one of them, you live. In another, you die. The choice, as they say, is yours."

I reach up with my free hand and undo the lock holding the bar gag in place, the knife held steady at his throat.

"Now," I say, rotating the bar out, "where is the Dream?"

"Fuck you, Claire," he spits. I'm surprised he remembers my name; I kind of figured he'd forget, though I did tell it to him when ordering my drink. He must have enchanted his own memory. Now that he knows I'm not just some random crazy girl with a fetish for ancient torture devices, he's no longer scared—the lines at the edges of his eyes are tight with rage.

I roll my eyes. Like I haven't heard *that* line a hundred times before.

"We're not really going down the road that sees you keeping all your blood," I say. "Which is fine with me. Winter's been rather boring lately."

"You'll have your hands full soon enough," he says. He starts shaking, and I can't tell if it's anger or laughter. "The snow will be red with faerie blood."

"And now you're threatening me," I say with a sigh. "This really isn't going to end well for you."

"Nor for you, assassin."

"Whatever you say. *You're* the one bound to a chair." I dig the blade deeper, just enough to shut him up and coerce a little rivulet of blood. "Now, I'll ask again: Where is the Dream?"

"Go to hell."

"According to Dante, I'm pretty much already there."

The witch smiles.

"You have a sharp tongue for a slave," he says.

"And you have a wry wit for a man about to die. Now tell me, where is the Dream and how much have you given to Oberon?"

The guy laughs. Oberon's the King of Summer and, thus, Mab's mortal enemy. They've been at war since way before humans were even a thing. I think that's just how the two of them like to operate.

"I don't serve Oberon."

His statement is rather unexpected. I mean, Mab sends me out here because her Dream is being diverted, which means Oberon's getting handsy with our resources. There's no other place for the Dream to go. Winter or Summer, dark or light, Mab or Oberon. When it comes to the Dream Trade, you pick a side and stay there for life.

Still, this guy's mortal. And mortals are notoriously bad at following the ancient rules.

"What do you mean?" I ask. "If you don't serve Oberon, where's the Dream going?"

Ludwig smiles.

"You don't know as much as you think, girl. You, or your queen."

And before I can ask him what the hell he means, he jerks his head forward, skewering his neck on my blade.

"Shit-sucking—!" I jump back, cursing, but it's no use; his blood is already coating my hands and splattering my black bomber jacket. I'm drenched. I reach out and pull my dagger from its fleshy sheath, and the man immediately starts choking on his own blood. He's past saving. Not that I was going to try.

Of course. My knowledge of his true name kept him from using magic against me or himself. But it didn't keep him from physical acts.

He chokes for a few seconds, and I stand, then kick him in the shin. I look down at my white shirt coated in blood. So much for going out after this.

I tune out the sound of his frantic gagging and look around, hoping *something* will catch my eye and give a clue as to where he's hiding the Dream. If it's still here. I'd already given the room a cursory once-over before Ludwig—oh hell, "Frank," since it doesn't matter anymore, and "Ludwig" almost seems like an insult to his character—arrived home from his closing shift. Nothing here.

Like most New Yorkers, he has a small place, a basement studio. Tiny kitchenette, standing-room-only bathroom, and a twin bed in the middle of his living room. The only things that set him apart are the fact that he lived alone on a barista's income (dead giveaway he was selling on the side) and the extreme tidiness of his living space. He definitely entertained some high-end guests. I mean, seriously, not a creature is stirring in here, not even a cockroach. There's an altar along the wall—a small steamer trunk covered in a scrap of purple silk and a few odd and ends: candles, an iron pentacle, an athame. And in the center, a shallow brass bowl containing the head of a pigeon (fresh) and a lock of hair.

He's still gagging when I walk over to undo the headpiece and throw it in my bag. A trail of blood streams from his lips and the hole in his neck, his eyes wide and rolling around in their sockets, trying to find something to cling to. Something to anchor him to life. *You're not going to find it, bud,* I think.

"What's the matter?" I ask, kneeling in front of him. I shouldn't taunt him, but he's pissed me off. No trace of Dream in his place and no clue from him. Mab *hates* it when I come back empty handed. The least I can do is funnel some of that rage toward this jerk. "Dying like a martyr not all it's cracked up to be?" I shake my head as one last gurgle comes from his mouth. His eyes don't close in that Hollywood way when he dies, but the light behind them goes out. I stand. Magic and faeries might exist, sure, but the dead don't talk. Sadly. My job would be *so* much easier if they did.

It's not often that I let myself admit defeat, but I'm an assassin, not a PI. I was sent here to scare the location of the Dream out of him and then send him on his merry way.

"Mab's gonna be pissed," I mutter.

The Winter Queen is many things. *Understanding* definitely isn't one of them. And now, apparently, there's someone else out there stealing her Dream? I can only imagine how lovely this interaction will be.

I head over to the door and pull a piece of chalk from my pocket, scribing a symbol in each of the corners. It's simple magic, and if Frank were still alive, I'd feel a little ashamed using it—not that I care now, since Frank technically died by my hand. When I open the door, I'm not facing a sweaty summer evening in Queens. Snow blows over my boots and the dark sky glitters, not with streetlamps, but with crystalline stars. The Winter Kingdom beckons, its spires of onyx and ice glinting in the darkness. It's not the most inviting sight, but that's sort of what makes it so appealing. I guess that's just the allure of home.

"Coming, Mother," I say under my breath, and step into Faerie to meet my queen.

Two

Snow stretches before me, a well-traveled path pressed into the eternal white. The footsteps permanently embedded in the snow aren't just mine, though I probably use the path more than most. Behind me, a long, low wall of concrete stretches for forty paces, the surface rough and windswept. There are hundreds of ways into Winter and the world of Faerie—knotted trees, particularly inviting ivy paths, and the ever-popular faerie mound—but this wall acts as a quick medium between the two . . . provided you know the right symbols and magic, of course. I trudge down the snow-swept hill toward the sprawling expanse of Winter.

If Frank wasn't selling to Oberon, I should at least have been able to sense where it was going. I should have had a hint of direction, or even of the person buying it. But his place was antiseptically clean, at least in terms of magical footprints. He knew he would be sought out. And, judging from his complete lack of reaction to my reveal, he knew it would be me.

I'm not about to say I feel like I'm being watched. I just don't feel as incognito as I used to. And I really don't like it.

There's nothing behind me but rolling hills and jagged mountains and swaths of black forest. The real heart of Winter lies within the wall that glimmers like a sheet of midnight up ahead. The wall stretches far off into the horizon before me, disappearing in the shadows on either side. The buildings within tower high up into the everlasting night, their angles sharp and cruel. Everything in Winter is built from ice and stone, and whoever laid the first building block decided that anything less than an acute angle was passé. It's a city of razors and frostbite, deliberately built to be as imposing as possible.

As far as I know, the walls have never been breached. I don't think anyone ever got that far.

I near the wall and place my hand on the freezing stone. It's smooth as glass and just as reflective; my mirrored image stares back at me. I try to rub off some of Frank's blood from my cheek. I'm only moderately successful. My reflection smiles and mouths the words *"Rough night?"*

I nod.

"You have no idea. Nothing ever goes as planned, does it?"

My enchanted reflection just shrugs.

"What did you expect?" she asks. Then she shifts in a blur of grey, and it's no longer my reflection staring back, but Mab. She points a finger at me accusingly, her green eyes glaring. The reflection is eerily accurate, from her wavy black hair and curving frame to the silver bone stilettos.

"Yeah," I mutter. "She's not going to be too happy. And she probably shouldn't be kept waiting."

My reflection shifts once more into my likeness—I look like shit, all sleep deprived and bloody—then she traces a large rectangle on the surface separating us. A brilliant white line of light trails in her finger's wake. When she's done, she steps to the side and vanishes.

Ever wonder what would happen if you touched a mirror and your reflection didn't press back? Mab managed to figure that one out.

I walk through the pane of obsidian glass, and it slides over me with a chill static, like a sheet of frozen gel—just a little bit of give, and then I press through to the other side.

I emerge in an alley quite unlike the one I hunted Frank down in Queens. Sure, there's trash littered against the buildings and rats scurrying between refuse piles. But here, everything is black and glittering like an oil slick. Light filters down from iron-ensconced globes that dangle above the alleys like some steampunk Chinese lanterns. Only, the light glittering inside the globes isn't fueled by electricity or gas, not like in the mortal world. I pass under one as I head toward Mab's castle, the shrill buzz of the lantern almost comforting.

It was admittedly jarring when I first learned those lights were captured Summer faeries doing penance in their iron prisons, but that's just how life is. Mab doesn't mess around with her punishment. She would let them go. Eventually.

I don't think too much about my surroundings as I head toward the castle; my feet navigate the twists and turns of alleys and avenues on their own. I've walked this way enough to know it by heart, and Mab ensured that I'm good at remembering my surroundings. Often, that's the difference between those who live and those who die after a hit—a quick escape route is paramount.

It's a good thing, too, that I don't have to pay attention. All I can concentrate on is my conversation with Frank. His words were like a curse. Not a real curse, of course—I had plenty of wards and charms against those—but his words were just as effective at knocking me off my guard. I'm used to my hits begging or lying their way out of a messy death. I'm used to attempts at bribery, at lame threats. But this . . . this was new. Normally I'd just figure that Frank was hoarding the Dream for himself, but he was a mortal: mortals can't use Dream, not in the same way the Fey can. To a mortal, a small dose of Dream is just a temporary high. In larger doses, it can be deadly. Frank didn't have the typical signs of a mortal Dream junkie anyway: his eyes were clear, he wasn't jittery, and he wasn't delusional. The mere fact he could hold a job meant he was clean. But he was bringing in a *lot* of Dream. Which meant he was selling to someone else, someone outside of Winter, which meant Oberon. It always meant Oberon.

I sigh. This was supposed to be a simple hit. Knock out the bastard, sever the vein to Oberon, come home and celebrate like always.

"Long day?" someone asks. I look up from my daze to see a banshee floating toward me. Her hair is brown and wild and her dress way too sheer for the cold. But, being half-dead and half-faerie, she doesn't seem to notice the chill. Her bare feet hover an inch or so off the ground.

"Something like that," I reply. I have no idea who the girl is, but everyone in this city seems to know me. The joys of being royalty. And feared. Not that the first was historically ever exclusive from the last. The Winter Kingdom cultivates their stock of Dream in any way possible, and that doesn't always mean flights of fancy or magic tricks. Fear is as good a source as any, and—unlike publishing or reality TV—it never goes out of style. "How's haunting?"

The banshee shrugs. "Fair. Just met my third exorcist. I really love screwing with those guys."

"I bet. Keep up the good work." And before she can try to make any more small talk, I start walking again.

I'm not certain if I'm a loner because of my job or if I'm in my job because I'm a loner, but it doesn't make a difference. I hate small talk. It means pretending to be interested. Right now, being social and pretending to give a shit about anyone else is beyond me.

The street I turn down is part of the club district. In many ways, it's like a darker Bourbon Street, with bars and dance halls crammed side by side on the ground floor and balconied flats above. None of the places serve alcohol, of course, but distilled Dream is as potent to the Fey as any liquor. I walk past a hookah bar, the front patio filled with patrons blissed out on vaporized Dream. A man in a sharp burgundy suit is passed out on a cushion, his head resting in the lap of the winged nymph beside him. She gives me a salacious grin as I pass and waves the pipe invitingly, but I shake my head and keep going. Definitely not the time, though the idea of spacing out on a Dream high is tempting.

Just then, a crowd of young satyrs bursts from the club opposite, the owner—a tiny, fluttering ball of light—screaming obscenities behind them. The satyrs just laugh and stagger drunkenly down the road. Unlike their Summer cousins, these guys look more like Krampus clones, with mossy black fur and glowing eyes and wickedly hooked horns. Not creatures you'd want to meet in a back alley, though their bark is definitely worse than their bite. I bite harder.

"Wanna take care of them for me?" the owner asks. She hovers up beside me, and I have to look away. Her violet light—normally cool and serene—is blinding with rage.

"You know the deal, Celeste," I say. "No murders within the Court."

"I don't want them dead," she says, watching the half-deer, half-college-jock drunkards leave. "Just roughed up a bit."

"I'm not so good at straddling the line between the two," I say.

Celeste chuckles. "From what I've heard, you're good at straddling other things."

Despite everything, that manages to pull a small laugh. "I've had my practice."

"Come in for a drink," she says, her light dimming to a more bearable intensity. "On the house. You look like you need it."

I want to. I've gotten triumphantly drunk at the Lewd Unicorn more times than I can count. At least her bar has high enough ceilings to allow me to table-dance. Celeste is one of the few people in this city I speak to, and one of the fewer still whom I actually consider an acquaintance. *Friend* might be an overstatement, but it's close. I suppose her being a bartender helps, as does the fact that she keeps a stock of bourbon behind the counter, just for me. She even puts it in one of those fancy bottles she keeps her Dream in, just so the other patrons don't stare.

"No thanks," I reply. "Tonight's hit went south."

"Then you definitely need a drink." There's a pause as she studies me. Faeries are notoriously good at judging mortal emotions, which is why I try to keep mine under lock and key. Tonight, I'm not so good at it. "What happened?" she asks. "I haven't seen you this upset in ages."

I glance away.

"He knew I was coming and was ready to die. And he had a message for Mab."

"Not a good one, I take it?" she asks.

"Not at all. And she won't want to be kept waiting. I'll catch you after."

Celeste knows me well enough not to push the subject. She pats me on the shoulder consolingly—which, her being a ball of light, is more of a telepathic thing—then heads back into the bar. I look around at the mess of drunk and high faeries, the revelry that will continue for eternity. I really wish I could join them. But Mab hates it when I enjoy myself on the job.

The street twists and rises, the black cobble slick and worn from centuries of boots and talons and heels. After a few blocks the place becomes more residential, with towering tenement flats and broad windows, everything looking like some masterpiece of basalt and ice. A few Fey wander the street, those interested in a more urban existence. Many, like the water-dwelling naiads or treelike dryads, live on the outskirts of the city. There are parks and icy streams and miles upon miles of frozen wilderness for the Fey that need a little nature to survive. Not that it's necessarily verdant out there. Winter isn't just a title—this place is frigid. Always.

Finally, the street widens into a boulevard lined with wrought-iron lamps. Great marble and obsidian statues stretch along the center, some static, some moving slowly. Years ago, Mab brought me down here and taught me the histories of each: A dragon devouring a knight. An oak dryad successfully locking Merlin within its chest. A plague doctor in his beaked mask delivering disease and feeding off the fevered nightmares of his victims. I pass them by without so much as a second glance. Until the one at the very end. It's newer than the others by a few hundred years at the very least, though the plaque attached to the base gives no indication of its year or purpose. That's partially why I like it—there's an enigma, a mystery.

It's a girl, maybe in her early twenties. Her features are hard to make out, and not from an error on the sculptor's part but because of the live blue flames that lick up and around her like a veil. Her arms are outstretched, and only one pointed foot rests on the pedestal. The plaque reads simply "The Oracle's Sacrifice." When Mab brought me to this one, she pursed her lips and said the Oracle was responsible for saving us all. No clue why she included me in that statement, since apparently the event was years before my time, but she refused to say anything else. It wasn't the first time Mab had made a point of withholding information from me, but it was—for some odd reason—one I found maddeningly annoying.

I pause before the girl, wondering if her sacrifice involved having to deal with frustratingly lock-jawed witches, before continuing up the boulevard, up the wide steps that lead toward Mab's castle. Two guards stand at the ready on either side of the massive door. They each wear gunmetal-grey armor and have halberds at the ready. Neither moves when I near; they know me by sight, and I'm pretty certain they're actually just pieces of armor enchanted to look like people. I've never seen them move. I've never seen them have a *reason* to move.

The door is probably the only thing in the castle that isn't stone. Instead, it's a thick, dark wood studded with steel and covered in intricate filigree. It's easily three times my height and twice as wide, but the moment I near it, the fleur-de-lis inlay before me glows silver and curls in on itself, the vines and knot work twisting away to reveal a small door hidden in the ornamentation. It opens silently. I sigh. Every single time this door opens, a part of me wishes there'd be a rush of warm air to accompany it. Nope. The air within the castle is just as cold as the air without. And sometimes, when Mab's throwing a shindig (or pissed), it's even colder.

No one greets me inside. No servants rush to and fro. The entrance is stoic and imposing, just as Mab intended it to be. About the only thing welcoming in here is the plush carpet that stretches from the door to the main chamber ahead. Everything else, just like the rest of the city, is black stone and sharp ice. Even the snow that occasionally piles up in the corners is gone. She must have had someone sweep.

My usually silent footsteps are somehow even quieter as I walk toward the main chamber, the carpet and the vastness swallowing up my very presence like a vacuum. It makes me feel small, insubstantial. Just how Mab likes all of her guests to feel before seeing her.

Then, the walls and ceiling of the hallway disappear as I enter Mab's throne room. My body immediately shifts into business mode—I stand up straighter, shoulders back, chin high. Just like Mother taught me.

Mab sits on a throne raised fifty feet in the air, the structure balancing on a pinnacle of twisted ice. Her throne is ebony and planes of crystal, a dark snowflake made of daggers and despair. Mab's black dress trails down the edge of the throne, dangling mere inches above the floor, its hem lined in white and silver fur.

"Back so soon?" she asks. Her voice is rich and deep, like a jazz singer's, and it fills the chamber like moonlight on snow.

"It didn't go to plan."

One doesn't mince words with the Faerie Queen. She's good at spotting lies, and to her, small talk to avoid the truth is just as bad as a falsehood.

Even just saying those words is enough to make the room go colder. My next breath comes out in a cloud of white, and there's a band around my chest, a constriction of frost that wasn't there a moment ago. It's not just nerves, either.

"What do you mean, *not to plan?*"

She slides from the throne as she speaks, drifting slowly down to the floor and landing a few feet before me. Even though she only comes to my chin, she holds herself high. I feel myself shrinking down from the sight of her. Her skin is pale porcelain, her hair black nightmare, and her expression unreadable.

I don't back down, though. Intimidating though she may be, I'm still her daughter, and she raised me not to cower; I look straight into her emerald eyes as I deliver my report.

"I did what you told me to. The guy's dead."

"But . . . ?"

"But he wasn't supplying to Oberon."

My statement is met with silence. One black eyebrow rises, but she is otherwise impassive.

"And you are sure you killed the right one?"

Okay, I know she's the queen and I know she could kill me without blinking, but her words are incendiary.

"Who the hell do you think I am?" I ask. My fists tighten in my bomber's pockets. *Don't hit her. Don't hit her. Whatever you do, don't hit her.* "Of course I killed the right one. You're the one who trained me."

That eyebrow rises just a little higher, and my chest warms. It gives me insurmountable pleasure to know I can still get under her skin.

"You're sure he was mortal?"

"He died like a mortal." I raise a hand still smeared with blood, forcing it inches from her face. If anyone else in the Court did this to her, they'd be dead. Instantly. She just looks at my bloody palm with perfectly composed calmness.

"Then where was the Dream?"

I drop my hand and shove it back in my jacket. So much blood. I think this jacket's past saving.

"He didn't have it," I say. "His apartment was clean. But he was definitely the guy. I could smell it on him."

"What did he tell you?"

"That the Dream was going to someone else."

She sighs. "You are sure he wasn't bluffing?"

"Positive. But the bastard killed himself before I could get on with the torturing."

For a while she just looks at me, and it's impossible to read what's going on behind those eyes. That's more dangerous than rage. With Mab, it's the hooks you think you're avoiding that will impale you later, when you think you're safe.

"There have been rumors," she says slowly. It kills her to divulge any information, especially gossip that makes her look like she isn't in control of everything. No wonder I'm the way that I am. She seems to reassess her words and continues on in a completely different direction. "If someone else is buying Dream, I need to know who is selling and how much is going unaccounted for. I need you to investigate."

"Whoa, hold on. I'm an assassin. I kill things. I don't do private investigation."

"You do now," she says. She steps closer to me. I half expect her to rise on tiptoes so she doesn't have to tilt her head back. She doesn't. When she speaks again, her voice is just above a whisper. "There are few people I trust in this world, Claire. At this moment, you are one of them. If someone besides Oberon or me is buying Dream from outside, I need to know who it is before the Trade is thrown off. And for that to happen, I need that mystery person to keep buying Dream so you may track them. If I hire anyone else, word will leak and the buyer will flee. We are already suffering from a decreased harvest. We cannot handle any more slipping through the cracks."

I blink, trying to absorb all this, because A) she doesn't usually divulge information, and B) I've not seen any hint of that within the city, or heard any rumor in the streets. Not that people really talk to me, but still, I have ears.

"So hold some more concerts or something," I say. "Frank wasn't pulling in *that* much Dream. What's it matter if that little bit goes to Oberon or someone else?"

Her lip quirks up to the side.

"I don't keep you around to ask questions," she says. Despite the grin, there's zero humor in her voice. "Or must I remind you of your place once more?"

Definitely not. The last time I crossed the line—and I mean *really* crossed the line, seeing as I take a step or two across it almost daily— she'd dropped me in her labyrinth without weapons or magic. The minotaurs had *not* been happy to see me, and I still have the scars to prove it.

"What do you need me to do?" I ask. I keep my voice as level as possible. It's not a trait I excel at.

Her whole face shifts into a smile—there's nothing natural about the movement. It is just a mask like all her other expressions. "I need you to ensure there is no leak in our main supply chain. Think of it as a reward for tonight's *job well done*. Tomorrow, you'll visit the circus."

Three

"Who am I going to kill?" I ask. Because, you know, that's sort of the name of my game. I can't actually remember a time when my trip was purely for pleasure.

Mab's smile doesn't slip, which somehow makes her more imposing.

"It's the *Immortal* Circus, Claire. I highly doubt you could kill anyone. And I highly recommend you don't try. I need you to go and check in on them for me. Make sure there are no Dream leaks, that sort of thing."

Great. A job I'm completely not cut out for.

"Why can't you do it yourself?"

Again, I feel that small note of pride for getting under her skin with no consequence to my livelihood. The twitch of her eyebrow is the only sign I get, but it's enough.

"Didn't I just tell you not to ask questions?" she says. "If I show up, it will raise a red flag. I haven't been in the show for years, and my appearance would not go unnoticed. The Dream I've received from them has been lacking lately, and I need you to ensure that someone isn't stealing from me."

"Is that even possible?" I ask. "Shouldn't it be against their contracts?"

She looks at me, really digs into my skull with that gaze, and waits a few uncomfortable seconds before speaking. "Even contracts can be manipulated. Which is why it must be you who does the investigating. You will sneak in as though it is a normal, routine checkup."

"One I've never done before," I say.

"And once you have made sure everything is running as it should, you will return to me for your next assignment. I need to speak with Oberon and see if he has heard of this new threat. Besides, I have a kingdom to run and you have nothing better to do. It is clear you can't even handle a simple hit without cocking it up—consider this your second chance to prove yourself."

"Not my fault."

"He died by your hand. Thus, it *is* your fault. If he were still alive, we could have questioned him and learned the identity of his buyer. Until we find another seller, we are dead in the water. And until that time, you will prove yourself useful by ensuring that there are no other leaks. Have I made myself clear?"

"Yes, Mother," I mumble.

"Good. Now, go clean up. I expect you there in the morning."

The morning, of course, was subjective, seeing as the barrier between Mortal and Faerie made timing as fluid as water. But I got the gist. She was giving me a chance to unwind and sleep before sending me out again, however long that took. No matter when I left this realm, I'd ensure it was morning in the mortal world.

A part of me expects her to call out as I leave, some final words of wisdom or warning, but when I turn and stalk out through a side hall, she remains resolutely silent. It isn't until I glance back that I realize she has vanished.

I make my way back to my room, through a series of twisting halls and tunnels that—like so much of this world—changes by the hour.

Tonight the trip seems to take an especially long time, and I wonder if this is the castle's way of expressing its own displeasure at my failure. I pass through a hall I've seen only once before, the carpet here blue and the walls of ice glowing as if the sun is beaming overhead, before heading back into the darkness of obsidian walls and flickering sconces. No doors here. Just an endless tunnel of wavering shadows.

"*You* don't have to punish me, too," I mutter to the castle. There's a distant groan, the sound of settling foundations. Which is just the castle's way of telling me it hears me and probably doesn't give a shit.

After one more turn and a spiral staircase that somehow leads to the same landing I just left, I find the door to my room. It's at the end of a long hall that is completely identical to the rest of the castle save for the tug in my chest that tells me it's mine. I lay my hand on the gilt frame. The stone is cold and smooth under my fingers, the door inlaid with ivy and twining dragons.

The first time Mab set me loose in the castle and had me find my way back here, I'd gotten lost for three days. If not for the statues that snuck me food or showed me where to pee, I probably would have died. When I *did* finally make it back, Mab was lounging on a settee before the door, eating grapes in a gauzy gown and looking like she could wait a hundred more years for me to show up. Tears formed in my eyes the moment I saw her, but even then I wasn't certain if they were from anger or relief or both.

"How did you find it?" she asked when I neared. No congratulations. No notes of worry. Just business.

I shook my head and told her I didn't know. *I just closed my eyes and walked.*

It was the first time I'd done something to make her smile.

"That's the greatest rule of magic," she'd said. "You can't control it. You can't understand where it comes from. But if you give in to it, you can allow it to work through you."

That was the beginning of my training. The moment I realized that basic fact of magic, that it was something you lived and sensed but probably never fully grasped, was the moment I understood Dream—how to track it, how to gauge it, how to manipulate it. That was also the moment I stopped being her daughter and started being her tool.

Maybe I should feel regret. Or coldness. Or something. Instead, my heart is empty. I've seen families in the mortal world, know how they're apparently supposed to work. But that sort of relationship is so far out of my realm of understanding, I can't even yearn for it. Mab's all I've ever known. I push open the door and step into the one place in this entire kingdom that actually feels like home.

Mab gave me free rein in here, and I crafted the room to be the antithesis of Winter. I might have spent most of my existence in the chilly hellhole she calls home, but I am mortal. And like pretty much every other mortal I've known (and probably killed in the greeting process), my nesting habit is strong. I step inside to a temperature that's almost tropical, shucking off my coat and throwing it over a rich velvet armchair beside a roaring fireplace. The walls are lined with bookshelves crammed with paperbacks and hardcovers and leather-bound tomes. The ceiling itself is vaulted and gold, a rich architectural style I stole from some churches in Scotland. There are sofas and oak tables, a liquor cabinet stocked to the nines, not to mention a fantastic vinyl player and sound system that's so state of the art, the mortal world hasn't invented it yet. I sigh and inhale the scents that make this place perfect: cinnamon and wood smoke, cardamom and clove. No matter how shitty my day has been or how bloody my return, stepping in here makes me feel like maybe things won't be so bad.

The place has changed over the years, though in truth I probably didn't have a typical teenage life or room to reflect it. No boy band posters, unless they were for dagger-throwing practice. No pink and gauze and sequins. My teen years had been Spartan, and my room had reflected it. It was only in the last few years, when I started . . . entertaining . . . that I began to cultivate a sense of style.

Trouble is, seeing as I'm the one in charge of keeping this place clean, it kind of looks like a horde of drunken satyrs blew through here. The tables are littered with books and bottles. My clothing is strewn everywhere. Hell, it's not even all *my* clothing. Books aren't my only entertainment, even though they tend to last longer and have more satisfactory endings.

The horde of drunken satyrs thing isn't just a phrase.

I head into the bathroom, stripping out of my boots and clothes as I go. Ass-naked, I flick my wrist toward the sunken Roman tub, which starts filling with water immediately. Magic isn't my forte, but I've rigged this place to make the most of what I've got. You don't have to be a witch to use the stuff. You just have to know the motions.

The massive tub fills in a matter of moments, lavender-scented bubbles frothing up and onto the bathroom tiles. Everything in here is gold and ivory and crimson, a lush indulgence. Mirrors glint on all four walls, amplifying the light of a few hundred candles that never drip or die. I stare at myself in that light, tracing the scars that line my body like scores to lost music. The gash on my hip from a werewolf that got a little too friendly. The burn across my shoulder from where an ifrit's fireball got too close for comfort. A hundred brushes with death. A hundred markers for my retribution. I'm proud of them, in a way. My little gold stars for surviving. For thriving. They aren't just mistakes. They're reminders that I have a purpose here. I'm worth something—at least, I'm worth more than the ones I've killed.

I turn and slip into the tub. The foam and water lap up around me. Perfect temperature, every time. Far away, I hear the scream of a banshee—maybe laughter, it's always hard to tell with them. One underwater twitch of a finger, and the vinyl player in my living room turns on. Enya blares through the speakers laced throughout my place. Don't judge. She's relaxing.

I know the water's turning pink underneath all the gossamer foam, but I don't pay attention to it. Blood's the least of my worries right now. I know Mab much better than she thinks I do. I know my little revelation worries her. Dream is more than just sustenance; it's strength. After all, a starving kingdom can't thrive. If someone's building up a reserve, someone outside of her or Oberon's control, she could have a new adversary. Someone who doesn't play by the rules she and the Summer King have stuck to since the dawn of time. Sure, she calls it a war, but I know that she would die of boredom if she didn't have their little game. They both would. I'm just here to keep things interesting, to be a little more of a threat.

An outsider, though—someone with an ax to grind—that could be a real danger.

I push the thoughts down. It's late by my biological clock. My body wants nothing more than a shot of whiskey and ten hours of sleep. The liquor cabinet in the living room promises at least one of those things. Sleep in my world is left for the dead. I close my eyes and lean my head back and try to tune out my thoughts. Mab's problems can haunt me another day. Right now I have foam and music and heat, and that's enough. I take a deep breath and let my muscles unknot one by one. The darkness behind my eyes pulls me down into a floating, shifting mass of comfort.

"Claire?"

The voice shocks me awake. Before I can push myself from the tub and execute the half-dozen crippling blows already running through my head, I realize there's no point trying to kill the intruder. He's not even technically alive.

"Jesus, Pan," I gasp. I try to settle myself back into the tub, but there's definitely no relaxing, not anymore. My heart's going a thousand beats a minute. Instead, I turn my attention and self-anger toward the faunlike statue in the doorway.

Pan bows his head. He's crafted after one of those cherubic satyrs, with tiny nubs of horns poking from his sculpted curly hair. Well, one horn. The other's chipped off at the base. Even though he was made to look young, he seems kind of the worse for wear, with little pockmarks and fissures all over his youthful body.

"I'm sorry," he says. He really does sound it, too. That's the problem with being angry at him—he always takes it to heart. "But I heard about your night."

"Word travels fast when you fail," I mutter. The foam in the bath has pretty much dissipated. I blow across the surface and it replenishes in a wave of froth.

"Only when you're listening," he replies. "May I?"

I nod and gesture him in. He takes a few steps into the room, his hooves clopping harshly on the marble.

"I take it you didn't just come here to offer condolences on a job shittily done," I say.

"It's not your fault he killed himself."

I sigh. "You might be the only one who thinks that way. So why *are* you here?"

"To warn you."

This perks me up.

Pan has been many things throughout my life—mentor, friend, and, more often than not, babysitter. I wish I could say we'd spent many fun evenings with kid-me trying to play dress-up, but from the stories he tells, it was more like me chasing him down with a pitchfork. Aside from Celeste, he's probably my closest confidant here, and he treats me like his kid. But he's never been one to question Mab's orders. I think I'm the only one who does.

"Warn me about what?" I ask.

"The circus." His reply is so blunt and earnest, I actually laugh.

"It's a circus, Pan," I say. "Unless you're worried I'll get trampled by an elephant, I'm sure I'll be fine."

He crouches on the floor beside me.

"Just . . . promise me you'll be careful. Trust nothing you hear, especially not . . ." He cuts himself off and looks away.

"What? Especially not what?"

He looks back to me. "Especially not what you hear from the magician. You can't trust him. Not with your heart."

I laugh bitterly.

"With my heart? Are you feeling okay? Because I'm wondering if you remember who you're actually talking to here. You know I'm the lust-and-leave sort. No heart-giving involved."

"Just be careful," he whispers. Something about the way he says it sobers me instantly, like he's saying his last good-bye before I'm sent before the firing squad.

"Always am." I try not to sound confused. Or worse, concerned.

He nods, as though that's consolation enough. Then he stands and leaves without another word, patting the side of the tub as he goes.

Statues. Not known for small talk.

I sink back into the tub and consciously try to undo the knots that re-formed the moment Pan appeared. The water's cooled down, but a push of magical intention and it warms back to its original temperature. Tomorrow's going to be a long day, and right now, I need all the relaxing I can get. Especially since I apparently have an amorous magician to contend with.

Won't *he* be in for a surprise.

*

The next morning, I walk up the dirt promenade leading to the entrance of the grounds for the Cirque des Immortels. The massive violet-and-black big top towers above the unlit entrance sign like a living entity. Silent, waiting. Hungry. As Mab demanded, the sun has just begun to stretch over the plains rolling out into the distance. Everything is quiet and dusty, the air smelling faintly of bacon. Which is really strange, since we're in the middle of Bumfuck, Nowhere. A few steps closer and I hear music, but it's not some organ-grinder BS. No, this is really bad pop music, the type you listen to on the way to some dull desk job to get yourself pumped up for another long day pushing papers. And it's not coming from the tent; it drifts from one of the smaller trailers off to the side, just beyond a partition of flags and fencing. I head toward it, brushing past the signs that say "Performers Only Beyond This Point" because, in a way, I own this place. Literally.

Besides, I learned early on that you can go anywhere unobstructed if you act like you're supposed to be there. Never show that you don't belong.

The area behind the fence is just as empty of people as the endless fields of corn beyond. There are long double-wide trailers lined up in orderly rows on one side, the grass in front mostly empty save for a few meticulously placed lawn chairs. And I do mean meticulous: everything back here, from the angle of the trailers to the line of porta potties, is arranged in a strict grid, lining up perfectly. It feels like walking onto a movie set, one where there's just been a grisly murder and everyone's trying a touch too hard to play it off. It's the circus—shouldn't there be some sort of chaos?

Pan's warning slips through my mind. I shove it down and continue toward the music. The scent of bacon grows stronger by the second, as does the allure of brewing coffee. The trailer in question is clearly the kitchen—there's a huge window on one side and picnic tables are set up out front. The sides are painted in rainbows and stars, Tibetan prayer flags and wind chimes hanging from every available eave. A man and woman bustle about inside, singing along to the music while they cook.

For a while I just stand there beside the trailer, out of sight, and survey the scene. I've been hearing of this place for as long as I can remember, but Mab never let me visit. Honestly, it's a disappointment.

No juggling clowns, no roaring lions. Just a quaint Midwestern sunrise and greasy cooking smells and a ridiculously precise floor plan. The chefs don't even have the decency to be making popcorn.

"You shouldn't be here."

The voice is right by my ear, and for the second time in twenty-four hours, it takes all my training and self-control not to scream. Instead, I slowly turn my head to look at the girl standing only a few inches to my right. How she got there, I have no idea.

She's a little shorter than me, maybe in her late teens or early twenties—it's hard to tell. Her hair is black and curly, with sharp bangs and a blue ribbon in it that matches the *Alice in Wonderland*–esque dress she's wearing. It's her eyes that snare me, though—they're bright green, almost lime, and they seem to glow with their own light.

It's not a comforting light.

I don't step back from her; I refuse to show I'm afraid.

"And who the hell are you?" I ask, as deadpan as possible. My heart's racing, but I keep my breathing slow and steady, keep my muscles relaxed yet ready to react.

"My name is Lilith," she replies, which is an awfully diabolical name for a girl who looks like she should be sitting on a tuffet somewhere.

"Well, Lilith, my name is Claire and—"

"I know who you are," she cuts in. She doesn't raise her voice or quicken her speech. Despite the growing warmth of the day, her presence gives me chills.

"Then you'll know who I work for. And *she* doesn't like to be told what she can or can't do. Neither do I."

Something about the girl tightens when I say that, like she knows full well just how vengeful Mab can be. Her face remains perfectly composed, no hint of emotion, though her stance is definitely stiffer. She actually steps back. I stand up a little straighter—not that it's hard to tower over her.

"Why are you here?" she asks.

"To check up on things."

"We are fine."

"That's not what I hear." Which, okay, is a slight lie, but I find interrogations go much better when the hit thinks you have some dirt on them. Guilty until proven innocent, as I always say.

"I was promised," she says. She looks at me when she speaks, but it sounds like she's talking to herself. "Promised she would never be here. Would never see her. Never again."

"Again?" I ask, something close to fear stirring in my chest.

"Is there are a problem?"

I don't know how I recognize the voice, but I do, and that freaks me out almost as much as Lilith's vague mumblings. I turn my head slowly, doing my best to retain my calm, because once more, someone has snuck up on me, and that's just not something I'm okay with or used to.

It's the magician.

And suddenly, I'm very aware of why Pan told me to be on my guard.

The guy is hot as sin, in that washed-out-rocker kind of way. Thick black hair that's currently pulled back in a messy ponytail; dark, brooding eyes; and a lean body wrapped with muscles that bulge beneath the sheer white of his tank. His eyes are locked onto mine, though I notice them flicker up and down quickly, and I'm grateful I passed over my usual work attire for a slightly more revealing purple bra under a sheer T-shirt and skinny jeans combo. I can still kick ass in it, but it makes my ass so much perkier. Magic boy clearly notices.

Trouble is, he looks like he's staring at a ghost. Maybe I need to tan more.

He doesn't move, but the grayscale tattoo of a feathered serpent twined around his arm does. It slides under his shirt and up his neck, its catlike eyes glaring at me.

"Who are you?" I ask, raising one eyebrow as coolly as possible, trying to convey as much holier-than-thou attitude as I can. Which is a lot. Mab taught me well. Besides, as far as he's concerned, he's working for *me*.

"I'm Kingston," he says. He inclines his head slightly, as though that little bow is ingrained. "And you are?"

"Claire." I can tell he knows who I am. This is all just formality. Whatever. I was raised on this shit.

He doesn't extend a hand. He holds his coffee cup in one and his other is shoved in his pocket. Just like Lilith, not one inch of his body language is welcoming, and the tattoo glaring at me isn't helping. Somehow, Kingston's eyes are even colder than the girl's.

"And why are you here, Claire? When Mab could just as easily visit herself?"

I shrug.

"She was busy and I needed something to do." I look to Lilith. "I'm here on official business. *Need-to-know* sort of thing. And this kid definitely doesn't need to know."

Kingston tilts his head to Lilith. The girl casts me a glare that could set someone on fire, then turns and stomps off. I look back to Kingston; the slam of a door tells me she's disappeared into a trailer.

"So," I say when she's gone and Kingston continues to be silent and unhelpful, "who does a girl have to kill to get a cup of coffee around here?"

I'm proud of myself. Kingston actually grins.

*

"You'll have to forgive us," Kingston says from across the picnic table, and I'm wondering if he's actually trying to be sociable now that he knows I can't be bullied. "We don't get too many visitors from Winter. And when we do, it's never good news."

I fondle the cup of coffee before me. All the magic in the world, and Mab's kingdom still sucks at making coffee.

"It's fine. I'm not exactly used to warm welcomes. In fact, they might cause panic attacks."

Kingston chuckles again, but stops quickly. He doesn't want to be happy around me. He doesn't want to show his human side.

Good. If he's trying to hide that, he'll be off-kilter, which will make finding out his other secrets just a little bit easier. Sometimes, playing with humans is too damn easy.

"So why are you here? I'm guessing it's not for pleasure."

I grin. "I take my pleasure where I can." I look him in the eyes when I say it. Sex can be the greatest weapon of all. "Though you're correct in assuming Mab didn't send me out here to see the show."

"What is it now?"

He looks haggard. Should witches look haggard? I thought they'd have some wicked magic to reduce crow's-feet and under-eye bags, but this guy just seems to stick to coffee. Which doesn't appear to be doing him any good.

"She thinks there might be a leak."

"A leak?"

"Someone outsourcing."

He pauses.

"Our Dream goes directly to Mab," he says slowly. "We've never had any problems before."

"Be that as it may, it doesn't mean someone else isn't skimming off the top before it even goes to ship. Maybe someone higher up?"

Things connect in his head, and he leans back a little once he realizes he's a prime suspect.

"I've been in charge around here since Mab left, and I'd appreciate you not implicating me in all this. I can't be stealing from the show. No one could. Our contracts prevent it."

"And those contracts have never been jeopardized before."

Mab told me all about the circus's history, and how one lone performer banded with Summer to manipulate the contracts every worker within the show had signed. The contracts were magical and binding, but someone named Penelope had figured out how to undo them. The resulting deaths and battles had caused a huge hit to the show's Dream intake and Mab's faith in humans. Penelope was Mab's prime example of why you shouldn't trust anyone whose word wasn't binding.

He looks away. I can tell he was hoping I'd be just another pretty face. Sucks for him.

"So you won't have a problem with me looking around," I say. "I'll need to see the show, of course. Front row seats. Y'know, royalty and all."

"You truly are your mother's daughter," he says. Is it my imagination, or does he sound a little angry about that? "But that shouldn't be a problem."

"Of course not."

He looks back to me, and for the first time in our interaction he looks at me like I might be something of an equal. I want to pat his hand consolingly and say *there there*, because he was right the first time—we *are* on different levels. They're just opposite of what he initially thought.

"Why are you really here?" he asks. "Mab wouldn't send an assassin to do an investigator's work unless she was expecting something bloody."

Pan told me not to trust this guy, and I don't. Especially because at this moment, the long line of tattoos that stretches up my spine starts to tingle. Bastard's trying to use *magic* on me. And once I see him smile, I know just what sort of magic he's trying.

Love spells. The oldest tricks in the book.

I smile back. Good. This is really good. I turn up my personal charm as my own literal charms keep his magic at bay.

"I'm not supposed to say," I whisper, dropping into a conspiratorial giggle. I glance around to make sure no one's looking and gesture him closer. He leans across the table, the scent of his musky cologne amplified in the growing heat. "But I know I can trust you. My last hit went south. The guy was hoarding Dream, but he wasn't sending it to Oberon. He was a free agent. And I think Mab's scared."

The truth is, I have no clue why I'm here. Frank was pulling in a small amount of Dream compared to the rest of Mab's Trade, and I can't imagine why it would actually scare Mab enough to send me here to check her supply chain. Sure, someone might be trying to rise against her, but the amount of Dream being skimmed is tiny—barely enough to feed a single faerie, let alone an army. There's something Mab isn't telling me. Which, I guess, isn't anything new.

That's not something I'll admit to him, though. If it got back to her that I was doubting her rule, there'd be hell to pay.

Kingston doesn't sit back when I'm done talking. Instead, he leans a little closer, his eyes looking deeply into mine. The only word to leave his lips is "huh."

"I know," I say. I move one hand closer to his, so our skin just brushes. It's electric, and I don't know if it's the magic he's working or my own imagination.

I can see why Pan told me not to trust the guy. My chest is warm, my heartbeat fast—it doesn't matter that I know the guy's an asshole and trying to magic me into liking him; he has genuine charisma.

"I was hoping you'd give me the full tour," I say, a little breathlessly. "You know . . . leave no space unexplored sort of thing."

"Yeah?" he breathes. Is he getting into it as well or is it just a front? Hard to say, but so long as I get him to trust me, it doesn't really matter.

"Yeah."

"I'll show you anything you want," he says. He leans in even closer, lets his lips brush my ear, and I almost chuckle. He thinks he's closing the deal. I close my eyes and let a tremor pass through me in anticipation of his final, lusty words. "I'll even show you what color your hair would be right now, if you didn't have so many wards against magic."

My eyes snap open.

He leans back, a shit-eating grin on his face.

"Hair?" I ask, still breathy, still thinking I can maybe salvage this, but I already know I can't. Damn it. Ruse is up.

"Yeah. Your hair. It should be purple by now." All breathiness is gone, but his chest is still heaving a little, and I can tell that whole fake seduction worked better on him than he wants to admit. "What, you don't think I'd try out a full-on love spell on Mab's prime assassin without checking to make sure you were susceptible first?" He takes a sip of his coffee. "I've heard the stories about you. I'd have been more shocked if Mab let you come here—anywhere, really—without at least a few magical wards. I'm not an idiot." He raises his mug in toast. "Still, that was some *excellent* acting on your part. You do your mother proud."

The way he says it, the bitterness in his voice, is scathing.

I take a sip of my coffee and roll with it.

"But you *would* have tried out a love spell," I say. I gesture to myself. "Because I mean, obviously."

He shakes his head and chuckles. "Probably. I'm assuming what you told me was a lie? The loose Dream and all that?"

"Actually no. I find it's often easier to tell the truth to my targets. Keeps them on edge."

"So you, what? Watch the show and make sure it's all going to Mab?"

"That's the gist of it." *I guess.*

"And if someone is skimming?"

I flourish my wrist and a small fan of throwing daggers appears like magic. Mainly because it is.

"They die," I say.

He laughs. "This is the *Immortal* Circus. You know that, right? I know French is hard to understand and all but . . ."

I gently toss a dagger at the table. It thunks into the wood not a millimeter from his ring finger. He shuts up. He might be immortal, but I'm positive he can still bleed.

"I'm good at what I do, magical contracts or no," I say. "Hopefully you don't have to find out just *how* good."

That's when I realize why I feel so out of place. It's not because I'm not necessary, not because everyone's doing their damnedest to make me feel unwelcome. It's because I feel like I'm here for *them.* I'm here to be seen. Like . . . I don't know, a prize pony.

Or bait.

*

After some pointless small talk about sales and marketing, Kingston tells me he has "other things to worry about rather than babysitting" and leaves me at the table. He doesn't sound pissed when he says it. Honestly, it sounds like a front. I must have gotten under his skin much better than he let on. A part of me is disappointed—he was fun when he was trying to get into my pants—but I didn't come here to make friends or playthings. This is just another job, circus tent or no.

The grounds start filling up as people leave their trailers and begin their day. Some head straight to breakfast; others vanish into the sur-rounding field with yoga mats in hand. A few people start juggling, and there's a low tightwire set up by one of the smaller tents that a young girl begins prancing across. But the people who catch my eye are the ones who look like biker punks, all denim and leather and tattoos, who leave their trailers with the bleary faces of the perpetually hungover. Their presence breaks up the stoic uniformity of the place—they drag their evenly spaced lawn chairs into semicircles and crack open six-packs. A few light cigarettes. Only one of them does anything remotely circuslike: some girl with a dreadlocked Mohawk begins juggling beer bottles high into the air, a cigarette dangling from her mouth.

Seeing as I've got a day to kill, I might as well start trying to learn what I can. And these are my type of people. At least, they seem more like burnouts than the ones stretching at seven in the morning, which means they'll probably be up for banter.

I head over, grabbing another mug of coffee on the way and wondering if I could steal the carafe on my way home.

You know those scenes in the movies when the new girl approaches the cool kids and the cool kids all stop and punch each other on the shoulders and nod at the new girl like she's fresh meat? That's honestly what I expect to happen when I step up to these people, especially since I'm not dressed in my usual work attire—a little leather goes a long way when meeting other ruffians. But they don't. They barely notice me. Save for one girl.

"What's up, buttercup?"

As with Kingston, there's something about her that's eerily familiar, and I wonder if maybe she's been by Winter to chat with Mab. She's got shoulder-length brown hair and is relatively petite, in that I'm-an-athlete-and-could-still-bench-you sort of way. She also doesn't seem to fit into this group at all—no tattoos, no dirty denim. Just a brown floral skirt and white T, both immaculately clean. About the only thing that ties her to them is the delicate septum ring in her nose.

"Hi," I say. I hold out a hand, but she ignores it. She's smiling at me like she's been waiting for me to arrive. It's a complete reversal from Kingston and that psycho-goth, Lilith. "I'm Claire."

"I know," she says. "I'm Melody." She steps over and gives me a hug. "It's really good to see you."

"Do I know you?"

I've faced down demons and murderers and worse, but her embrace sends my body into shock. Hugs aren't exactly common fare in the Land of Ice and Horror.

"Oh, sorry, no." She backs off when it's clear I don't subscribe to the touchy-feely brand of interactions. "It's just I've heard a lot about you."

"Uh-huh." Okay, so maybe this Melody girl is just as unhinged as the rest of these performers. But at least she's nice about it.

"Anyway," she says, "these asshats are the tent crew."

A few of the closer ones nod, but the rest don't even notice the introduction.

"I'm sort of the head of them," she says. "Though I also do admin."

"You look like a performer."

Her expression goes from happy to pained in a millisecond, but then she's back in control. "Not anymore," she says. "Anyway, enough about me. What brings you here?"

*

I spend the rest of the morning and afternoon bumming around, trying not to get in the way. Melody's a gracious host at first, but even she has her limits with my antisocial nature, and after twenty minutes of us hanging around the tent crew and discussing the tour, she admits that maybe I should just go explore for myself. Which I do.

Trouble is, without a show going on, there's no influx of Dream, so it's impossible to trace any leak. I can feel small traces of the stuff lingering in the air, can taste the excitement of last night's haul, but it stays safely on the circus grounds. If someone's stealing from the show, they clearly aren't interested in mopping up the small stuff. It's maddening, waiting around, knowing I could still be asleep or could have manipulated time to arrive just when the show started. Mab wanted me here now for a reason, but I sure as hell can't figure it out beyond punishment-by-boredom. Because, like I said, I'm not a PI—I'm not about to interrogate every performer in the troupe. Tact isn't my forte, and I highly doubt Mab would appreciate learning I had to maim her main source of Dream just to find out that no one had a clue what was going on.

Instead, I wander the grounds and watch people practice and feel like a general creep. I'm sorely tempted to head back to Winter, speed up time between the worlds, and come back when it's dark. But I don't, because I'm a masochist . . . and not interested in incurring Mab's wrath.

I save the big top—the *chapiteau*, Melody reverentially called it—for last, having made my way around the trailers and booths and changing tents. The air is hot and humid as I stand outside the flap to the black-and-purple tent, small gusts of warm wind bringing scents of hay and dirt and manure. But as I stand there, staring up at the dimmed neon sign for the Cirque des Immortels, I can't fight the shivers racing across my skin. Every once in a while a light breeze flickers out from beneath the curtain. It feels cold and dusty, like a grave.

I reach out and touch the thick vinyl to push it aside.

Pain sears across my eyes, a bolt of heat that drops me to my knees.

"And this is the chapiteau," comes a voice behind me. I turn my head, and there's Mab, leading a girl with blonde hair and bloody jeans toward the tent. Both of them waver in the sun, light filtering around and through them. My vision tilts . . .

"I don't know if I should stay," the girl says. Why is her voice so familiar? Nothing about her stands out besides the blood.

"Nonsense. You're safe here. I swear to you, within this tent, nothing will befall you."

I open my mouth to ask what Mab's doing here, but then they step forward and pass straight through me.

I nearly vomit as another wave of pain hits. I drop my head to my knees and squeeze my temples with my hands, willing the ache away before it crushes me into a bloody mess.

Then it's gone.

"This place has ghosts." It's not the happy-go-lucky Melody. It's Kingston.

I look back slowly, fully expecting the world to swim and for it to not actually be him. *What the hell was that?* I think. A vision? I don't *get* visions.

He is silhouetted by the sun, and I can tell he's not certain whether to back away or bend down to help me up. He picks the middle ground and just stands there like a statue. At least the statues where I come from are helpful.

I force myself to standing and wipe the dust from my jeans. I still haven't even made it past the entrance. The tent feels colder now that I'm closer.

"Places like this . . ." He shakes his head. "Sometimes you can't escape the memories."

"I don't know what you're talking about," I say. Now that I'm standing, I feel a little light-headed, but thankfully I don't faint or sway. "I was just a little woozy. Not exactly warm where I come from."

"Right." He takes a small step toward me then, and I can't deny there's some sort of magnetism there. Maybe it's magic or maybe it's the fact that it's clear he's used to getting what he wants—he has charm, and a part of me wants to get lost in the illusion. Something about him promises the act of forgetting. "That's why you're seeing things."

"How did you . . . ?" I begin, then catch myself. *Shit.*

"I'm a witch. I know these things." He hesitates. "What did you see?" It doesn't actually sound like he wants to know.

"None of your business." I take great pleasure in the subtle physical reaction he has, the slight lean back. Oh yes, he's used to getting exactly what he wants. Too bad I'm used to the same thing.

He shakes his head and turns, muttering "Just like your mother" as he leaves.

I'll take it as a compliment.

I look toward the tent warily, then remember it's just a damn tent, and brush past the curtain to step inside.

Four

I'm back in one of the castle's many courtyards. Grey cobblestones arc out from a central fountain made of sharp planes of ebony, stretching toward waist-high black bushes that lean heavily against the castle walls. The fountain looks like some sort of intergalactic laser, but rather than a beam of light shooting from its top point, there's a cascade of water delicately frozen in its downward spiral.

"What did you find?" Mab asks.

"Nothing," I say, sitting down on the rim of the fountain. There are tiny azure fish in the basin, ensconced in the ice. Not that they're dead. They somehow swim through the frozen block like it's water. They don't even know they're trapped in there, that there's a whole new world on the other side. The metaphor is way too apt for my liking. I tap the surface and watch them dart off. "The place was a dead end."

Mab sighs and examines the bush beside her, cupping a delicate crystalline rose in one hand. She's in her usual evening wear, meaning a velvet riding cloak trimmed with white fur and a sheer black dress beneath.

"Kingston's a charmer, eh?" I continue. Mab's not in a talkative mood tonight, which honestly isn't that different from any other night.

Something about her is a little more reserved than normal, though. It has me on edge.

"Not a single lead?" she asks. Something in her voice seems smaller than before. She doesn't look up from the rose.

"Nope." I cross my legs and stare at her, watching my breath puff about me in small clouds. With the wave of a finger I make it change shape, turn into ships ghosting through the night air. It passes the time for a few moments while she continues to slowly walk around the hedges, examining the roses in silence. Even though I'm used to the cold, I'm not dressed for this, and my skin flecks with goose bumps. "Why did you send me there?" I ask. It's all I can do not to let my teeth chatter.

"To see if there was a leak in Dream."

"Bullshit."

She looks at me. I can't tell if she's about to chastise me or smile. I continue before she can do either.

"You knew the show was safe. No one in the troupe can leave to deliver Dream without your express permission, and even if they could, treason is a death sentence."

"Contracts can be manipulated," she says.

I laugh.

"Which is precisely why you keep them in your bedroom."

Oh, that shocks her. Her delicate black eyebrows nearly disappear in the fur of her hood.

"Yeah, I've snuck in there. What kid wouldn't? And it's kind of hard to miss a book bound to a table with enchanted chains."

Because damn, that thing had been protected. It had been years since I'd been in Mab's room, but even then I knew the runes burned into the wood and the pulsating green chains meant business. That thing wasn't going anywhere.

"Nothing in the troupe can change," I say, thinking back to the boredom everyone seemed to emanate, the perfection of the placement of *everything*. "You've made sure of it."

She plucks a rose and glides over to me. I'm pretty certain she's actually floating, because when she nears me, she's at eye level, and she's not that tall.

"When did my little girl become such a petulant woman?" she asks.

"I learned from the best."

Her slap makes my teeth ring. I resist the urge to punch her back, and then the second impulse to put a hand to my cheek in shock. She's yelled at me, threatened me, locked me away. But she hasn't smacked me since I was eight and trying to juggle my throwing knives.

"This may seem like a game to you, Claire." Her voice is dangerously quiet, and it makes a fresh wave of goose bumps race over my skin. "But my kingdom is in danger."

"We found one stray witch selling Dream." My jaw makes an unhealthy popping noise. "It's not that bad. We don't even know if there *is* someone out there buying. The guy could have been bluffing to throw us off. One final *screw you*."

She doesn't answer. She just crushes the rose in one hand, not breaking eye contact. I see it spiral to the ground from the corner of my eye. As the ashes twist, so, too, does the courtyard. The world breaks apart into crystalline shards, and the next time I blink, the courtyard is gone.

In its place is a room as large as a football field, the ceiling—if there is one—high beyond the reach of the few torches spaced below. Even though the light is gold and warm, the air in here is even colder than outside. I really, really should have brought a coat.

Mab sits beside me, and it's only then that the vertigo hits. We're sitting on the head of a massive gargoyle jutting from the wall, easily a hundred feet from the floor below.

The room is nearly empty. Bolts of fabric are scattered throughout in haphazard rows, some in rolls and others folded thick. Between them are rows of iron stands covered in glass jars with multicolored liquids. There are small pyramids of stacked gold and silver and ebony, mammoth tusks whose points disappear into the shadows above. Beautiful though they are, it's what they contain that makes them truly valuable. Even from here, I can feel the Dream infused into every object—it's woven in the thread of the tapestries, distilled into the vials, forged into the precious metals. The contents of this room are worth more than anything else in the kingdom.

But despite all of the things strewn about, the room feels empty. There's too much space between the objects, a sparseness that settles into my bones. Because the room looks like it was made to be filled to the brim. The fact that there are only a few rows, a few piles of affluence, is harder hitting than if it were completely barren. It's like those enormous houses I occasionally saw in the mortal world, all glorious facades and immaculate furniture in the windows. But once inside, I realized there's nothing in the pantry, no clothes in the five walk-in closets. The money was spent on showmanship, and everyone suffers for the indulgence.

"What's this?" I ask, fully knowing where we are.

"Our storeroom," she says. "Where we hold all the Dream in Winter."

She says it sadly, her words swallowed up by the void. That can't be right. This can't be all there is. Winter is *vast* and this could barely feed the castle for a week.

"But it's so . . ."

"Empty?" she asks. I look over, and somehow, with her hood pulled up and her hands in her lap, Mab looks like a little girl. One being chased by a particularly nasty wolf.

"Yeah. What happened?"

She shrugs and continues to look out at the expansive room.

"It was a slow transition," she says. "In the years after the Oracle's War, after I lost one of the few aces I had up my sleeve, Oberon began taking more and more of the Dream from the mortal world. I thought it a natural transition at the time, an evening of the scales. One my kingdom could handle and eventually overturn. But every year we gained less and less; Oberon's kingdom has flourished in the aftermath of the Oracle, and mine has slowly slipped into disrepair. The world should be ripe for Winter—the darker dreams are rampant, and yet even they don't hold the same weight as they used to. What we *do* gather is nearly impotent."

My skin prickles. Mab's never told me anything about the Oracle's War, only that it happened and—like anything else in Winter's history she doesn't approve of—it should be ignored. She gestures to the room as though she hadn't just dropped a history bomb.

"We may have found only one rogue trader, but even that is a crippling blow. Oberon and I have always lived in balance. Even in the grips of our worst war, we knew we needed each other to survive. Summer needs winter, night needs day. Our workings even the scales of life. If there are more leaks in the system, more Dream going to something outside of our carefully crafted system, the balance of all life will be thrown. This will go beyond the world of Faerie, Claire. Faerie and Mortal are twined together. Should Faerie starve, so too will the humans. Dream is more than just food for us. Dream is power. Life. Strength."

I look around the empty room. How have I not noticed this earlier? I decide, rather than take my oversight to heart, to ask.

"How the hell are you keeping this secret?"

"Never show weakness, Claire. I'd hoped I'd taught you as much. If my kingdom knew what was happening, they would begin to lose faith in my rule, which would make us ripe for an attack."

"An attack? You really think someone's going against you? I thought Oberon and you were at peace for a few more years."

"Oberon and I have a temporary agreement, yes. But if someone else is stealing *my* Dream, then it is clear to me they mean to pose a threat."

"You think they're building an army. To what? Overthrow you? That's ridiculous." Mab's a veritable force of nature. Like storms or the season of winter itself, she's not something you could just overthrow, not without dire consequences.

"I think the wisest defense is a sharp offense; cut out the threat before it truly becomes one. And that is why I have you."

*

We don't linger in the storeroom. Mab waves her hand and suddenly we're sitting on my bed. Moonlight streams through the curtains behind her, making her a darker shadow against the night, her eyes glowing like Saint Elmo's fire.

"You will return to the mortal world in the morning," she says. "Take Eli. You may need an extra set of eyes."

"Really? Eli?"

"Do you know any other fit for the job? You will track down those who are stealing Dream, from me or from Oberon. I have no doubt there are others out there—the deficit we've noticed lately can be due to nothing else. Interrogate when you can. Use whatever means necessary. And when you are done, kill them. We cannot risk them turning back to their Trade."

"Can do, boss." My voice is deadened, just like the rest of me.

The ghost of a smile touches her lips, now outlined in the light of the moon.

"Good night, sweet child," she says. Then she closes her eyes, and the darkness behind her swallows her whole.

I don't know what's more unsettling—the fact that she referred to me as *sweet child* or that, for the first time in my life, Mab is genuinely relying on me to keep her and everyone else safe.

My hits up to this point have all been minor. Yeah, I'm great at what I do, and yes, there's no room for error. When Mab tells me to kill, they're as good as dead, no sweat. I'd always assumed the targets were of some political import—usually, they were tied to Summer or the unclaimed Fey who inhabited the Wildness between the kingdoms. Important kills, to be sure. But I always figured the world would continue to function if I messed up. Which really just meant "died in action."

But this? This is a weight I can't shake. This is more than Mab's kingdom on my shoulders. This is the world.

I head into the bathroom and start the bath, even though a part of me is too tired to even soak in the tub. I feel ridiculously worn-out considering I did nothing but wander around and stand behind the scenes of a circus show. I didn't even watch the show, despite my joking with Kingston. Instead, I spent those two boring hours wandering the backstage area, tracing Dream and making sure it was being stored and sent out properly. It was. I stare at myself in the mirror, at the shadows under my eyes and the frazzled hair that probably needs a cut seeing as it's now reached my shoulders, and wonder if I'll ever look like I'm not one step from the grave. Probably not. Especially not with my current job prospects.

Eli? Really?

The tub is filled and ready before I even strip off my clothes, but I head back into the living room and grab a bottle of bourbon and bring it back with me. No fancy cocktail tonight.

I slip into the tub with the bottle in hand and take a long pull, settling back amidst the suds. It's only then, when the first wave of heat and tingle of alcohol wash over me, that I remember just why I feel so off. It wasn't just waiting at the circus or talking to Mab.

It was the vision.

"What the hell is going on?" I ask no one. A part of me wants to call Pan and talk to him, but I know this isn't something he would understand.

I don't have visions. I'm normal, mortal; my skills are from the runes and glyphs traced down my spine like a long black scar. Not one of them has to do with having visions of . . . of what? The past? How long ago? Mab looked like she always did, and the girl with her . . . I shake my head. I can't remember the girl's face. Just the blood on her jeans.

This place has ghosts. That's what Kingston said. So had he known the girl? And why was I getting a vision of that? I mean, of all the useless things to have some sort of psychic flare-up over, a girl with bloody jeans is pretty far from impressive. It could have at least been about whoever is stealing the Dream.

The question flashes through my mind. *What if it's her?*

I take another swig of bourbon and submerge deeper into the tub. I may not know who this mystery girl is, but she's the closest thing I have to a lead. I'll find her. It's what I do.

And when I *do* track her down, she'll have a lot of explaining to do. Mostly about how she managed to get into my head.

*

I wait until after breakfast the next morning to get Eli. And oh, how I draw it out.

I soak in the tub until I wrinkle. I shave my legs (manually, no magic, because sometimes you need an excuse to spend more time submerged). I take way too long to do my hair and pick out my outfit. Not because I actually care about any of it, but because these are my last few moments of Eli-less time, and those are precious. He's not a bad guy, per se. But as I said before—I'm a loner. Eli knows this, and he delights in being the wrench in those gears.

Finally, after eggs Benedict and a plate of bacon and some bland black water that barely tastes like coffee (it has to be the water in Faerie; I get my grounds fresh), I can't hold off any longer.

There's a wall in one corner of my study that's devoid of books. While everything around it is chaos, that wall and the space before it remain clear. Always. It's exposed brick, and I'm not talking Winter obsidian brick, I mean New York Hipster Loft brick, with a semicircle of concrete like a hearthstone at its base. A single line of white chalk is drawn in an arc on the floor, the exterior scribbled with runes and glyphs that refuse to smudge or fade, no matter how many times I sweep or walk over them. A tin bucket filled with chalks of all colors sits to one side. The wall, however, is remarkably clean. No markings. Just a swath of red brick.

It's funny. Kids in the real world think monsters come from the closet or under the bed. Which I suppose is true. Mostly. But the fact is, monsters can come from anywhere with a flat surface. We just need a door, and if it's a flat plane, it can be a door.

Chew on that the next time you're reading a book about demonic possession. Pages are flat planes, too.

The sensation of chalk scraping against brick makes my mind go silent. It's about as meditative as I get, really, and as I draw the rough shape of a rectangle on the wall, I feel the power build within me. It starts as a vibration in my fingertips that could just be mistaken for the rough brick, if you weren't attuned to that sort of thing. Then it spreads up my wrist and through my arm, loops over my shoulder and into my chest, until every breath is gravelly. Magic *feels* different, depending on the goal. And this magic is heavy, earthy. It's the magic of dirt and cobwebs and layers of pressurized stone.

When the pale blue door is complete, I sketch out the symbols for travel, visualizing my destination with every stroke. Some are old—Norse runes, Masonic equations, Hebrew numerals—while others are so modern they're laughable—GPS coordinates, a street address, the color of the floor ("concrete," which I know isn't a color but it works).

When I'm done, my body is practically quivering with power. There's only a tiny nub of chalk left. I step back, my toes touching the circle on the floor, and grind up the chalk in my palm. Then I raise it to my lips and blow.

The feeling of power leaving my body is immense, like a coat of concrete sliding to the ground; only rather than leaving me feeling freed, it renders me exhausted.

Chalk dust floats through the air in a cloud. Slowly. Much too slowly for normal physics to allow. It dances and expands in the space before the door, forming shapes I've long since given up trying to understand. Some particles attach to the markings I made, thickening them or filling in blanks to equations and words. The rest twine down to the floor in a serpentine show, making new marks, new sigils, ones I cannot and will not ever write or try to discern.

Then the dust settles. Spell done.

That's it. No flash of light, no Hollywood glow around the corners of the door. The brick is still bone-crushingly solid.

I grab a second piece of chalk—purple, because Eli hates purple—and slip it in my pocket beside one of twelve butterfly knives I'm carrying.

"What fresh hell awaits?" I mutter.

I step over the line on the floor, and the world of Faerie melts away.

*

The warehouse—or what used to be a warehouse—rises up around me like the ribs of a decaying dragon. In the late-evening sunlight, everything is rust and rot, all reds and umbers and grey. And it's cold.

Of course, this being southern Vermont, evenings are always cold, even in the summer. Summoning demons is best done at transitory times—dusk or dawn, preferably on some equinox or solstice—and, since I'm not really interested in mingling with Eli all day, I'm going with dusk. The joys of being able to manipulate time between the worlds. I zip up my leather jacket and step forward, kicking a small stone before me as I go.

The place used to be part of a cotton mill. The complex stretches along a lazy river, the trees garishly green against it all, foothills rising in the distance. It's silent and oppressive in a way that only empty buildings can be—the empty space, the weight of history. It's almost like being in some ancient cathedral. If you ignore the graffiti and beer cans, that is.

After last night, all I can imagine is Mab's storeroom, and how it's going to look in twenty years. Empty? Covered in Fey graffiti? Hell, at the rate we're going, it may only take twenty days.

Trouble is, I can't even feel that bad about it. I know Mab. She didn't need to show me that. She knows she just has to point and I'll kill. The storeroom was a ruse; she wanted me to forget that she never actually answered why I was sent to the circus. She wanted guilt to outweigh my desire for knowledge.

Whatever, she can keep her secrets. I'll do the job like I always do and save the day and no one will know there was ever a problem to begin with. Like a good assassin. No statues made in my image, thanks. I'll be lucky if I get a tombstone.

I kick the pebble a little harder across the broken concrete. It skitters straight ahead, then hits a point near the center of the warehouse and changes course entirely, veering off to the right to knock into a beer can. A few pigeons burst from the rafters at the sudden noise.

Bingo.

My brain slips back into business mode as I walk over to where the stone changed course. It's no different from any other place on the floor, no debris to have caused the stone to ricochet. Just dusty, relatively smooth concrete. I grab the chalk from my pocket and kneel at the point where the ley lines converge. A crossroads of energy. The perfect place to summon an astral creature.

"Okay, Eli. Time to say hello."

I've heard that the ability to draw a perfect circle freehand is a mark of insanity. If that's the case, I'm outright demented. Then again, I kill for a living and live with faeries—I can't imagine too many institutions passing that off as normal. The circle I draw is absolutely perfect, damningly so. Mab taught me everything I know about magic, which still isn't much, and remembering the months she forced me to practice drawing circles of varying sizes still makes me want to rip my hair out. Circles every day, every hour, at every angle. I didn't shy away from the work, though. On day one she showed me what happened if you tried to summon from an imperfect circle.

I didn't sleep for weeks.

And even then, I only relaxed after Mab let me change rooms. To one not covered in blood and . . . well, whatever else the summoned monstrosity had left behind.

After the circle comes the series of markings ringing it. These are a little more archaic than the portal spell—summoning spirits has been around since mankind recognized that there was something bigger than them in the universe. I lay out the symbols carefully, first drawing a large serpent eating its own tail around the perimeter, then a half-dozen god names in Aramaic. Technically speaking, if I were a ceremonialist, there'd be incense and candles and probably some blood, but I don't have the time or patience for that. Besides, Eli and I have a . . . rapport.

The first time I'd dredged him up from the netherworld, it had taken half a moonless evening and two sacrificial lambs. Thankfully we're okay forgoing that formality now—livestock get expensive. But there's one thing astral creatures *do* need, no matter your relationship.

I reach into my pocket and grab a butterfly knife, flipping it open with a small flourish.

"Dinnertime," I mutter as I stand. Then I slice a triangle on the palm of my hand.

The crescendo of power in my body is almost more painful than the cut. Eli's *very* hungry today. I reach toward the rim of the circle and press against a wall of energy. The invisible barrier hums under my hand, but as the blood drips down, it doesn't fall to the floor—each drop bursts into flames that twist and spiral, caught in some inner whirlwind, and soon the space before me is a tunnel of flame, a whorl of silent heat and ferocity. I don't remove my hand as more and more blood fuels the fire. The inferno spirals up toward the sky, raging in a pillar brighter than the sun, but somehow dark, as though it isn't a light that exudes, but instead consumes. Sweat breaks across my skin as my knees go weak and more power pulls from me. *Damn it, dude, stop being a dick.*

Then a hand slaps against mine, palm to palm, and the flames spiral down, sucked up into the form of a man standing in the circle.

He's tall and suave, and this time around he's decided to wear the skin of a Japanese pop star. Lithe and angular, with mussed black hair and sunglasses. And a very fitted, very lavender suit. That's one small quirk of using chalk to summon a demon—they appear in whatever color you used. Explains why so many demons of old were red and black. All that charcoal and blood.

"Purple, Claire? Really?" His voice befits him, but there's a hint of crackling under it, a power slowly subsiding.

"It's a good color," I reply. Neither of us moves a muscle. Our hands are still pressed together, my palm now slick with blood that drips to the concrete in quiet pats. He examines me for a while, and once more I'm hit with the question—what side of the looking glass am I on?

"What do you need?" he asks.

I don't tell him anything about Mab, not yet. This is the negotiation phase. And like with all contracts with an otherworldly creature, I have to be numbingly specific.

"I need you to be my ally and follow without question. I need you to do exactly as I say and nothing more. You will be bound to me and only me, to serve as I command for as long as I need you and no longer."

"Is that all?" His lips quirk in a smile.

"And I need you to not be such an ass."

He chuckles.

"You are always a delight to do business with," he says. The embers from his voice are gone now, and his tone slowly slips into something a little more human.

"Your terms?" I ask.

"One human soul," he responds. "Of my choosing."

"Of *our* choosing."

"Too many hands in the kitchen. But fine. If you make it two."

I sigh. This is getting pricey. Too bad Mab was so intent on me having him around.

"Fine," I say, pushing that train of thought down. Losing steam now could be deadly. "But no kids."

"You ruin all the fun."

But he doesn't change the terms. Instead, he curls his fingers around mine. I do the same. A lancing pain shoots up my arm and through my heart, a power that makes my eyes burn and my blood boil. I bite down the gasp. A second later, our terms are signed and sealed. The pain vanishes in a blink.

I drop my hand and pull a rag from my back pocket, wiping clean the now-cauterized cut.

Eli brushes the blood off on his pant leg, leaving a smear that fades by the second. Not the most charming, but it's much better than the show he made the first time we met. Apparently licking off the blood of your host is considered good manners. Especially creepy when he's standing between two dead ewes.

"So," he says, stretching his arms up. "What brings you my way?"

I try not to notice as his black T-shirt becomes untucked, revealing smooth abs and the wing of an angel over his hip. How ironic. Eli's not necessarily a sex demon. But he's also not necessarily *not*. He clearly sees where my mind is going; he steps closer and brushes aside a strand of my hair.

"Or is it *that* sort of visit?" he whispers.

I bat away his hand and begin brushing away the summoning circle with my foot. I'd hate to have a drunken teenager accidentally summon something. And by *hate* I mean would hate to miss seeing it.

"You wish," I say.

"I do," he replies, fast and smooth as silk. Ugh. His voice is taking on a distinctly Japanese accent, and it's maddeningly hot.

"We're in trouble, Eli." When I turn back to him, I've pushed down the petty emotions, just like Mother taught me.

"Trouble?" He tilts up his dark glasses, revealing pale blue eyes that glow like the hottest part of a flame. "You know how I enjoy trouble."

"Someone's stealing Dream. And they're siphoning it off to a buyer in the Wildness. Mab's worried there's someone out there building an army, trying to overthrow her and Oberon."

"So why are we not venturing into the Wildness?"

I shrug. "Mab wants us to root out the traitors here. You know how the Wildness is—if something doesn't want to be found in there, it won't be. Not even her magic can change that."

"That's because *she* has no power there." The way he says it, it's almost like he's suggesting *he* does. He strolls casually around the warehouse, examining graffiti and dead pigeons with equal amusement. "Still, her logic is sound. It is best not to meddle in the Wildness. The denizens there take much less kindly to strangers than even your dear mother does, and there's no use dying without a good cause. So where do we start?"

"Seattle," I say. "We're going to see a show."

Five

Large influxes of Dream are relatively easy to find, and just as easy to foretell. Every major concert, every movie theatre, and even some of the less pretentious art openings are assured Dream generators. If it gets a mortal's imagination going, it's a source of Dream. And the kingdoms of Winter and Summer have their stakes laid pretty clear—have had for centuries. You know that elderly usher who doesn't look like they should be up that late for an EDM concert? Probably a faerie and, most likely, one from Winter. That really big author reading that somehow sells out? That's Summer's territory. Every major event will have at least one representative from the Fey to skim the Dream off the crowd and send it back to their monarch.

When you consider just how many venues and concerts and openings there are all over the world on any given day, it's a little overwhelming. Finding that *one* concert whose Dream isn't going to Winter is like finding a needle in a haystack. Even with the tricks Mab taught me, and Eli as a bloodhound, I'm stretching my skills on this one. Normally Mab points someone out and has me attack—I'm not usually searching for them on my own. I'm going on a hunch with this one. I've heard reports that this place isn't funneling as much Dream to

Winter as it used to, which potentially means we're missing a harvester or two. Either that or the shows are starting to suck.

Personally, I'm leaning toward the latter.

I'm not going to say the place is Seattle's oldest or classiest venue, but it's definitely one of my favorites. If I'm going to start on this wild goose chase, it's going to be somewhere I can at least enjoy myself before the killing begins. Which, of course, is when I *really* start enjoying myself.

Plus, this place is crawling with creatures from the otherworlds, Fey and astral. Something about the gloom draws them in. Must remind them of home.

When Eli and I emerge from a small alley, Seattle's giving us its usual charm. The night sky is heavy, and rain falls in a constant mist, everything wet and glistening and a hair on the cold side. Eli produces an umbrella from somewhere and raises it above our heads, like he's trying to be a gentleman or something. Perfectly courteous, until you realize the silver handle is in the form of a bound and screaming child.

I start walking down the street and he keeps pace, expertly navigating puddles so his expensive Italian leather shoes don't get wet. I mean, they look expensive. I'm sure they're human flesh. Probably an Italian.

"So we're here in this beautiful weather because?"

"Because this is the last place that reported a leak." Which, after saying it, I realize sounds kind of funny, but I don't correct the language.

He glances over at me, and I catch the faintest glimpse of blue flame from behind the glasses. A group of drunk college students skirt around us. *Seriously, how are they already drunk? It's like nine on a Tuesday.*

I'm jealous.

"You keep speaking of secrecy, keeping our actions hidden from this third party. But won't killing off their suppliers be a red flag?" he asks.

I stop in the middle of the sidewalk and glare at him.

"Do you remember our terms? *Without question.* Explicitly stated."

"I'm not questioning," he says. "I'm just trying to learn more about your plan."

"My plan is to do exactly what Mab says and get it over with. She knows more about what's going on than I do and that's fine by me. I'm the weapon, not the mastermind behind it."

"It still surprises me you're okay with that," he muses, but he doesn't press the subject. Probably because he knows I'd send him back missing a limb.

This is why I hate having him around. It's not the advances or sarcasm—those I can handle. Hell, those I *enjoy.* It's the fact that he questions. And when he questions, I start to wonder what I'm doing as well. The rage inside me grows, but it's not at him, not really. It's at this third party, the one who's threatening my livelihood and making me question everything.

"Suppliers die all the time," I finally mutter, continuing down the sidewalk. "It's part of the job. We just need to find one who will talk and direct us to their buyer. Then we're done."

"Then perhaps tonight will be our lucky night." He holds a hand out and watches the rain collect and sizzle on his skin. "It's already going so fortuitously well."

*

The exterior of the venue is pretty nondescript, jammed between a pizza place and a shady-looking convenience store. There's your usual marquee announcing tonight's show—Roxie Rhode and the Long Island Truckers—and a ticket booth out front, a line of college kids smoking shitty cigarettes and wearing beanies stretching around the block. It's Seattle's University District, which explains the red eyes and bad fashion choices and scent of pot that drifts through the crowd like a ghost. The main drag—The Ave—is teeming with bars and corner stores and vegan restaurants, all a little dirty and run down from the rain and soot and clientele. And in some strange twist of irony, it's probably one of the few places in the mortal world I feel at home. It's shabby in a fashionable sort of way, the faintest layer of grit coating everything like a teenager pretending to be tough. Phone poles are covered in peeling posters and decades of staples and nails, the gutters flowing with leaves and trash and dark water. It's kind of disgusting. But it's crawling with magic, and like so many places where "the youth" gather, it's infested with Dream. Mostly the darker kind.

Eli and I don't bother with the line, nor do we pretend with tickets. From what I can hear, the show's already started, and these kids are either just loitering or the opening act is really bad. I walk right up to the ticket booth and wink at the cashier, an older woman with salt-and-pepper hair and a green shawl.

"Business as usual?" she asks.

"You know it. They any good?"

She shrugs and looks to the line behind me. The kids are eying us suspiciously. Eli's dressed like some skeezy music manager, and I could easily be his mail-order bride. Or escort. They must think we're some sort of famous.

"They seem to think so," she says, and waves us on.

"Thanks, Val," I say, and head inside.

Eli and I settle ourselves up in the balcony, near the back. The opening band is already in full swing, and truth be told, they suck. The guitar's too loud to hear whatever the singer's screaming, and they're all jumping around like they took a little too much coke beforehand. The music doesn't really fit with the old opera-style room, with its high domed ceiling and velvet seats and dramatic aqua uplighting. No wonder there were so many kids smoking outside.

Still, it gives me time to get ready for tonight's kill. About a week ago, our contact here dropped off the face of the earth. Or, more likely, was dropped into Puget Sound bound in iron chains. Again, nothing too unusual for the line of work, but *someone* has been taking in the excess Dream. The stuff tends to collect and grow stale if no one gathers it. And, according to my senses, this place is spotless. Dream has this feel to it, almost a scent—it's like the tingle right before a lightning storm, that scent of rain and electricity. It had taken me four years of training to be able to feel it, and two more to be able to trace it and judge its potency.

"Anything yet?" Eli asks. Being from the netherworld, he's attuned to Dream like a bird is attuned to the magnetic fields. But I appreciate him deferring to me. Maybe I finally *had* worked out the language to our contract.

"Nothing," I say. Not surprisingly, the band's not generating enough Dream for even the most eager scavenger to skim.

I glance around the room, staring at the backs of heads and wondering who here is working for the Fey. Sometimes, the skimmers are faeries themselves, but more often than not they're humans with some sort of magical proclivities—creatures from other planes attract too much attention. Take Eli, for instance. To most mortals, he looks like a normal guy. But I can smell his otherworldliness, the tang of ether and sparks. I can feel the heat of him, radiating like a furnace of wrongness. Creatures from other planes never feel like they belong, which is why so many earthbound Fey are solitary.

There are maybe a dozen or so creatures scattered throughout the crowd. I sense a few Winter Fey, and one outcast from Summer who's wearing way too bright a pink coat for a night like this. The rest are unclaimed—Fey or supernatural creatures with no ties to Summer or Winter. Some might be from the Wildness, but others were born on Earth, or on some other plane altogether.

Mab tried to train me to distinguish them all, but with literally thousands of planes of existence, it was a vain attempt.

I keep my eye on pink-coat and the Wild Fey over in the corner, just in case.

Finally, the lights go up and the opener leaves the stage amidst halfhearted clapping. As many of the patrons stand to stretch or leave, Eli and I linger, watching faces, looking for traces of Fey attempting to go unnoticed—a stray flicker of light from an eye, a feather hat that's not really a hat, that sort of thing. Because of course someone out there made charms to hide Fey from those trained to seek them out. Thankfully they're really damn expensive.

"We better find them during the next act," Eli mutters beside me.

"Excuse me?"

"You heard." He looks over to me, then goes back to scanning the crowd. "I didn't come here to listen to crappy music. And you still haven't fulfilled your part of the bargain."

"Help me bag a traitor tonight and you'll eat. In the meantime, do yourself a favor and shut up."

He chuckles. But he doesn't talk.

There isn't anyone suspicious in the crowd, and by that I mean everyone looks a little bit suspicious in my paranoid state. Then the next band—clearly Roxie—takes the stage, and I think I know precisely who's stealing the Dream.

Everyone but the singer is Fey. And they're all unclaimed.

The musicians are all men, wearing fifties-style suits and fedoras and sunglasses. No doubt the glasses are to hide the glow from their eyes, which means they're probably ifrit or some other dangerous variation of elemental faerie. But even though they're Fey, it's the singer who looks truly otherworldly.

She's in a tight leopard-print dress that reaches her thighs and wears thick white wedges. Her dark hair is swept back, her bangs done up in a large pin curl with a red flower on the side. She is curvaceous and dark-skinned and gorgeous, and when she takes the stage, I can practically feel everyone's attention narrow in on her. It's not just her beauty, though. There's something about her that demands attention. Something not entirely human.

"Good evening, folks," she says into the mic. Her voice is smooth and deep, and her red lips part in a huge smile. "It's so good to see y'all out here." There's a small twang to her words, but it's concealed. Girl's been learning to hide where she's from. "My name's Roxie. Roxie Rhode. And these boys are my Long Island Truckers."

Applause ripples through the audience, along with a few whistles, which just makes her smile wider. She turns around and claps for the band as well, and that's when I catch it, a tightness to her eyes. I may be in the balcony, but my senses are amplified with my runes. She's eating this up, yes—but a part of that is an act. When she turns back to the audience and starts snapping out a tempo, I feel the energy of the room amp up. She's drawing quite a bit of Dream already, and she hasn't even started playing. Impressive. And impossible.

I don't take my eyes off her as the lights dim and the band begins to play. It's only halfway through the jazzy song that I realize Eli's no longer by my side.

I curse loudly, making the couple in the row in front of me turn around and glare, probably more from the noise than the cursing. I flip them off and storm away, following Eli's bond. Being summoned and bound means he can't just run off and hide—we're connected by a thread that's stronger than steel and ridiculously easy to follow. It's just annoying when he up and leaves like that. I can't tell if I'm frustrated because he left or frustrated because a part of me really wanted to watch Roxie. Watch her sing, that is.

I head down the stairs and through the lobby, toward one of those "Staff Only" doors that doesn't dissuade people like me. To my extreme frustration, not even my anger toward Eli can dislodge Roxie's image from my mind. Even now, when she's out of sight, she seems to grow larger in my thoughts: her legs, her voice, the part of her lips. She's gorgeous. And yeah, I've dealt with (and played with) some gorgeous girls in my time, but something about her snares my attention and refuses to let go . . . I shake my head and force my mind back in the game.

There's no use finding her attractive when I'm just going to have to kill her later.

Eli's in the wings, talking to the drummer of the first band. They look so casual back there—Eli leaned against an amp and the drummer twirling a stick between his fingers, both with arms crossed over their chests and watching the band onstage—that it's easy to ignore the fact that Eli's clearly enchanting the guy. When I sidle up to them, the drummer's halfway through some diatribe about Roxie's tour manager and how he's tired of being second-rate. The glow behind Eli's glasses is just a little brighter—easily hidden by the stage lights flashing over the lenses—and his palms emit a muted blue shimmer.

"Learning anything?" I ask.

"Not yet," Eli replies.

"You shouldn't have gone off."

"I saw an opportunity. And you were too busy ogling."

"I wasn't—" I begin, but stop myself. Unlike the Fey, I *can* lie, but Mab raised me not to—doing so invoked the worst type of punishments she could imagine. And she has quite the imagination. Even now it's hard to do so much as fib. "Fine. There's something about the singer, though. I think she's our girl."

Eli nods while the drummer continues to ramble on about money and ingratitude and other things I can barely hear. I can just make out Roxie's silhouette from here. She's dancing across the stage, playing to the crowd and singing to her band in turn. I've never been a fan of rockabilly music, but she could convert me.

"Clearly," Eli says. "She's enchanted."

"What?"

Eli nods to her.

"She's enchanted. Some sort of glamour. To make people fall in love with her."

"You think she's a witch?"

"I don't know what she is," he says. He elbows the drummer, who doesn't cease his rambling. "And neither does he. Apparently, though, the band wasn't playing anything bigger than a bar show two months ago. Now they're doing an international tour that's selling out fast."

"Instant fame?" I muse. "Sounds like a witch's work to me."

"It would make sense," he says. He leans closer to me and whispers in my ear, "I think I found my first meal."

I look past his shoulder to the drummer, who's probably in his midthirties and is covered knuckle-to-neck in tattoos. None of which are very good. He's got gauges you could stick a tennis ball through and a backwards baseball cap. And red flannel. Sleeveless, of course.

"Really? Didn't you want a debutante last time?"

"Tastes change," Eli says. "Besides, this little spell will leave him addled and probably a little brain-dead. It's really for the best you let me take him."

"Damn it, Eli." There's not much vitriol behind it. I can't make myself care about the drummer, not while Roxie's out there singing about a guy in a bar with a broken heart. "We were supposed to collaborate."

"And we are," he says, giving me a devilish grin. "You get to choose whether I take his soul or let him live as a vegetable."

I roll my eyes. "Fine. He's all yours."

"Yesss," he hisses, doing that annoying bro fist-clench thing that really doesn't suit his current persona.

"But not until after we get *her* to talk," I say, nodding to Roxie. "I don't want you distracted."

"I don't think I'm the one getting distracted."

I glare at him. "Excuse me?"

"I said, *as you say, boss.*"

"Damn right you did."

I turn my attention back to Roxie, who's now singing at a horn player who's echoing her refrains. Dream flows around her like a whirlpool. I don't know how they're collecting it, but they're definitely bringing in a lot tonight. Whoever killed off our collector here must have known they were coming in advance—hell, before they were even really popular. *A score this big could feed all of Winter for a day,* I think. It's more than a music show should realistically bring in. It's almost like they're pulling it from the crowd, which shouldn't be possible. If you could just rip Dream from mortals, Mab would have set up a factory centuries ago.

Roxie sings along like she's the center of the world. Her skin practically glows. I can't take my eyes off her, off the curve of her waist and the pucker of her lips, and something in me twists every time she glances toward the wing, when her eyes blindly pass over the shadows where I lurk. I force the feelings down as my fingers clench around the knife hidden in my pocket. She's beautiful and she knows it.

It's a shame she won't be that pretty when I'm done with her.

*

After the encore, Roxie exits through the other side of the stage, and Eli and I head to the lobby, leaving the drummer behind.

"He'll make a good midnight snack," Eli tells me as we leave. Hopefully that means I won't need to be around to see it. Watching an astral creature rip out a mortal's soul isn't a pretty sight. Coming from an assassin, that's saying something.

It takes far too long for the crowd to disperse; Roxie and the rest come out to sign autographs and CDs and T-shirts, and Eli and I head up to the balcony to survey the lobby in secrecy and wait it out. I try to just watch the mortals and Fey milling about the band, but my gaze keeps snapping back to Roxie. I clearly need to get laid soon, before it starts interfering with the job.

"Do you think they know we're here?" Eli asks.

"Probably," I reply. I have a half-dozen charms and wards against detection from Fey, but Eli's a veritable beacon, even though part of the summoning circle included some wards for stealth. "Does it matter?"

"No. I'm just curious if they understand the danger they're in. They seemed so enthusiastic up there."

I shrug. For once, I don't really enjoy the idea of taking out a hit. There's something about Roxie that's hard to hate. Maybe it's her smile. Or her giggle. Or even those stupid little personal narratives she told onstage about growing up in Tennessee and dreaming of seeing the world. Whatever it is, it goes beyond my training. And I hate her for it. I grab a dagger from my pocket and practice scratching small summoning circles on the banister.

Finally, the crowd's mostly gone and the ushers are going through the place to make sure it's cleared out. Rather than try to explain myself to a mortal or charm the wits out of them, I twist an onyx-and-bone ring on my right pinky finger twice. A chill breathes over me, like a billow of cold air. The ring's made from the bone of a thief who was buried under a new moon. Simple trick, but effective against mortals.

"Lame," Eli says the moment I go invisible. He can still see me, or at least the ghost of me. He doesn't even bother making himself invisible; all he has to do is will it, and humans look the other way. Mortals don't often see what they don't want to.

We head downstairs, past a few clerks arguing about some obscure band I've never heard of, and out to the alley where the tour bus is kept. Roxie is traveling first class—the bus is sleek and black and clearly brand-new, with tinted windows and the band name written across the side in white curving script.

I twist the ring the other way. Don't need the stealth; the rain is heavy and pounding against the bus like a drum, and a club down the street is blaring really bad death metal. Or really good. I never could tell the difference.

In any case, there's no one in the alley and no way the band inside the bus can hear us approaching through the din. I grab two butterfly knives and flip them open the moment we're a few feet from the bus door. Eli, umbrella open and sheltering only himself, just smiles at me. I've never seen him use a weapon. I've never seen him need one.

"Ready?" I ask.

"Of course. I'm starving."

We step forward and I press my ear to the door, a finger on my lips. Before we go in guns blazing, I want to make sure they didn't bring back any mortals. Casualties aren't something I want to deal with tonight. I can hear muffled voices inside, but with the rain and the death metal that's pretty much it. So I reach up to the bronze hawk locket around my neck and press my thumb against the moonstone in its eye. Despite the cold, the stone is almost hot to my touch.

"—be happy," comes a masculine voice. "Easily our best take yet."

A sob. Wait, someone's crying?

"Does that mean I can go?"

Shit. It's Roxie. What does she mean, *go*?

The only answer to her plea is laughter.

I look to Eli. "Leave the girl to me," I whisper.

I expect him to make some sort of witty comeback, but he just nods and takes off his sunglasses, folding them in a breast pocket. Rain flashes in the light of his eyes like faerie lights. I've heard enough to know that the band is, in fact, stealing Dream, which is punishable by death. Conscience clean as far as the musicians are concerned. Roxie, though . . . she's a potential conundrum. One I'll worry about when it comes to it. Time to dance.

Taking a deep breath, I grab the door handle and burst inside.

There's a momentary pause as the band members try to figure out what the hell's going on. They freeze and stare at me and Eli, and then they catch on to the fact that he's clearly not human, and I'm clearly not a fangirl, and they leap into motion.

The guy closest to me—bald, still in his suit—grabs a beer bottle from the table and swings.

I'm covered in charms for slowing time or speeding my reflexes. It's why I wear so much jewelry when going into battle. But it's clear when the first guy attacks that none of that will be necessary. Hell, the fact that I have time to think any of this while he leaps is indicator enough.

I duck and jab my knife into his ribs, angled toward the heart, and the iron blade goes cold as ice in my grip. Leaving it in his side, I twist around him just in time to meet the horn player, who's suddenly covered in talons and spikes that shred through his suit. Sadly for him, the scales haven't reached his neck yet, and one quick stab just above the shoulder drops him to his knees. Before he's even gasped his last breath, I have the next two knives in my hands.

Turns out I don't need them.

Eli's lounging on the sofa with one arm around Roxie, the other held before him as he examines his nails. The other three musicians are dead on the ground. Eli brushes an imaginary bit of fluff from his pant leg and winks at me.

"Took you long enough," he says.

I flip the butterfly knives closed and flip him off. Black and blue blood pools on the floor, which tells me they were all born in the mortal world. Those born in Faerie don't bleed, just vanish in a puff of leaves or glitter or smoke. Very dramatic.

Roxie is frozen on the sofa. I mean, not literally: she's still shaking, and tears are running silently down her cheeks. But save for that, she isn't moving, and I know it's not just Eli's nearness or the death of her band that's causing her stress. I glance down. My clothes are splattered blue and black, like some grotesque yet oddly apt Pollock painting, and with the blades in my hands I know I look like a madwoman. Sadly, I don't have any magical trinkets for that. The stains, that is. Looking like a madwoman is just a fact of my life.

"We're not going to hurt you," I say when I look back to her. She's trying her hardest not to touch Eli, which is pretty much impossible.

"Yet," Eli says. He gives her a friendly squeeze and she cringes. "If you play your cards right."

I gingerly step over the bodies as I make my way toward her—not that I care about respecting the dead, but because I don't think it would give her the best impression of me. That's when I realize—why the hell does it matter what she thinks of me? And for that matter, why are there butterflies in my stomach?

I chalk it up to the effects of her enchantment or whatever the hell it is and leave it at that.

"Are you one of them?" she asks. Her voice doesn't shake. I'm impressed; the girl knows how to put on a front. She also knows what she's dealing with. Not entirely innocent, then. Her eyes don't leave mine. We hold that gaze for a moment while my chest burns, and to my complete embarrassment, it's me who looks away. Who *is* this girl?

"Something like that," I say. When I glance back at her, there's a small grin on her face, one that slips away immediately. "Though I play for a different team."

She and Eli are on the sofa, so I grab a seat next to the small dining table. The bus might be big for a new band, but it's not *that* big. I have to push the horn player to the ground before sitting.

"The question is," I say, propping my feet on the table, "how are *you* involved with them?"

"They're my band," she says slowly. "Or, *were*. Until you came along."

Oh yes, please do play a little hard to get. It just makes my night more entertaining.

"But they weren't always your band," I say. "And barely a minute ago, you were crying over them letting you go."

She opens her mouth, and I raise a hand.

"Before you think of lying again," I interrupt, "let me just inform you that the man sitting next to you isn't actually human, and I've killed more people in the last year than you've met on tour. Neither of us are interested in mercy. We have a job to do, and you're going to help us do it or you'll die. Maybe both if you keep pretending to be innocent." My words are cold and stoic, completely at odds with the emotions warring within me. I don't want to hurt this girl. I don't want to intimidate her. Which makes absolutely zero sense.

Eli leans in and sniffs Roxie's neck. She flinches. It's a perfectly creepy yet completely unnecessary touch, and a small part of me is jealous that he gets to be the one doing it. "You reek of magic, my dear," he says. "You've been playing with forces you shouldn't and stealing Dream from someone you *definitely* shouldn't."

And, quite surprisingly, Roxie's cool facade shatters as she bursts into tears. Now it's Eli's turn to flinch; he withdraws his hand and slides over on the seat a little, making more space between them. There's a small part of me that wants to comfort the girl, but this is an interrogation. Business mode. And business-me doesn't have emotions. At least, not usually.

"What did you get yourself into, Roxie?" I ask. I try to keep my voice firm yet comforting. Seeing as I grew up with Mab as a role model, I'm not so good with that last part.

She cries harder. All I can do is watch her and wait for her to collect herself. It's cold, sure, but I'm not here to offer comfort. I'm here to collect debts.

Finally, with a very unbeautiful sniff, she collects herself enough to look up at me and wipe the tears from her eyes. Her mascara is magic—it doesn't smudge in the slightest. Somehow, she makes distressed look glamorous. Once more, she doesn't take her eyes off of me, and this time I resist looking away. I'm not going to give in to my own whatever this is—attraction or magic or whatever. Even if she is looking at me like maybe a girl covered in blood is right up her alley.

"A few months ago I was trying to make my way in the world. You know how it is for a young singer."

I don't, but I don't say anything. I don't want her to stop talking; she smiles a little when I nod.

"I was working bars and nightclubs and waiting tables on the side. Anything I could do to get by. Anyway, I was drinking one night after a show. All of five people in the bar, and that was the second week running where I couldn't bring in a crowd. So there I am, having my one free pity drink, and this guy comes up to me. Says he heard me sing and liked what he heard, and I told him he must be crazy or have bad taste because no one else thought so."

She takes a deep breath and bites her lip before catching herself.

"I guess it's kind of cliché, you know? He asked if I loved singing, if I wanted to make a career out of it, and I said yeah, I'd do anything for it. I didn't think much of it at the time. He was well dressed, didn't seem like a creeper, and besides, what did I have to lose? It was my last gig and I figured I was going to have to give up my dream. And then he grabs one of the cocktail napkins from under my drink and slides it over to me.

"*I can give you all that,* he says. *Everything you ever dreamed. Just give me your autograph and I'll make you a star.*

"I laughed at him. Right in his face. But you know what? I figured why not—it's not like he can do anything with an autograph. So I grabbed a pen from the bartender and signed my name. Next thing I know he's folding it up and dropping it in his pint. He raised the glass and we toasted and I remember thinking it was strange, because he downed the whole damn thing and when he slammed the glass down, the paper was gone. I figured he actually was just a creep with some weird fetish, but he left right after that and I forgot all about it."

My gut drops an inch with every word. I know this story all too well. Too many mortals have gotten caught up in shit like this, especially now that no one believes that faeries or magic exist. They make a silly wager with a stranger, and a few days later their house is on fire or their family's murdered because they didn't uphold their end of the bargain they'd forgotten about entirely.

I'm pretty certain the creatures of Faerie are assholes at heart. They love nothing more than screwing over humans, especially if they can get a good deal and a bit of Dream out of it. Because no matter their breed or social standing, any deal with a Fey is binding. Permanently. And no amount of begging can change it. The only thing the victim can do is continue bartering. Which, spoiler alert, never works out in the mortal's favor.

"So let me guess," I say. There's an untouched bottle of beer on the table, so I grab it and pop off the cap with my teeth. I glance at Eli in that motion—he's watching the entire interaction with a little grin on his face. "You woke up the next day and were headlining."

Roxie nods slowly. The beer's warm and practically impotent; I grew up on faerie wine—*that's* some powerful stuff. Right now, I'm mostly drinking for the effect.

"Precisely," she says. "I don't even *get* the paper, but there it was, slipped under my door. And an hour later there's five strange men in my apartment, saying they're my band. I thought I was going insane. Tried calling the cops but the line was dead and they said they weren't there to hurt me. Asked if I remembered anything about last night. And that's when the guy showed up, the one from the bar."

"Did you get a name?" I ask. "Any defining features?"

She shrugs. "He was Caucasian. Wore sunglasses and a nice suit." She glances at Eli when she says this.

"Don't look at me," he says. "I'm not Fey. I was happily sunning myself in hades."

"Nothing else?"

"No," she replies. "He came into the apartment and told me that this was my band, and he gave me my tour schedule and said I was now in his employ. I asked what he was talking about, and he said this was what I'd asked for: I was going to be a star. So long as I did what he asked, I'd be famous."

She shakes her head.

"And you know what? That night, I was. We were *sold out*. That night, and for every gig after. Fans poured out of the woodwork and after just a week we were on the road, traveling America. I had no clue where it was all coming from and I didn't care. The moment I took to the stage, I was a star."

"So when did it go south?" I ask. It's not enough for Fey to make horrible deals with mortals—they like to get hopes up, make their victim think they're on top of the world. Right before sending them crashing to the ground.

"Last week," she says. "He showed up again. We were in Vegas, taking a day off, and he comes up to me while I'm at the pool. Sits down, orders himself a drink on my tab. Doesn't say anything else for a while. Then he asks if I'm enjoying myself. I said yeah, it was great. And he just responds with, *good. Because you'll be doing it for a while.*"

Eli shakes his head at me, in what's clearly a *stupid mortal* gesture.

"I ask what he's talking about and he doesn't answer. Instead, he hands me a tablet with a doc opened on it. It's saved as 'Roxie's_ Contract' and I start scrolling through it. And under the section titled 'Duration' there's just one line: *For Life.* I actually laughed when I read it. I looked at him, but he wasn't smiling. He was just sipping his drink and watching people swim. He said it wasn't a laughing matter. I would perform until the day I died. And if I tried to cut my contract, he'd send someone to cut me apart."

I glance around to the dead band members. Well, this definitely wouldn't look good to whoever drafted the contract.

"Are you sure you can't remember anything about this guy, anything the band might have said about who employed them?" I ask. "Anything at all. We need a lead."

She shakes her head, and that immaculate pin curl falls out and bounces by her cheek. It would be cute, if we weren't surrounded by dead bodies.

"They never said anything," she mutters. I can't tell if she sounds lost or pissed or some cold combination of both. Maybe that's why I feel for her—I know what that's like better than most. "They only appeared when we were going onstage and they didn't like small talk. I tried to get them to tell me something about the guy who hired them. Anything. But they wouldn't. Said it was my problem, not theirs. They were just doing their job and collecting Dream."

"Well then, my dear," Eli says, sliding to standing. "I'm afraid we've hit the end of our discussion."

"Wait," I say.

"What? She's a dead end. Emphasis on *dead*. Now we kill her and I go to dinner and you do whatever you do after you finish a job. Take a bath or something." He grins. "I might even join you when I'm through."

I ignore the pass and stand. "We're not killing her. Not tonight, at least."

"Why? Don't tell me you're attracted to her. The allure's just whatever enchantment her contract granted her. It's not real."

Again, I ignore him.

"She's bait," I say. I walk over and hold out my hand. She looks at it, but doesn't take it. Smart girl—she's learned not to freely accept help anymore. But I can't help the small curl of regret that unfolds in my stomach; a part of me wants her to trust me, wants her to take my hand without hesitation. I force the thoughts down. I'm not her savior. I'm just not about to kill someone who seems innocent. Not until I know the truth. I drop my hand and shove it back in my pocket, pretending I don't feel slighted. "Whoever made that contract is going to come after you. And they're linked to whoever's stealing Dream."

"How can you be so sure?" Eli asks. "Any Fey could be the buyer. It might not be this evil third monarch. For all we know, Oberon's trying his hand at the music industry again."

"Oberon doesn't deal in the shadows like this, and besides, if he was pulling this much in, he'd be holding it over Mab's head. So whoever this is, they're new. I highly doubt it's coincidence."

Eli sighs. "Fine then. But I'm going to eat."

"Whatever."

He turns and bows low to Roxie. "It was a pleasure meeting you." Like he wasn't just threatening her life. Then, with a pat on my shoulder as he passes, he leaves. Roxie and I stay there in silence, the only sound the rain pattering down on the roof.

"So you're not going to kill me?" she finally asks. I'm impressed by how calmly she says it. All traces of tears are gone. She holds her head high and shoulders back, like any answer I give will be met with the same stoicism. Another point in her favor.

"Not tonight. Come on, I need to take you somewhere safe. Before whoever did this to you comes back."

"I thought you wanted me as bait."

"I do, but not right now."

She still doesn't move.

"Look," I say. "You don't have to trust me. I wouldn't either, honestly—you might live longer if you don't. But if you stay here, you'll either be dead or roped into a new contract before morning. You can't run from the Fey."

"So where are you taking me?"

Oh, I don't want to be doing this . . .

"To the one place you can be moderately safe. Winter."

She raises an eyebrow. Right, she thinks I mean the season.

"It's a kingdom. In the faerie world."

"So . . . to save me from the Fey, you're taking me to a place where I'll be surrounded by them?"

"Something like that." I glance to the door. Whoever drafted that contract will be here soon—they'd have felt the death of the band members immediately. "Now come on, before they get here. We can discuss the intricacies of faerie politics later."

"I don't go home with girls when I don't even know their name," she says. There's definitely a hint of a grin now, and it's too forward a statement to think it's just me. Maybe this wasn't such a bust of a night after all.

"Claire," I say. I begin fishing around in my jacket pocket. The one without all the knives.

"And how are we getting to this other world, Claire?"

It sounds so silly when she says it, like she can't believe it even though her band members are currently dead and lying in pools of multicolored blood. I pull out a piece of chalk and hold it up with a grin.

"Magic, of course."

Then I turn and start drawing a portal on the back of her bus door.

Mab is going to kill me for this. She hates it when I bring pets home.

Six

Roxie's clearly been dealing with some supernatural shit.

She doesn't seem at all perturbed by the chalk portal I draw on the bus's wall, nor does she freak out when she steps toward it and finds herself standing in my study back in Winter. About the only thing she does to reveal any surprise is shiver. I can't blame her—she's not wearing anything beyond that leopard-print dress, and that was definitely made for sweating it out on a stage. I flick a wrist and fireplaces roar into life. There are two in the study, each with a lintel carved to resemble a crouching griffin and roaring dragon respectively. Warmth immediately floods the room, but I know it's a relative term when living in the land of eternal winter.

"I should have let you grab a coat," I mutter, suddenly remembering just how messy the rest of my space is. The study's about the only place that's sacred to me, at least in terms of cleanliness. "Wait here for a moment."

I head into the living room. There are clothes all over the place, and I sadly have yet to get Mab's jewelers to craft me an Amulet of Cleaning or something awesomely useful like that, so I pull the college bro maneuver and run around, tossing bits of clothing into piles, throwing blankets on said piles, and trying to make it look like this place doesn't double as a frat house. (And no, I've never been to college, but I've taken down enough Fey on college campuses to know what they're like.)

Then I run into my bedroom and do much the same, though in here at least there's less clothing and more weaponry. As for getting Roxie something warmer . . .

I rush over to my cabinet and throw it open. She's a lot curvier than I am, but a bit shorter, so I grab a velvet nightgown and some soft, stretchy pajamas that will hopefully do the trick. When I head to the study to meet her, she's already in the living room, examining one of the many weapons racks along the wall.

"I wouldn't touch that, if I were you," I say. Her hand hovers a few inches from a large bastard sword, the blade of which is a sickly acidic green. If that doesn't scream *poison*, I don't know what does.

She drops her hand and turns, looking at me suspiciously.

"What did you say you do for a living?" she asks.

I walk over and hand her the clothes.

"They should fit," I say. Then, "And I didn't say. I'm an assassin."

"So you use these. To kill people."

I shrug. "Mostly. Some are just for show. Spoils of war and all that. That bastard sword's a bitch to try and wield." She doesn't say anything, but I can tell that's because she's holding back.

"Are you judging me?" I ask. I almost laugh. "I just saved your life and you're judging me?"

"I never said that."

"Yeah, but I can tell you're thinking it." And I usually can, too—part of Mab's training was learning how to read emotions. Mortals are ridiculously easy to figure out. Well, most of the time. Maybe it's the enchantments she's wearing, but Roxie doesn't give anything away.

"I highly doubt that," she says. She takes the pajamas from me and slips on the nightgown. I hate to admit how good she looks in it, like some housewife pinup. I half expect her to smile and ask *What are you thinking now?* but instead she looks back to the weapons and bites her lower lip. "So you're an assassin. Of faeries."

"And for a faerie," I say. "My mother is the Faerie Queen."

"Shakespeare?"

"Something like that. But a little more scandalous."

"So that makes you a faerie, too?"

If I were being dramatic, I'd take my blade and cut a line in my palm to show her I bleed red, but that's a little too Hollywood for right now and besides, she probably wouldn't get it.

"No. I'm mortal."

"So how are you . . . ?"

I flop down on the sofa and grab a bottle of bourbon from the table. A snap of my fingers and two tumblers appear. I fill one with a few fingers and hand it to Roxie. She shakes her head, so I fill it to the brim and drink half in a gulp.

"I was stolen," I reply. The bourbon won't kick in fast enough to make this conversation bearable, but at least I can swim in the taste.

"Stolen?" She sits on the other sofa and curls her legs under her.

"Stolen. At least, that's what I assume. Mab won't tell me much about it."

"Who's Mab again?"

"My mother. The Faerie Queen. Shakespeare's muse."

"Right."

"Anyway," I continue, downing the rest of the bourbon, "I quickly learned that I didn't fit in here. I mean, it was pretty obvious—I had to sleep, for one thing. And I aged. I think I was ten when Mab finally told me she wasn't my true mother. That's honestly how the conversation went, too: *That was a good kill, love. And you should know you're not truly my daughter.* She wouldn't tell me anything else. So I dropped it. I learned early on with her that trying to fish out information is impossible."

"So that's been your whole life? Training and killing? What about, I don't know, human things? Like friendship. Or—"

"Or love?" I cut in. I know where this is going. "Not really. I had what you'd call a 'fucked-up childhood.'"

She laughs to herself. "Haven't we all?" But she doesn't press the subject. Instead, she leans over and grabs the bourbon and pours herself a three-quarter glass. Definitely my type of girl.

"You know," she says, "for being some heartless assassin, you don't seem half bad."

She's been holding my gaze the entire conversation, but the moment she says that, she glances away. Is she flirting with me? And for that matter, am I flirting back? The alcohol is slowly kicking in, and I feel warm for what feels like the first time in days. I'd kill for another bath—literally—but there's still work to be done.

"Thanks," I reply. "But you really haven't spent any time with me."

She looks back. "From what it sounds like, that will change. I mean, I'm sort of a wanted girl, aren't I?"

"You are." I can't help it—with the warmth of the bourbon and the warmth of the butterflies, I let myself grin. I so want to hop over to that sofa and put an arm around her and kiss her neck. If this were any other situation, any other seduction, I would have. But for some stupid reason, I don't want to sleep with her. I don't want a one-night stand. I want to keep her around.

"Anyway," I continue, before this can veer into territory I might regret—which again is strange, as I don't usually regret any of my actions, "I have some more work to do before calling it a night. You can stay here for now. We'll figure out something more comfortable tomorrow. You okay with the sofa?"

She nods. I can tell she's a little disappointed, but I don't trust myself around her. Which is yet another strange situation, because I definitely shouldn't be trusting *her* right now. She's still a suspect.

"Okay then. I'm going out for a while. The bathroom's through there and there are snacks in the fridge if you're hungry." *Fridge* might be a misnomer. It's more an icebox, with a literal chunk of enchanted ice. But she'll get the drift.

I force myself to standing and turn toward the door.

"Claire," she says softly.

I pause. Why does my heart leap when she says it? Maybe I should eat something—it's the only explanation I'll admit to myself for why my brain isn't responding to any of this properly.

"Yeah?"

"Thanks for saving me."

"Of course. I try not to kill unless ordered to."

Which is why I'll talk to Mab tomorrow. Otherwise you won't be thanking me for long.

*

I close the door behind me and lean against it, trying to collect my thoughts. Roxie shouldn't be here. She should not be a part of this equation. Having her here in my room makes no sense; neither does leaving her alone. If she were a normal fling I'd have my way with her and get it over with like all the other boys and girls and playthings in between. I have a job to do, and she's getting in the way. If I were thinking straight, I'd send her back home and use her as bait to find her employer. I shake my head.

"Get ahold of yourself," I mutter.

I turn to my door and run my hand along the doorframe, funneling a small amount of power into the magic embedded in the stone. Glyphs flare to life under my fingertips, and I feel the magic race through my room, sealing off all the exits, rendering any magic used inside moot. It's a dangerous magic, but I made it so only I can trigger it—otherwise I know Mab would use it against me. Hell, she's the one I learned it from as a kid. Had to keep me in line somehow.

Once I know Roxie's safe and secure, I turn and stalk off down the hall. I know Pan will want to chat, and I definitely know Mab will expect a debrief. But they're both used to my nature—I've never been the most talkative after a hit. At least my years of being a hermit have helped with something.

The joys of living in an enchanted castle are many, but the main one is the ease with which you can escape. Getting around inside? Tricky as sin. But getting out is cake.

One door later and I'm outside, in one of the many back alleys that stretch out from the castle wall like a spiderweb. I can't get Roxie out of my mind as I head toward the bar. I try every trick I've been taught, every meditative practice and mantra. I even try jabbing my finger with a dagger to focus on the pain. But it doesn't work. As I trek through the cold streets of Winter, all I can think about is her curled up on my sofa, her changing into my pajamas, her wondering what's to become of the rest of her life.

I should be focusing on the job at hand. On the logistics. Someone out there is clearly funneling Dream, and they're not afraid to be bold in their strokes. They're infiltrating our usual sources and creating new ones—big hitters. So whoever this is isn't interested in hiding. They want to make an impression. They want to show they mean business.

I should care. I should be worried. Or plotting. Or actually giving a shit about who is behind all of this. But I don't. I can only think about Roxie. And as everything else in my life feels like it's falling apart, I can't help but admit that I like it.

The Lewd Unicorn's pretty dead for this time of night, not that any of the other bars along the strip are faring any better. Now that I know just how dire Winter's resources are, I can't help but feel a sort of desperation here—the need to forget what you can't afford to waste. I wonder how many of the citizens here are actually feeling the pinch, or if Mab's keeping up a lavish air right up to the very last drop of Dream.

In any case, the regulars are still there, all lined up at Celeste's bar. The place has a cozy sort of feel to it, as cozy as you can get when your building materials are ice and onyx. Everything in here is smooth black stone laced with veins of crystal and silver. From the bar to the floor to the twisted columns supporting the ceiling, it all glitters like a disco paradise. Purple light comes from icy chandeliers that drip from the ceiling, but even that light is mainly there to cast shadows for Winter denizens to hide in.

Celeste perks up the moment I step in. You'd think that for a glowing ball of light she'd be a shit bartender, but her skills are renowned throughout Faerie. She's simultaneously mixing a cocktail and pouring some draft Dream as I walk up to the bar—she uses some sort of telekinesis, which makes the bar look like it's haunted when she's really slammed.

"Claire!" she calls out, hovering toward me. "How's it going?"

"Royally," I reply. Which is shorthand for *royally screwed.*

"That good, huh?" she asks. Oddly for a tiny ball of light, she doesn't have one of those Tinker Bell helium voices—it's deep and sultry and sounds exactly the opposite of what you'd expect. As with all things in Faerie, appearances are deceptive.

"That good."

I settle onto one of the stools and cross my arms, resting my forehead atop them. The bar top doesn't smell like stale alcohol—it smells minty, almost.

"Well then, you definitely need a drink. On the house," she says. I don't look up at the clink of glass, nor do I glance at the patrons on either side. I recognize all of them, and like me, they're often at this bar because they don't want small talk, unless it's with Celeste.

"Make it a Daydreamer," I mutter.

The glass stops clinking.

"Seriously?" she asks. I can feel the regulars staring at me, or maybe it's just my imagination.

"Seriously," I reply.

"Okay. But you know what happened last time."

"Only because you told me after," I say, grinning into my hands in spite of myself. Apparently it had involved dancing naked outside before picking a fight with a brood of vampires. And then trying to make out with one of them.

A few seconds later there's the familiar clink of glass on onyx, and I look up to the tumbler sitting before me. It's the rich amber of bourbon, but there's something else dancing inside of it, a thread of blue and purple that glows but never coalesces.

As I said, she keeps the bourbon especially for me. The Dream is top-shelf shit. Combined, the two pretty much guarantee that Roxie will no longer be on my mind. I'll be flying. Maybe literally.

"Do you need to talk?"

Celeste's voice resonates inside my head. She's at the other end of the bar, pouring shots of green Dream for a group of punk dryads that just walked in, their bark branded with tattoos and their leather jackets roughly tanned skin. Another reason she's a good bartender; she can converse with everyone in the bar at the same time, and no one would be the wiser.

Just a rough night, I think back to her. *And it's not going to get any better for a while.*

"I know how you feel," she replies. *"It's starting to feel like the Dark Ages all over again. What happened?"*

I brought back a straggler.

There's a pause, and I don't know if it's because she's focusing on the dryads or because she doesn't know how to answer that. We all know how well having humans in Winter goes over; they're usually just brought in for food or cheap—albeit short-lived—entertainment.

"Why?" she finally asks.

I take a small sip of the drink. The bourbon burns sweetly. Dream sparks against my tongue and sends images of lounging on a white sand beach through my mind, the smell of salt in the air and the waves a relaxing rhythm. That's the magic of Dream. To the Fey, it's food. To mortals, it's a really vivid hallucination. It could be anything—flight, fame, even fear if you're twisted enough. It's been ages since I've seen her break out beach Dream for anyone. I must look worse than I feel.

She was in trouble, I reply, mentally stretching myself out in the lounge chair. *I don't know, but I felt like I should save her.* Then, as an afterthought and clearly not fast enough to pretend it was otherwise, I add, *And I think I can use her to track down my next hit.*

"Sounds dangerous." She hovers over and pours more bourbon into my glass. *"Mixing romance and business is never a good thing. Especially in your line of work."*

I never said anything about romance.

"You didn't need to."

I don't have a response to that. Thankfully, she doesn't expect it. I take another, bigger drink and let myself float in a world of blue skies and warmth. I need a real vacation. One with poolside-drink service. And cute cabana boys. And no worries about whether or not an entire kingdom is going to fall down around me if I don't play Little Miss Supersleuth. I force that thought aside and try to focus on the Dream—the shit's expensive and in short supply, and I don't want to waste it to worry. The heat is decadent, even if illusory. I can feel the stress I've built up slowly ebb away with the surge of the tide . . .

"Am I interrupting something?"

Eli's voice crashes me back into the bar, where I'm sitting with a ridiculous grin on my face and my arms stretched over the bar top like I'm trying to expose as much surface area to those imaginary rays as possible. This is why I combine Dream with alcohol—ideally, by the time the Dream wears off, I'm so blazed I don't actually notice the transition to reality, or care what sort of fool I made of myself under its influence. Flying Dream is the worst. I've broken many bones—mine and others'—that way.

I grunt and sit up straighter as he sidles onto the stool beside me.

"Finished with your drummer already?" I ask.

He nods and graciously accepts the drink of yellow Dream Celeste slides over to him.

"Put it on my tab," I say. Not that Eli's ever set a precedent of paying for his own drinks. It's my way of paying him back for, you know, being summoned and held here mostly against his will.

"So," he says after a moment. "How's our damsel in distress taking it?"

I take a sip of my drink and fight off the beach scene, which is ridiculously hard because it's ridiculously tempting. I'm definitely starting to feel the second bourbon. I also don't give a shit. Tonight's a night for obliteration.

"Managing," I reply.

"You like her," he says bluntly.

"I'm intrigued." It's almost a lie, but there's enough truth in it to convince myself. "And protective; she's the best lead we've got."

"She's a mortal. She won't know what's going on, and unless you're planning on dangling her like bait in the mortal world, you're wasting your time. No one's going to try and get her while she's in Winter. So don't try that utilitarian BS on me."

I sigh. "I know. I know. I panicked or something. But unless you have another idea, this is what we're doing."

He downs the Dream in a single drink and shudders happily.

"I'm just the sidekick," he says. "You don't pay me enough to have ideas." Another drink slides across the bar toward him. He grabs it and brings it to his lips. "But, if you did, I'd tell you that you can't keep her here. Even if Mab was okay with it. The girl can't grow soft, and she can't think she's safe. Take her back to the human world and let her see firsthand what sort of shit she's gotten herself into. A few threats on her life will get her talking."

"And if she doesn't know anything?"

"Then we get some fun out of her." He takes a drink. "Besides, eventually, you kill enough of the cannon fodder and the boss will reveal himself. Or someone who knows the boss. You just gotta get through the underlings first. It's a waiting game."

"I'm not going to say that's brilliant. But it doesn't suck."

"I try."

"One problem: I'm not about to sit around and babysit for the next few weeks. I'm still on a job. Mab's convinced we don't have much time."

"So find someone you can trust to watch her while we go about our dirty work." He finishes the drink.

"I don't trust anyone," I reply. "Why else do you think I'm working with you?"

*

Roxie's fast asleep by the time I stumble in. Against expectations, I didn't have more than two drinks at Celeste's—as much as I wanted to lose myself, a part of me kept a firm grip on reality for fear of what I'd do if I let go. As for Eli, he was back in the mortal world, probably lingering in the drummer's hotel room and playing with his meal. Draining someone's soul didn't necessarily equate to death, unless the demon was careless. And I know that Eli is far from careless; he'd have known he'd need a place to stay and a distraction for his sleepless night. He's not allowed in Mab's castle. Period. Something about not letting the dogs in.

I stand there watching Roxie sleep for a while, partly feeling like it's sweet and partly feeling creepy, depending on the wave of inebriation. She's changed into the pajamas, which miraculously fit her, and is curled up on her side on the giant leather sofa, a fire smoldering in the hearth. For the first time since we burst into her tour bus, she looks peaceful. And I know that's a stupid observation because everyone looks peaceful when they're sleeping, but she seriously looks like slumber might be the only time she isn't trying to run from something.

Can Mab feel Roxie's presence? Faeries don't dream, which is part of the reason they need ours, and for as long as I can remember, I've been sleeping with talismans and dream catchers that snare and funnel my nighttime dreams to Mab. Always in service, even while asleep. Roxie's wayward dreams can probably be tasted for miles. Another reason I can't keep her here. Summer and the unclaimed may be unable to reach Mab's domain, but that doesn't mean Winter Fey won't be tempted to grab her for themselves.

There aren't any regulations or safeguards for humans in Faerie. As far as anyone's concerned, mortals are trespassers, and they're to be dealt with however the Fey wish. Usually not in a way the humans appreciate for long.

Why do you want to protect her? I ask for the hundredth time tonight. And, for the hundredth time, I don't have an answer. I just do. I want to feel like the good guy for once. Maybe it's the alcohol and lingering Dream, but there's something about having her here that makes me feel the flicker of possibility, one I've never dared entertain before. A normal life. A mortal life. With a partner and a family and what the hell am I even thinking right now? I'm not falling for her. She's not my type.

Damn it, Claire, you're drunk. And you always do stupid things when you're drunk. Remember that group of shape-shifters in Manhattan?

I take a breath and calm my thoughts. It's just the enchantments surrounding her. It's just my intense desire to not be dealing with all of Mab's shit—Roxie's a nice little distraction, and I need to remember that that's all she'll ever be. Protecting her is just part of the process, rather than the end result.

She must feel me watching, because she murmurs and rolls over, pulling the blanket tighter. It takes all my self-control not to walk over and brush her hair from her eyes. But that would definitely jump the line into creepy territory.

Before I can pull that card, I turn and head into my bedroom. I keep the door open. Just in case I'm needed.

*

By some magical coincidence, I'm up before Roxie the next morning. I amble into the kitchen and grab some eggs from the fridge. Obviously, there aren't any farms or groceries in Faerie, seeing as I'm the only resident who actually eats anything, so I have to import from the human world. But I think everything's fresh. Ish.

I brew some lackluster coffee and scramble the eggs and about halfway through, Roxie shuffles in.

"Breakfast?" she asks.

"Gotta keep my hostage happy," I say, flashing her a smile.

Clearly she doesn't catch the humor.

"How long are you planning on keeping me here?" she asks. I can hear the subtext: *Will I see my world again? Will I have a normal life?*

"Until you've cleaned your plate." I stir the eggs with the spatula. "Like I said last night, I just brought you here to keep you safe while we figured out what to do with you. You're not a hostage."

"And you've figured out what to do with me, have you? I appreciate you collaborating."

Ooh, sarcasm. Someone needs her morning coffee.

"You kind of gave up your negotiating rights when you signed your life away," I say. I know it's a low blow, but I'm not in the mood today. Not like I'm ever in the mood to feel guilty. Still, I appreciate that she has a bit of backbone left in her. She'll need it. "You'll be happy to know that you're going back home. Wherever your home actually is."

She steps farther into the kitchen, and I hate how it's like she's practiced this—entering a kitchen in someone else's pajamas, looking tired and beautiful at the same maddening time. I turn back to the eggs and scrape them onto some plates before they burn. I hand her a plate and mug.

"It's not gourmet," I say when she takes them. "But it won't kill you, either. Hopefully."

I grab my own food and head into the living room, collapsing on one of the leather armchairs.

"So," I say when she settles across from me. She does so delicately, cross-legged, her plate balanced in her lap. "Tell me about yourself."

"Is this an interrogation?" She's smiling while she says it, though. Clearly her anger is short-lived. Either that or my cooking's better than I thought.

"Definitely. The fingerprinting comes after."

She chuckles, which is a good sign since that was clearly a shitty joke. "What do you want to know?"

I shouldn't be playing getting-to-know-you games right now, but I'm starting to realize everything surrounding Roxie is one big *shouldn't*. I can't actually remember the last time I had a conversation with someone that wasn't about killing, which means I have no clue how to navigate this sort of congenial small talk. But I've watched plenty of mortals interact. I can fake it.

"Why singing, for one thing? I mean, what made you want that lifestyle so much that you'd give up so much for it?"

She raises an eyebrow at me over her mug. "For one thing, that was a figure of speech I didn't expect anyone to take literally. That aside, haven't you ever had a dream you'd do anything to achieve?"

I honestly haven't, but thankfully she's not looking for a response because she just keeps talking.

"That was singing for me. I was lucky. My parents supported me all through school. I had to work for it, but they helped send me to private lessons, supported me through college. Singing was my everything. Trouble was, they were the only ones who seemed to believe in me. No matter where I went or what I tried, I couldn't get a gig. Tried starting my own band three times before going solo, but even then it wasn't easy. And, well, you know the rest."

It's not exactly a life story.

"What about you?" she asks. "How does someone get tied up in"—she pauses, gesturing to the weapons along the wall, her finger lingering at the stuffed unicorn head above the fireplace—"in all of this?"

"It's all I've known. Mab brought me here when I was a kid. My first memory is waking up and walking down the hall in tears, and then Mab appearing out of nowhere to tell me it was all going to be okay."

I glance at Roxie. She's stopped eating and is watching me intently.

"I'm sorry." She actually sounds like she means it.

"Don't be. I can't miss what I don't remember. Anyway, Mab isn't one for keeping useless things around, so she started training me immediately. Said she needed someone like me, that I was important. And that's precisely what I needed to hear. I didn't want to make her proud, really. I just wanted her to want me around."

"She called you useless?" Roxie asks.

"It's just how she operates. I quickly learned that you're only worth something here if you're working, and you're only kept around if you're worth something. That's why I don't debate my role. I've never known anything else, and I don't think I could *do* anything else. I know how to kill. And I'm damn good at it."

"Don't you ever feel bad about it?"

"No. Because if I didn't do it, someone else would. I'd rather be on my end of the blade."

She nods.

"You seem like you've had a rough life," she adds.

I shrug. I don't really like this, this reverse interrogation. But there's something about the way she asks that makes me want to answer, rather than close up like I usually would. No one's ever actually taken an interest in my feelings before. I can't tell how it makes me feel— beyond odd.

"It's just a side effect of growing up here," I say. "I didn't know anything else, so I've never really had room for comparison. Though, that said, watching mortals bitch about the little things is endlessly fascinating. I don't know *how* you guys manage."

She picks up on the sarcasm and laughs.

"We're good at making the worst of anything. I've tried to take a different approach. You know that saying, *when life hands you lemons.*"

Once more, I don't, but I'm not about to tell her that. I just nod knowingly. I can get the gist.

"Anyway, back to you," I say. "Singing was your everything?"

"It was . . ." she begins. She looks into her mug for a moment. I just wait, patiently. I'm good at waiting. When I need to be.

"I don't know anymore," she finally says, speaking to the coffee and not to me. "The last month has been great in so many ways. I mean, all that adoration. All that applause. But none of it feels real. I don't feel any happier at night. I still wake up alone and go through the motions and go to sleep wondering if there's something else out there, some- thing bigger. I thought that singing would fill the void, but it hasn't. And maybe it's just the circumstance. I don't know. A part of me knows I was made for the stage. But the rest of me wants more than that." She laughs and looks up. "Is it stupid to say I just want to be happy?"

"Normally I'd say yes," I reply. "But in this case, no."

"What about you?" she asks. "What do you want? Once all this is over with, what happens next?"

"Ideally I live."

She raises an eyebrow over a sip of coffee.

"What? When you kill for a living, that's the best reward—getting to wake up again." And no, I'm not going to tell her that yes, a part of me is tired of waking up alone, too, because that part of me was killed off years ago through Mab's training and a lot of other people's blood.

She doesn't say anything, though, which is a clear sign that she's not taking me at my word.

"I'm serious. I'm not like you. I didn't grow up with the American Dream or whatever—I was never told I could be or do whatever I wanted. My life was set in stone the moment I set foot here, and there's really nothing I can do to change it."

"Are you contracted to be her assassin?" she asks. The question is so innocent, yet so straight-to-the-heart, that I actually pause.

"No," I finally admit. "I've never signed anything. I'm technically a free agent."

"Then you could still change your future."

"No. You wouldn't understand. Things don't work like that in Faerie."

"Maybe. But you're still human, magical powers or not. You could still always just go home."

Home. The word is a bomb I prefer not to handle. This conversation's veered way too close to personal territory.

"Speaking of," I say, "we need to get you back home."

"Why?" she asks. "You said yourself that faerie contracts can't be broken."

"They can't. But if you kill the faerie holding the contract, it's void."

"But . . . won't others hear about it?" she asks. It's the first time in this conversation that she sounds timid. "I mean, this guy seemed like a big deal. Will I ever actually be safe?"

"I'm not going to let anyone hurt you," I say, looking into her eyes.

The surprising thing is, I'm positive I actually mean it.

Seven

About an hour later we're standing outside the door to Roxie's Brooklyn apartment. She's not on the top floor, but we're pretty high up, and I know this place is more expensive than it should be. You can tell from the ridiculous modern art on the communal hallway walls. It's in one of those fancy condos with a bellhop or whatever you call them at the front door. All that newfound success has been good to her.

"I used to live in a shared apartment in Queens," she explains to us. "Three roommates. All artists, so obviously no one cleaned and they rarely paid the rent on time. It was hell."

Us being me and Eli, of course. And Pan. Though he's not very talkative right now.

Roxie glances to the satyr statue in front of her door. It definitely doesn't look like it fits in, but this is New York—if nothing else, her neighbors will just label her as a little eccentric, if they notice anything at all. I pat Pan on the forehead as Roxie opens her door and leads us inside.

I can't tell if the space screams *Roxie* or if it's one of those pre-furnished condos that make such good showpieces: White walls with multicolored accents—red in the kitchen, sage in the living room, chocolate in the dining room. Eclectic art, with ceramic vases and African statues, Impressionist portraits and urns filled with colored grasses. It's antiseptic in its beauty. New money, clearly not lived-in, nothing that says *personal* or *keepsake*. Compared to my messy nest, this place makes me feel like I should be wearing gloves before touching anything. About the only nod to someone actually living in here is the bottle of wine on the glass coffee table, a single glass beside it. I also can't help but notice all the truly important things: the number of windows, the alarm system, the furniture that could help hide or impede.

"So, you know the drill," I say, turning back to Roxie. She looks much more natural now that she's in her element. She nods and watches as Eli goes around to all the windows, a piece of orange chalk in his hand. He draws sigils of warding and protection on every corner of every entrance. I turn and start on the door, which is slightly more complicated.

"Yeah," she says. "House arrest. I don't leave unless you tell me to."

She does *not* sound happy about it, either. The fear she showed yesterday is gone, and either she's really good at rolling with the punches—which I guess she'd have to be after what she's been through—or she's currently acting pissed to hide her uncertainty about her safety.

I don't react to the emotion in her voice. With Eli here, I can't exactly show that I care about how she feels. He'd never let me live it down.

"Exactly," I say. "Pan will be out front to protect and alert you. Remember—don't let anyone in. *Anyone.* Even if they look like your best friend or mother. Shape-shifters are very, very good at their craft and the moment you invite one past the wards, you're screwed."

With Pan out there, it shouldn't be a problem—the guy can sense faeries and mortals just as I can, though shape-shifters are some strange mix of both.

"And you're sure those things will keep me safe?" she asks, nodding to the symbols.

I glance at my handiwork and almost laugh at her concern. Seeing it through her eyes, I can imagine just how childish this all looks. The Aramaic is indecipherable, but there are symbols even she can recognize—a few triangles for elemental binding, a sunwise spiral, and even a heart with an eye in the center, for seeing through illusions. Yeah, it looks like a kid just scribbled over her pristine walls. But it's potent. Nothing even vaguely supernatural can cross the thresholds without her express permission.

"I'm positive," I say.

I stand from my crouch and head over to a spot along the sage-colored wall. I made sure to tell her all about the boogie men the Fey might employ to bring her back, just to keep her from thinking it would be smart to dust off any of the symbols. I begin drawing a large rectangle that will link to the portal in my room. The wards I've drawn in here prevent spontaneous travel into this place, but I need a way to get in. Roxie watches this all in silence. Then I pull out a tiny awl from inside my boot and gesture her over. She comes. Slowly.

"Hold out your finger," I say. She does. Despite her reservations, she doesn't shake. I like that about her—she doesn't flinch from reality, even if reality is about as unreal as you can get. I take her hand and ignore how soft it is, how her pulse flutters, strong and steady. One quick prick and a small drop of blood bubbles up on her finger. She doesn't even gasp. "Press it here." I point to a blank space in a rather long string of hieroglyphs, between a falcon and two palm fronds. The only thing that seems to bother her about all this is the fact that she's smudging blood onto her wall.

I prick my own finger and leave a trail of blood right beside hers. The colors are the same. Is it wrong that that seems kind of romantic, us both being humans who bleed the same color? It's funny, the things you take for granted when you live among the Fey.

When done, I draw another series of hieroglyphs right below it, then encircle the entire thing in a symbolic cartouche, binding the blood and the glyphs together. Now, no one can enter or leave through this portal, save for her and me.

"How rude," Eli says, examining it all from behind us, knowing full well he isn't allowed into my room. "I don't get a key?"

"No way in hell." I smile—I mean that figuratively and literally. "You can go through the front door like everyone else."

"So trusting."

"And still alive because of it."

I go around and inspect the windows and vents and every other opening he's surrounded with wards, just to be sure. It's against his binding to do anything beyond what I say, and since he was expressly told what to do, he shouldn't be able to cock it up intentionally. But even centuries-old astral creatures can make mistakes. Especially if those mistakes are convenient.

"Looks good," I say when I've made my rounds. I look to Roxie, who's standing beside the sofa like she isn't certain what she should be doing, an actress who can't figure out what to do with her hands. "Do you need anything before I leave?"

"Not now. But if I do later?"

"Knock twice on the door if you need Pan for something, you know, not life threatening. Knock any other number of times if you're in danger. He'll relay any messages to me and I'll be here as soon as I can. Just don't open the door. Ever. Even if it's just to chat with him or accept a pizza. I'll deliver whatever food you need until this blows over. And don't. Touch. The chalk."

She nods. Eli's disappeared somewhere in the back of the apartment, probably searching the bedroom for anything scandalous, because he's a perv like that.

"What happens if . . . if they get in?" she asks.

I don't want to tell her that she's screwed if they make it past my defenses. If *my* magic can't hold them, nothing she can do will save her skin. But she's looking at me like she needs me, and that makes me soften. I pull out a tiny folding dagger and hand it to her.

"That's iron," I say as she tests its weight. "Poison to faeries, and it's magicked strong enough that they can't sense it on you. I added a few enchantments in there to bring them down fast. Just be careful—it'll work on you just as well."

"I know how to wield a knife," she says. She grins when she says it, and I have to admit, that's a huge turn-on.

"I bet you do," I say. "But hopefully you won't have to. I know I don't need to tell you how dangerous these things are, Roxie."

"You don't."

Then, after slipping the knife in her pocket, she steps forward and wraps me in a hug. She smells of a deep perfume I can't place. And, unlike the few times other people have tried to hug me, I don't flinch from it. But I don't hug her back, either.

"Thank you," she whispers. "Thank you for everything. I owe you my life."

"Am I interrupting something?" Eli asks.

Roxie steps back hurriedly.

"Oh, no, no need," Eli says. "I was just going to make some popcorn if there was a show to catch."

I fight the blush that rises—*what the hell? I don't blush*—and turn to the door, not looking to see Roxie's reaction.

"We're going, Eli," I say.

"Oh, I didn't mean to ruin the fun."

"And Roxie," I say as Eli heads toward me, "that blade will work just as well on assholes like Eli. Just make sure to stab them in the dick."

Eli doesn't say anything. His chuckle is enough.

*

Snow swirls around us. It's not a blizzard, but it's damn well close. Because Mab doesn't appreciate having Eli enter her kingdom through anything besides the front gate, we trudge through the gale toward the kingdom's wall. I have my coat zipped up and the collar pulled to my ears. Eli looks like he's out for a casual jaunt on a sunny afternoon— I'm surprised he's not whistling happily to himself as his unbuttoned jacket flutters in the wind.

The gate rises up before us like a plate of blackened glass, a monstrous feat of engineering that looks deceptively delicate. The material is maybe half an inch thick and stretches a full two stories above the wall itself, the top a sheer slice of glass as sharp as a knife's edge. No guards out here, no patrols on the wall itself. None of that is necessary. Even though the wall is reflective and smooth, there are more glyphs and wards and golems hidden within than there are snowflakes in the city. As Eli and I approach, I momentarily wonder what it would be like to try attacking this place. Everything about Mab's kingdom is deceptive and imposing, a tantalizing mix of satin and steel—you know it will bite, but the temptation to try is still there. We near, and a long line of runes in old Celtic Ogham blazes into life, a turquoise brilliance that stretches from the top of the gate to the bottom. I feel my own markings tingle along my spine. The gate opens silently, wide enough to admit Eli and me side by side. It closes silently behind us when we step through, immediately blocking out the wind and the snow.

I've been doing that for years, but every time I do, I still feel a little badass for having the key.

Everything within the walls is silent. There's a long, wide avenue of black stones leading straight up to the castle, but that's not my destination. We head up the ave for a while, my footsteps silent, Eli's shoes clopping against the tile like gunshots. Normally there'd be *someone* out and about right now. The Fey don't sleep, so it's not like they're all taking a nap.

"Why are we here again?" Eli asks. "Unless you're expecting to find the mastermind within Mab's walls. That would be a fantastic twist." He pauses and grabs my arm dramatically. "Ooh, you don't think it's actually Mab, do you?"

I shake off his grip. Now that Roxie's safe, I can get down to business.

"This is bigger than one Fey," I say. I try to keep my voice down, just in case someone's listening in. Mab would kill me if her kingdom found out there was a crisis. "Even if Roxie's contract holder is involved, he's not the one behind all this."

"How can you be so certain? Don't they say that the most convenient answer is often correct?"

"If they do, they're idiots. Besides, Roxie didn't smell like Frank."

It sounds like an irrelevant statement, but people take for granted how potent smells are. Especially magic—there's a tang to it that's nearly imperceptible, yet it brands the power like a calling card. Anyone who uses magic or Dream leaves their own personal impression on it. The magic binding Roxie was completely different from the magic lingering in Frank's room. So either there's a bunch of people smuggling Dream for disparate reasons, or there's someone in charge who hasn't shown their hand yet.

Either way, my job is far from done. And I need to figure out where the next leak will be. I can sense where Dream originates and trace where it goes, but tracking down the end points for every thread of Dream in the world would be an endless task. The Seattle gig was a shot in the dark, but I haven't heard of any more venues losing their revenue. Which means this buyer either is very crafty, or is going off our usual grid.

"So," Eli says, "where are we going?"

"The jewelers," I say. "Mab put in a special order for me."

We take a side alley that leads past shops out of a fantasy nerd's wet dream. There are apothecaries with bubbling vials and jars of literally everything you could imagine, magic shops with pentagrams in the window and magical artifacts predating Jesus, and even a bookstore that stretches for five blocks, every window crammed with books stolen from the mortal world or handcrafted in Faerie. I've spent months of my life wandering through here, picking up odds and ends, learning the histories of people and places no one else had even heard of. It was my first real introduction to the mortal world, before Mab actually let me venture there. Just being here makes a weight settle in my bones, a history that ties me to something larger than myself. It's honestly the only place in Faerie besides my room that feels inhabitable. Probably because it's the largest collection of things taken from humans.

A few shops in, I stop outside a nondescript door—anyone wandering through here would pass it over as residential, as it's crammed between two shops and looks to be made of old wood. Only, on closer inspection, the door isn't wood at all, but finely hammered silver, tarnished with age.

I knock three times, and barely a second passes before a small window in the door slides open. The eyes looking back are not human. Not by a long shot.

"Who goes there?"

The phrase is so cliché I want to laugh every time, but the deep rumble of the golem's voice strikes a primal nerve within me, one that says laughing would be a very bad idea.

"Hello, Hephaestus," I respond. "It's Claire."

"Claire?"

"Yeah, you know, Mab's daughter and all that?"

The golem's smoldering orange eyes turn to Eli. "Not all."

"Yeah, a friend of mine is with me, too."

"He stays."

I look at Eli. "Mind waiting?"

"Do I have a choice?"

I shake my head and he sighs dramatically.

"Fine," he says. "I'll meet you at the Unicorn."

The golem doesn't open the door until Eli's wandered off around the corner.

"We all sorted now?" I ask. The golem doesn't answer, just slides the window shut and opens the door.

I don't know how the thing manages to walk up and down the cramped hallway. He's hunched over so much his back is brushing the top of the obsidian ceiling and his shoulders nearly touch each side. The hulking humanoid is made entirely of metal, a great clockwork thing of brass gears and steel plates. Even though the cogs that drive him are intricate, nothing about Hephaestus's creation says *delicate*. He's a beast, and every step he takes as he ambles down the hall makes the ground tremble.

"Why here?" he asks as he walks. The hall is long and appears slick, every surface glinting with false wetness, the only light coming from a warm glow deep within the golem's chest and a few panes of teal glass along the walls.

"William," I reply. "He's got a piece for me. Or should."

Hephaestus doesn't answer. His master never gifted him with witty banter. The hall slopes down, leading us deeper and deeper under Mab's kingdom. I glide a finger along the wall and smile at the runes that flash from my touch like ripples in a pond. The walls are heavily enchanted, some of the runes so old I don't even know if the jewelers know what they're for. With every step, the airborne tang of copper and solder gets thicker.

Finally, the golem gestures to the second offshoot hall we've seen, this one noticeably warmer than the rest of the place. Golden light glows near the end of the hall, heavenly if not for the sound of hammers and the hiss of steam and flame.

"Thanks, Heffy," I say, patting the golem on the arm as I pass. As expected, he doesn't respond.

I head down the side hall on my own, leaving Hephaestus towering behind me silently. He'll probably be there until he's needed to escort me out again.

The workshop is a masterpiece in and of itself. The room is filled with worktables and stools, racks of hammers and pliers, shelves of copper and gold and platinum. There are dressers filled with gemstones, crates of bones and teeth, and in the corner, a giant meteorite sits by a kiln, the black stone glinting. You'd expect the place to be grimy, but the surfaces here are polished to the same luster as the rest of the hall. The floor is an inlaid spectacle of gold and ruby and tiger's eye, a great mosaic with hundreds of patterns. The tang of metal is strong in here. It's the one place in Faerie where iron is used, which is why it's so deeply hidden. Iron is kryptonite for the Fey and thus left entirely to the mortals to forge.

I head over to William, who's hunched over a table with a sanding file and what looks like a small golden bird. He has the pale pallor of those who never see the sun, his shirt covered in soot and glinting gold shavings. He doesn't even seem to notice I've arrived, which wouldn't be surprising if not for Hephaestus's booming footsteps.

"Morning, William," I say. I don't know if it's actually morning by his inner clock, but it's a fair enough greeting.

William's head darts up from his work, his tired eyes locking onto mine. I half expect him to drop the bird to the floor in that moment of skittishness, but his work is his life—literally—and his hands don't move a millimeter.

"Claire," he says. His voice belies a bit of breathiness. Looks like I startled him a bit after all. "It is good to see you."

"Likewise," I say. I sit on the bench opposite him and look down at the bird in his hand. It seriously looks like a living creature, albeit one missing a full side of its body. The feathers are soft and delicate, the feet intricate and tiny, and the space within is filled within mechanisms so small I can barely discern them. Clearly he's been working on this for some time. "Please say that's for me."

He smiles. I'm pretty certain I'm the only one in this kingdom who's ever made him smile. Probably because, when I was ten and tired of killing things, I came down here and demanded he make me a jeweler like him. Mab would have nothing of it, of course, but he'd taught me little lessons on the side. In secret.

"I am afraid not," he says. He holds the bird up so I can see it and taps its beak. The eyes glow blue and it makes one soft chirrup, fluffs its feathers, then goes silent once more. "Just a side project of mine. Your piece is over there."

He carefully sets the bird on the counter and stands. When he turns to go, I can't help noticing the line of black tattoos inked along his spine, the markings like a bruise beneath his thin white shirt. Many of them are similar to mine: runes to prevent treachery or subversion, wards of protection, and sigils of strength and steadfastness. But I have many, many more. I've never been able to tell how old William is. Something in his mannerisms makes him seem antiquated, but he doesn't look any older than an uncle. If I had an uncle.

I don't move from the bench. I've been chastised enough for sticking my nose in places it doesn't belong, and I know he enjoys having the big reveal be his doing. So I watch him go to a curio cabinet along the wall, then studiously look away when he turns and makes his way back.

"This is for you," he says when he's settled in.

I look to him, and then to his hands on the table, which hold a tiny black box. For a moment, my eyes snag on the single ring he's wearing. It's crappy and silver, an amateur creation hammered to within an inch of its life. I made it for him after our first and last official lesson, before Mab caught on and threatened to break my fingers. Before I can get sentimental, which I seem to be doing too much of lately, I focus on the ribbon-wrapped box.

"You shouldn't have."

He chuckles, and I take the box gingerly, as though whatever's inside could be fragile or alive—and to be honest, it could be. Though hopefully he built something that can withstand a beating; if I'm using it, a beating is almost a guarantee. I slide off the ribbon and open it slowly. I can practically feel William's anticipation growing with every millimeter unveiled.

Inside the box is a golden pocket watch. The exterior is perfectly plain, and even a little tarnished. I grin. Perfect. I've often found that, with William's craftsmanship, the more subdued it is on the outside, the cooler it is on the inside. When I open it, I discover I was right.

It's not a watch face looking back at me. Instead, a series of silver rings covered in runes and symbols and constellations form the face, each of them moving at different speeds and in different directions. Three hands of varied lengths sit completely motionless.

"How does it work?" I ask.

"In stages." He plucks the watch from my hand and holds it up to me. "Mab said you needed something to pinpoint Dream that wasn't flowing to Winter or Summer. Is this correct?"

I nod.

"As you know, both Courts lay claim to their Dream before it is even manifest, by staking out certain territories as their own. The Dream is imprinted by the Courts, and that's what channels it back to the respective kingdoms. That sort of Dream is what these two larger arms show," he says. "The silver arm is for Winter, the gold for Summer. They trace the largest nearby sources."

"And the third?"

"Unclaimed Dream," he says. He sighs. "I'm afraid it's impossible to find Dream that was, say, claimed for Winter but hijacked in transit. The best I can do is have it suss out sources that haven't been claimed by either Court."

"That's still helpful," I say. I kind of feel like right now, *anything's* helpful. "What about the rings?"

"They will spell out the location of the unmarked Dream. Well, they should. I haven't had the ability to test it out down here."

"I'm sure it will work perfectly. How can I repay you?" I ask. That's the one issue when working with William and the rest of the jewelers—technically, they're employed by Mab, so technically, they have to do whatever I ask. But that feels a little too close to slave labor for my liking. Especially since the only thing I've ever seen them compensated with is living longer.

He smiles. "When my bird is complete, will you take it to the human world and let it fly? I would like nothing more."

"Of course," I say. It seems a little Hallmark for my liking, but I think a few centuries down here have addled his brains. I'll play along the best I can. I reach over and put my hand on top of his, which is probably the most touchy-feely I get with anyone. I can't help it; William feels like family. "Thank you again."

"My pleasure, Claire."

Then, before I let the moment linger any more, I pocket the watch and leave.

*

Eli's waiting for me back at the Lewd Unicorn, as expected. What's not expected is the fact that he isn't alone, even though the bar is empty save for him and the woman sitting next to him. Celeste's nowhere in sight.

Eli's companion is Mab.

I almost don't recognize her at first—she's wearing all white. The color switch is almost as much of a shock as seeing her in a bar. It explains the reason everyone else left; no one wants to be drinking and unguarded around the feared matriarch.

She turns around when I open the door. Eli glances over at me as well, his eyes no longer hidden behind his glasses.

"Welcome back," he says.

Mab says nothing. *Great.*

I walk over slowly, each step feeling like I'm about to spring a trap. Ah, screw it, the trap's probably already been sprung without my knowing. Might as well get the blood and gore over with.

"I hear you brought a human into Winter," Mab says when I sit down. I sit beside Eli, so he acts as a buffer between us. If she kills him, I can always just bring him back.

"I did," I reply.

"And you thought it unwise to ask me first?"

"I thought it unwise to let our only living lead die while asking your permission." A small tumbler of bourbon slides across the bar toward me. Celeste's still not here. She's probably in the back hiding, but at least she's still considerate. "Besides, it was just for the night. She's back home now. Where she'll be staying."

Mab lifts the long-stemmed wineglass to her lips. I'm not sure if it's blood or Dream or wine or some combination of the three, and I'm not about to ask. Her lips are already red from the lipstick, and when she sips, they go an even darker crimson.

"And what has this lead brought you?" she asks. "Besides more trouble?"

"Nothing yet."

"Do you think she is working for our buyer?"

I shake my head and sip on the bourbon, truly wishing Celeste had added some Dream to it. Maybe some emboldening, you-have-superpowers Dream.

"It's not the same guy as Frank, that's for sure. So either there are more players on the field than we thought or this is just a fluke. You know which I'm leaning toward."

She nods over her wine.

"Eli tells me they were storing Dream in their bus, but that the vehicle has disappeared without a trace. The trail is dead. You will use the girl to find the buyer."

"That was the plan." I glance over to Eli, reminding myself to thank him for going back and checking for stored Dream. So *that's* what he'd gotten up to last night. I pause. "Why the hell did you come here, anyway?"

Eli actually leans back a little, making room for me to glare over at Mab. She wouldn't have come out just to make sure I was doing my job, or even to chastise me for bringing Roxie here. She hates being seen among the—how did she put it?—*unclean.*

Mab's eyes narrow, but she doesn't reach over and slap me like I know she wants to.

"I am here," she says quietly, "because I have recently heard from Oberon."

I glance around out of habit. No one discusses the Summer King in the open. It's as close to treason as you can get without ending up in iron chains. The place is empty, and it's not like there's anyone above Mab to get her in trouble.

"Oh yeah?" I ask. Another sip of bourbon.

"Indeed. Apparently our little dilemma is worse than we had initially expected. His kingdom is feeling the effects as well."

Again, I glance around. Hadn't she sworn me to secrecy?

"What's your point?"

"Only that our situation is dire. We don't have time for you to be waylaid with thoughts of protecting this girl. Eli tells me you don't yet have another lead, and here I find you, drinking when you should be out there finding who is behind all of this."

I open my mouth to argue that I'm only drinking because she's here, but it doesn't seem worth it.

"I was getting that amulet from the jewelers," I reply coldly. "So I could *find* the next trail. You haven't made this easy, you know."

"I would if I could," Mab says, and for once I actually believe she means it. Which tells me just how dire the situation really is. She likes it when I sweat a little. "Will it work?"

"I haven't had the chance to try it out." I look to Eli. "You ready?"

"Always," he says. Which is true. Astral creatures like him never tire. He pushes himself from the stool and bows to Mab, who barely takes notice of him. "A pleasure," he says. Then, without waiting for me, he turns and leaves the bar.

"I'm doing the best I can," I say quietly, when he's out of earshot.

"Then do better." Mab turns back to her drink. Clearly my exit cue. I sigh and down the last of the bourbon and leave. Eli's waiting for me outside the bar. He doesn't say anything at first, just pushes off from the wall and falls into step at my side.

"Well," he eventually says as we make our way toward one of the kingdom's many exits, "that was pleasant."

"Can it."

"I see where you get your manners. Where are we off to, anyway?"

I open the tiny locket and study the small hand.

"No idea. But we're about to find out."

Eight

The pocket watch works.

After I've landed in the mortal world and asked where the greatest leak of Dream is, it spells out the coordinates to a conservatory in Chicago. I'm not certain which conservatory it is, but thankfully I don't need the name for my magic to work. I hastily sketch a portal on the wall of some dingy hallway in what looks like a middle school, using the coordinates from the amulet and praying it actually works and doesn't lead us into, I don't know, the heart of a volcano or something fun like that. It must be my lucky night—the portal lets us out in a hallway that definitely isn't on fire. I hear the murmur of an audience down one end and silence down the other. Judging from the photos and plaques on the wall, this is the right place. The tiny watch hand points dead ahead. I sniff once and feel my skin crawl.

"This is Summer territory," I whisper. The magic ringing through this place has the telltale whiff of lightning and cut grass. And, sure enough, the gold hand on the watch is spinning around wildly. I thought the amulet would only track unmarked Dream. Or has someone found a way to smuggle right from underneath our noses? Not by hijacking claimed Dream, but by stealing it before it could be branded . . .

Eli nods silently. I twist the dead man's ring and the tingle of magic washes over me. I have no connections here, and if I'm found out, I'm as good as captured—Oberon's made it quite clear that I'm not welcome on his turf. I guess he's pissed that I've killed off so many of his "best and brightest."

Even though I'm cloaked, I stay close to the wall as I head toward the stage. The music coming through the hall is classical, which is so unlike last night's show I almost laugh. Whoever's stealing Dream clearly isn't playing genre favorites. It's not a concert, though. That's readily apparent when a bunch of lithe men and women run past wearing nude shorts and nothing else—not even the women.

"Modern dance? Really?" I whisper. Eli just shrugs.

It figures that Summer would have stakes on this place. Personally, I'd rather be getting my teeth drilled.

We head to the stage wing and stay in the shadows. Onstage, the dancers twist and dance and leap, making circles with legs and hands, throwing billowy sheets of silk into the air. It doesn't make any sense to me, but I can tell from the influx of Dream that the audience is eating this shit up. Like with Roxie, there seems to be more getting pulled in than should be possible—I mean, in a situation like this, I'd expect most of the Dream to be occurring because the audience is falling asleep. It's also readily apparent just who onstage is siphoning the Dream.

It's a young man, maybe twenty-three, with short auburn hair and a single black ring tattooed around his right ankle. He's clearly the lead ballerina or whatever they call it in modern dance foo-foo land—he's the one dancing in the center of the stage, doing a duet with a girl I could probably crush with one hand. I watch him lift her, the muscles in his arms and back flexing quite nicely. Why is it always the hot ones who get mixed up in this shit? I can't even pretend to be excited about killing this guy—I'd much rather seduce him in a bar and take him back to my place to show him how we dance in Faerie.

Like Roxie, the guy's not Fey, but there's a magic surrounding him similar to hers. I sniff again, and sure enough, the scent's the same as the magic binding Roxie to her contract. Bingo. But if this place is run by Oberon, I'd think he'd realize there is an interloper on his own grounds. Unless the contact here was recently killed off as well and Oberon hasn't caught on yet. Unlike Winter, Oberon's kingdom isn't known for being bloodthirsty; I don't think he has anyone like me, and I don't think he'd know what to do with an assassin if he did.

I glance at Eli and gesture to the lead dancer. Eli nods. Usual drill—find the bastard after the show and make him talk, by whatever means necessary. I just hope I don't have to suffer through another hour of this mess before that happens. That bourbon can only take the edge off for so long.

Thankfully, I only have to stand there another ten minutes or so before the final act—a very "rousing" number that involves all the dancers running into each other repetitively to ambient piano music. Then the lights go dark and rise again, the whole cast standing in line for a few bows. I'm practically tapping my toes in eagerness. After a day of being shit on, I'm ready for someone else to pay for it.

The cast leaves and heads toward the dressing room. Just to make sure my senses are right, I click open the watch William made me; sure enough, the short hand follows the auburn-haired dancer like a bloodhound. He smells so strongly of magic when he runs past that I nearly gag. Maybe I was wrong; maybe he's not like Roxie. The magic surrounding him feels different, even if there are threads of the same faerie bindings. But something tells me that—unlike her—he got precisely what he wanted from whatever agreement he made. There's a smugness to him no magic can alter. It reminds me a lot of that barista witch from Queens, Frank.

Eli and I follow closely, heading straight into the dressing rooms. I guess I'd normally feel like a creeper as we stand there, watching the guys undress and congratulate each other. But I can't take my eyes off our man, a guy the others are calling Henry (which in reality is not the most sinister of names, but then again, a modern dancer doesn't seem like the most sinister of people). I watch him like a hawk, examining him for any tells or weaknesses. He undresses slowly, and once again I'm in awe of his perfect musculature, the way his entire body seems to glide through the motions. I've never been too fond of the willowy types, but there's a power under his skin that's a huge turn-on. And when he slips out of his shorts, it's clear it's not just his legs that are long.

I'd blush, if I were that sort of girl. Instead I just watch as he walks around the changing room ass-naked, clearly in no rush to get into normal clothes. I can't say I would be either; if I were in his skin, I'd be showing it off to the world. I'm no longer as torn over having to kill him—something about his cocky nature completely switched off that trigger—but I can still appreciate his beauty. We just need to get him on his own. To start the interrogation, that is.

For that, I have a few different tools at my disposal. I have rings to paralyze and a pouch of faerie dust in my pocket that could put them all to sleep. Eli alone could probably weave a quick spell to knock them all out at once. But as we watch and wait, it becomes readily apparent that none of that will be necessary. The dancers all leave one by one. Henry stays behind, slowly changing into street clothes.

When the rest of the dancers are gone, Henry goes over to the dressing room door. I clench my fists, ready to leap at him and start our dance, when he does a tiny motion over the doorknob and I hear a click.

No wonder the guy feels like Frank. Henry's a witch.

"You can take off the enchantments," he says as he turns. "I know you're there."

I chuckle to myself. Thank gods. I needed a fun one to help relieve the stress.

It's really boring when they don't put up a fight.

I twist my ring and let the enchantment roll off. Eli clearly does whatever he does to be visible to mortals.

"How long have you known we were watching?" I ask.

"Since you teleported here," he replies. He smiles at me. It's a very *bedroom* sort of smile. "And I could feel you watching me."

"What can I say? I appreciate confidence. Especially when you've got the goods to back it up."

Eli chuckles beside me. I have no doubt he was enjoying the show as well.

"You from Summer?" Henry asks, looking the two of us over. He's wearing baggy sweatpants and a loose V-neck T-shirt, the neckline of which dips below his sternum. Not a look I'd normally find attractive, but he's somehow pulling it off.

He might be in the know, but at least he's not *that* in the know.

"Not even close," I say. "But it's nice to know I won't have to explain anything when forcing answers out of you."

Henry laughs. "Babe, I don't think you know who you're dealing with."

I cringe at that word. "*Babe?* Really?"

He just smiles. I shove down the revulsion and flick my wrist, a small piece of magic. A long sword slides from the ether, appearing in a sliver of black mist. "I don't think you know who you're dealing with, either."

"I really hope that's not supposed to scare me." He definitely doesn't look perturbed by it.

"Not really," I say. "That's what this guy's for."

Eli takes off his glasses then, sliding them back to rest atop his head.

Still, Henry doesn't flinch. He looks Eli over coolly and says, "I was wondering why he felt off."

Overall, this isn't going as well as I'd expected. Why aren't these people as timid as they should be when staring death in the eyes?

"You know why we're here, yes?" I ask.

"I'd assume because I'm not playing for your team." He winks at me. "They told me the Courts wouldn't be too happy when they found out about me stealing Dream."

"And yet you're still onstage," I say. "Seems pretty stupid to me. It's not like you've made yourself hard to find."

"I wasn't trying. I've played my part. And all parts have to end eventually."

"How poetic," I say, rolling my eyes. I take a step forward. "So this is how the rest of this game goes: You're going to tell me who's buying your Dream. If you do, I might actually let you live." Again, it's a good thing I'm not bound to telling the truth. There's no way this guy's getting out of here alive. "If you don't, I will make the next few days of your life a living hell."

Eli chuckles. "As someone who's been there, I can personally attest to this."

Henry spreads his arms wide. "Do your worst."

"I was hoping you'd say that."

In the next blink I'm there at his side, my sword slicing clean through his Achilles. He goes down with a grunt, and then I'm behind him with my hand in his hair and my blade to his neck.

"Now," I say, "let's try that again. Who is buying your Dream?"

"Fuck you," Henry says through gritted teeth.

He actually puts up a fight. Or tries to. My spine scalds with power as the glyphs protecting me from magic flare to life. A folding chair beside me bursts into flame, and the room quickly fills with the scent of burning plastic and sweaty clothing.

"That wasn't very nice," I say. "But I appreciate you trying so hard. It's cute."

Henry's blood has formed a small pool at my feet now, and I know he won't have too much time left before he bleeds out or faints. So I stamp my foot over the slash in his leg and send a few small enchantments down there, let his flesh stitch back together. I don't want him to fade just yet.

For his part, Eli just stands there with his hands clasped behind his back. Watching and waiting.

"I'm not going to tell you anything," Henry says.

"Oh, but you will. You'll tell me who's buying and who else is selling before I actually start to get pissed."

Henry just laughs. "No, I won't. Contractual impossibility."

I yank his head back and look into his eyes. He's just smiling at me.

Of all the times in the world I could use a charm or something to sever a faerie contract, now would be it. But there isn't one. Faerie magic can't be broken, not like a witch's curse.

I let go of Henry and take a step back, look to Eli.

"What do you think?"

"He's telling the truth," Eli says. "I can taste it."

"Fuck," I say. I kick Henry in the ribs. "What do we do now?"

I can't go back to Mab empty handed again.

"Let me talk to him," Eli says. His blue eyes blaze.

"Be my guest," I say, and step away.

Eli walks over and kneels in front of Henry, who still has that ecstatic martyred look on his face. The guy grins even wider as Eli takes his head in his hands and forces him to look in his eyes.

"I want to show you something," Eli whispers. He leans in close, their noses almost touching. It would be borderline erotic, the intimacy of it—the blue of Eli's irises reflected in Henry's, the hush of his voice. Until, that is, Henry starts to scream.

Quickly, I grab hold of an amulet around my neck—a horned moon holding a bloodstone—and send a small riff of power through it, my other hand going to the wall. Magic pulses through me and through the wall, a quick ripple that I should have done the moment we got here. A spell to keep out prying ears.

I actually have to plug my own ears once that act is done. I've seen Eli do this before, but that doesn't make the knot in my gut any more pleasant. After a while Eli pushes Henry back and stands, wiping his hands on his pants.

"Well, that was fun," Eli says, smiling at me. He slips the glasses over his eyes and walks over to my side. "He's all yours."

Although effective, Eli's basically taken all the fun out of tonight. Henry just stays there, kneeling, staring at the wall with wide eyes and a completely vacant expression on his face. He's goneso. Nobody home.

Staring into the netherworld has that effect on people.

I walk over and kick Henry in the crotch to get his attention and anchor him back to reality. The guy's response is slow, just a grunt and a closing of the eyes. I kneel down in front of him and grab his shoulders to keep him from falling to his side.

"Let's try this again," I say. "I want to know who your buyer is."

"Can't say," he whispers. His words sound like they're being dredged up from the bottom of a well. Or, in this case, some hellish black hole.

"Then how do you know Frank?"

They shouldn't know each other—it's not like there's some international witches' coven or something. Though there might be some sort of social network . . . I should really look into that.

In any case, I know the two are connected. There's a tang to their magic, a similarity that tells me they've crossed paths. Maybe even learned a thing or two from each other. Which doesn't make sense, seeing as they live a thousand miles apart. Frank and Henry have been sharing magic, while Roxie and Henry are branded by the same faerie. Too convenient. I'll have to ask her about it.

"Frank?" he asks dully.

"Ludwig Fennhaven," I reply. Henry's eyes tighten. "Yes, I knew his true name. Just as I know yours, Alistair. I'm just trying to give you the benefit of the doubt here. How did you two know each other?"

He opens his mouth. No words come out. Just a thin trail of smoke.

"Fuck," I curse. I jump to my feet and step back, standing next to Eli.

Henry coughs and another plume rises from his lips. The truly terrifying thing is the vacant expression on his face and the terror behind his eyes, like he's watching it all but isn't close enough to do anything about it.

"Cross a line in the contract?" Eli asks.

I nod as we watch Henry sputter. "Must've been the true name thing. Damn it."

"Don't worry, there was nothing in there anyway."

Henry gasps loudly, as though he's just now regaining control over his body. He locks eyes with me, even as his irises burn up from within.

"My goddess will rise," he wheezes through the smoke. "And when she does, even your Winter Queen will tremble."

And before I can get anything else out of him, he collapses in on himself, his skin and bones disintegrating into ash as the fires of his contract consume him.

"Well," I say after a while. "That's just great."

"Less to clean up," Eli replies. "Just get a waste bin . . ."

Despite myself, I chuckle.

"How about this—I clean up and you go tell Mab that there is, in fact, someone out there opposing her rule."

"No, thank you."

"That's what I thought."

My goddess will rise. Great. Not only are we dealing with a rogue ruler, she thinks she's a god. And so do her followers.

Mab is *not* going to be pleased.

Nine

I don't tell Mab about Henry's dying words. I think too highly of my own life for that. Instead, I tell her the rest of the truth—that her fears were founded, that there is a new figure out there vying to take control. She takes it better than I thought. She doesn't even scream.

All told, the interaction takes about two minutes, and then I'm headed back into the streets of Winter. A small part of me wants to go check in on Roxie, but I won't. Not tonight. Not so soon. She has to think she's on her own, that I'm not playing savior—because that's not a role I can play full-time, even if it's something I'm gravitating toward. I have to keep my eyes on the job. The job I'm currently failing at.

I head down the main avenue from the castle, not really looking where I'm going. Until I get to the statue of the Oracle. Something about the waver of fire reminds me of watching Henry burn, and I pause there for a moment, looking up into the blank face. I brush my hand against the plaque, wondering what "The Oracle's Sacrifice" actually was, what the whole war was about and why Mab won't talk about it. I can't tell anything from the statue itself, but it's definitely feminine. Maybe my age. What did she do that was so important she got a statue, when here I am saving Faerie from apparent destruction and no one even knows it's happening?

Maybe, when I die in the midst of all this, I'll finally be deemed important enough to recognize.

I continue down the avenue, suddenly embarrassed for feeling sorry for myself out here, not that there's anyone around to see it. But as I go, I get a flash of memory, the faintest hint, probably from the flicker of fire in the statue's stone hair. It reminds me of the girl in my hallucination, the blonde chick with bloodstained knees. I glance back to the statue, trying to compare the two. Maybe it's something in the cheekbones? I shake my head. I'm losing it, trying to pull connections where they don't exist, and it doesn't even matter—the Oracle has nothing to do with this. She's dead. And the lost girl I saw with Mab in that vision wasn't exactly world-saving material. She wasn't even wearing leather.

I don't encounter anyone on my way to the Lewd Unicorn. The bars I pass only have a few patrons lounging inside, and the usual sound of faerie music and pleasures are muted, distant. Maybe people actually are feeling the Dream shortage . . .

Celeste's bar is practically empty. Only a few regulars scattered throughout, keeping to the shadows. No one's talking, so she's got some ambient rock playing through the house speakers. Apparently everyone's had one of those days.

"What'll it be?" Celeste asks when I sit down.

"The usual," I say. Because I never say anything else in here. This interaction is basically rote.

This time, though, there isn't a tumbler immediately in front of me.

I look up and see the hesitation in her aura, the faint flicker of light like clouds over the sun.

"Can you pay?" she asks in my head.

I actually laugh.

What? I ask.

Another pause. She starts pouring the drink, but there's definitely a bit of a tremble there.

"You know I hate to ask this," she says. *"But things are kind of tight around here."*

Wait, seriously?

I've never paid for anything here. I don't handle Dream; everyone knows that. As a mortal, I'm not allowed to use it as currency. "My tab" is just a running joke. I assumed she billed Mab for whatever.

She slides the drink over without answering.

Celeste, how bad is it? I know you told me things were getting rough but I thought you were just making small talk.

"You haven't heard? No, of course you wouldn't. Mab keeps the castle stocked."

I play it cool. I don't even think about knowing anything, because I want her to keep talking.

What's going on?

"There's a Dream shortage. People are starting to leave the city. Some are even forswearing their allegiance and heading into the Wildness."

That would explain the empty streets.

"You have no idea. Have you been outside the central district?"

I shake my head and take the tumbler, making a mental note to get my hands on some Dream to pay her back.

"It's a ghost town."

Where's the Dream going? I ask, playing dumb. *I mean, why would everyone go to the Wildness? They don't have any stock in the Trade.*

Another hesitation.

"That's not what I hear," she says quietly, as though Mab can hear our thoughts.

You mean someone's pulling in Dream? Someone not tied to the kingdoms?

It's nearly impossible to keep playing stupid, but I'm tired enough that it's working.

"*That's not all,*" she says.

What are you talking about?

She doesn't answer. Just pours me another shot and hides the bottle back behind the counter.

"*I can't say. You should go see for yourself.*"

*

So, after finishing my drink and promising to bring her back some Dream the next time I'm by, I make my way to the outer edges of Winter.

The city stretches on for miles within the great wall separating civilization from the frigid wasteland beyond. Tenement-style flats line each side of the narrow cobbled street, their facades black and covered in shadow. There are only a few stragglers out here, and even they seem to walk with a purpose, with the desire to get away. Needless to say, no one's talking, and the farther I walk, the fewer people there are to talk *to*. A few blocks down and the flats surrounding me don't just feel empty like Winter usually does, they *are* empty. I walk up to a door left slightly ajar and push it open, peering inside. The place is dark, but my eyes adjust quickly as the runes along my spine flare into life.

The flat is tiny, nothing more exciting than your average one-bedroom. There's a sofa and table and, in the other room, a rather uncomfortable-looking bed. Some Fey are lavish in their abodes, but whoever lived here clearly had a more Spartan outlook—no art on the walls, no personal objects. Just a vacant room ready for someone else to move in.

I don't know what I'm looking for. It's not like there's going to be "Come to the Wildness" propaganda posters lying around, and there's no one here to question. I also know that no one in their right mind would ever admit to having heard of some sanctuary offer from faeries in the Wildness, let alone consider moving there themselves. But I wander through the room anyway. And when there's nothing there, I leave and continue down the street, peering into the houses as I pass. None of them holds any answers. They're all empty. No one on the streets, no lights in the windows, no music in the air. The place is completely dead.

It's maybe my sixth or seventh house when I actually find something interesting. And that's still pushing the idea of "interesting."

I almost miss it. Really, it's just dumb luck and not skill that I see it poking out of a leather-bound book on the nightstand. There's no light for it to catch, no rustle of intuition. It's just a bookmark, and if I hadn't been so bored from all the other rooms, I probably wouldn't have opened the book in the first place.

But it's not a bookmark. It's a ticket. It's about the size of a business card, and the front is covered in fleurs-de-lis—I can't make out the colors in this darkness—and *Admit One* in swirling script. I turn it over. It's for the Cirque des Immortels.

I can feel the magic laced through the card. It's infinitesimal, but it's there, lurking in the ink, waiting in the fibers. I can tell it's one of those dormant spells, the type that requires just a little magic to open. Faerie magic, most likely, judging from the taste.

Thankfully, that's what I'm good at.

Faerie magic is fueled by Dream, which is why it's such a necessary resource. My own supply is linked to Mab's, seeing as I'm not allowed any of my own. *You don't need it to survive,* Mab had said, *so why would we waste any on you? You may take what you need, when you need it, and only the barest minimum.* I use only the tiniest amount. Seeing as Mab is in charge of my supply, she also knows when and where and probably why I'm using it. She won't be happy to learn it is to track down why her own people are willing to risk exile or death to flee—I don't think she wants me to know people are abandoning ship. If anything is to be her downfall, pride would be my number one guess.

The moment my power touches the paper, my vision shifts. It's not images, per se, but lights and colors and shifting shapes. It doesn't make sense. Flickers of orange and red, flashes of yellow, and curls of shadow, everything moving like light through a jungle's branches. It's strange and dazzling, but it's not the fireworks that make my hair stand on end and my heart race—it's the smell. For any other human it would be unnoticeable, but I can taste it: cloying, rich and powerful, a scent that fills my lungs and my blood with heat and power, a scent I know all too well. Dream. Pure, unfiltered, undistilled, unadulterated Dream. Whatever or wherever this place I'm seeing is, Dream is rampant there.

I could float in this forever.

Then a voice—feminine, ageless, and terribly angry—twines from the scene and roots into my skull.

"Come home," it whispers. *"Come and take back all that should be yours."*

Another flash, the image of Mab's castle from on high, the wooden gates of Oberon's kingdom. The smoke and flame of war.

Then the vision's gone.

I drop the card to the floor and lean against the wall, staring at my hands, which burn and tingle with power.

"Well shit," I whisper, looking past my fingers to the card on the floor.

People aren't just leaving Winter because they're hungry. They're leaving because they're being recruited.

*

I don't bother exploring further, and I hesitate for a very long time over whether or not I should bring the ticket back to my room. Mab's not going to like it, but she's going to want to see this. I slip it into my pocket and hope the next time I see her, she's in a good mood. When

I leave and make my slow way back to the castle, I actually start to feel the weight of our situation.

Why the hell is someone sending tickets from Mab's circus from the depths of the Wildness? How are they circulating without the higher-ups noticing? It's not until I reach the castle and am heading toward my room that a dangerous question arises . . . What if Mab sent me to the circus because she already knew about these tickets? She's always been one step ahead, even when she pretends not to be. So what in the world could her angle be?

None of it makes any sense, and once more my tired thoughts drift to Roxie, and I realize that for absolutely no reason whatsoever, I want to talk to her about this. The fact that I'm even thinking that makes me pause—I've known her for all of a day.

But that's also the longest time I've ever spent around a mortal.

"You shouldn't be thinking about her," I mutter. "She isn't important."

And yet, she's tied to this Henry guy. So maybe, in some purely business way, she is. I reach the door of my bedroom and press my head against it. I don't want to go in there, not for another empty night waiting for the morning to come. My body is completely thrown off from all these time jumps—I don't know if I'm hyper or exhausted or what. All I know is that I'm ready for this job to be over and done with. Back to your regularly scheduled killing, thanks.

There are dozens of enchantments that make my door accessible only to me. And Mab, I guess, but that's obvious since she owns the place. Which is why, when it opens without me turning the knob, I go from introspective to attack mode in a heartbeat.

My blade's against the neck of whoever opened the door—whoever is *inside my room*—before the shadow becomes clear.

"Were you planning on waiting out there all night?"

I don't remove the blade. It's the magician. Kingston.

"What the hell are you doing in there?" I ask. I peer past him, then back into his eyes. My knife stays on his neck. "And how the hell did you get in there in the first place?"

He grins. I hate to admit just how sexy that smile is, the perfect rebel-without-a-cause charm.

"Magic," he says. He wiggles his fingers.

"Give me one reason not to kill you where you stand."

He just laughs. "You wouldn't be the first, let me assure you." His eyes grow quizzical. "Come to think of it, the last time was just like this, too. What is it about my neck that says *please cut here*?"

Despite his attempts at humor, I don't chuckle. Mainly because I'm more and more confused with every word he says and am intent on not letting it show.

"Why. The hell. Are you in my room?" I bite down the words as my blade bites against his neck. Just a little more pressure, I know, and I'll break the first layer of skin.

"Because I wanted to see you. Obviously." He doesn't break eye contact when he says it, and there's something about that smoothness that sets my nerves on edge and relaxes me at the same time. Those are eyes you could fall into and disappear completely. And he knows it.

"Why?"

"You know, it's really hard to talk with this pressed against my neck." He points to the blade. "Don't get me wrong, I like it a little rough. But this might be crossing the line."

Again, that nonchalant charm, like his life isn't hanging in the balance. Which, to be fair, it probably isn't, seeing as he's under contract to live forever. Though maybe that doesn't extend past circus lines . . .

In any case, I withdraw the knife but keep it open.

"One wrong move, magic boy," I say, "and you're going to learn what your intestines look like."

I can see the flicker in his eyes, the inner acknowledgment that I am, in fact, being serious. But that's it—the smile doesn't shift and he doesn't apologize or swear he'll play nice. He just steps to the side and sweeps his arm out, inviting me into my own damn apartment.

I push past him without giving him a second glance, making sure to elbow him in the side as I go.

"I like what you've done with the place," he says as he closes the door behind me. "Very homey. You wouldn't even know we're in the depths of Winter in here."

The last thing I want is to let him know he has me on edge, even if I did kind of blow that cover at the front door. So I hop over the back of the couch and lounge on the cushions. A wave of my hand and the embers in the fireplaces roar into life, along with a dozen candles scattered throughout the room. It probably looks romantic. I just want to appear like I don't give a shit.

He pauses by the door, clearly a little crestfallen.

"I was wondering how to do that. Not normal magic."

I shrug and stare at him. Of course it's not normal magic—I was taught by the Motherfucking Queen of Winter, not some mortal witch. Duh.

I don't say anything while I look at him. Let him keep making the first moves—so long as we're in my territory, it should keep him on edge. He's wearing tight blue jeans tonight, along with a white button-down that looks like it's been through the Dark Ages and a beat-up leather jacket I can't help but envy. His hair's pulled back in a scraggly man-bun, and I hate to admit that—paired with the scruff he's clearly been tending—he looks pretty damn hot. The Quetzalcoatl tattoo twined around his neck definitely helps.

And it's then, right then, that I know what tonight's going to entail. I feel the inevitability crashing toward me like an avalanche, one I don't think I want to avoid. My chest feels warm at the thought; Kingston's the perfect way to spend the evening—the perfect focus to forget everything else, the ticket and Dream and even Roxie. He might be here to coerce me or something, but I'm going to use him like he's never been used before. And he's going to love it.

Clearly he notices the shift in my mental energy, because he clears his throat and actually looks away, toward the case of weapons. He doesn't look back to me. Score. After everything else today, it feels great to be back in control of something.

"I haven't been able to stop thinking about you," he finally says. It's the first time words have left his lips that haven't felt calculated. There's something raw to them, almost bitter. Though I still don't doubt for a second that it's all an act, even if it's a very good one.

"That's a shame," I respond. *Is he really making it this easy?* "I tend to have that effect on weaker men."

He does glance over then. Good. Let him see I'm not going to be won over by some vain show of self-loathing.

He opens his mouth to say something, then stops, leaving his lips slightly parted. I really, really want to bite that bottom lip, to give over to lust and just forget about everything else. And I will. But first: business.

"Why are you here?" I ask. I funnel as much cold into my voice as I can, using Mab as my muse. It sounds more like an accusation than a question, and the slight flinch in his eyebrows tells me I pulled off Mab's rendition flawlessly.

"Why do you think I'm here?" he responds.

"No. We're not playing that game. You're on my turf, you answer my questions. Or you get the fuck out." I grab an empty wineglass from the table and circle my finger lazily around the rim, letting its crystal chime ring out. As it does, the glass fills with red wine. A very nice old-vine zin. "So, last time: Why are you here?"

"I'm here to warn you."

"Ooh very dramatic." I take a sip and pointedly don't offer him a glass, even though there's another waiting on the coffee table. "Let me guess, *end of the world* or something like that? I already know."

"No." He doesn't move from his spot by the wall. "How safe are we to talk in here?"

"I enchanted the place myself. So pretty damn safe."

He grins again, a little more uncertain than before. "In that case, I should probably give it another coating."

"No magic." *I don't trust you not to weave in something else.*

"Okay. Well. What you're getting into . . . it runs deep. And you shouldn't be setting foot there, not if you know what's good for you."

"I'm not *getting* into anything. I'm already there. But thanks for thinking of me. Was great seeing you and all."

Because yes, I want to screw him, but I also want him to work for it.

"No," he says. "You're just starting."

I take another sip, letting him know his revelations are far from, well, revelatory.

"If you know something, you will tell me. To do anything less would be treason, and you know how well our dear ruler takes to that."

He shakes his head. "It's not that. I told you, I have no idea who's stealing Dream and if I did, I'd be as far removed as possible. I'm not coming between Mab and her Dream."

"So what are you warning me about?"

"You. Your life. What you're about to embark on. What you've already seen, even if you don't understand it." He looks torn when he says it, like he's not quite supposed to tell me. I wonder if it's against his contract somehow. I perk up inside but try to appear disinterested. The conversation's finally getting interesting.

"Thank you, Mr. Enigmatic. What are you, a fortune-teller now?"

He actually winces at that. Huh. Must not like being associated with charlatans.

"Jesus, Claire," he says, running his hands over his hair. "I'm trying to keep you from getting in trouble."

"Then just spit it out."

"I can't!" he yells. He looks like he wants to punch something—both fists balled up and his tattoo writhing around his neck angrily. "I'm trying but I can't. Listen, you . . . you're not . . . Ugh!"

He does punch the wall then. Not that it does any good, since the wall is solid stone, but the thud is oddly pleasant. Something about the sound of smashing flesh trips a trigger. Kingston doesn't shake his hand out, just takes a deep breath and clearly tries to collect his thoughts. It doesn't seem to work.

"What do you know about your . . . your family?" he mutters to the stone.

"Why?"

"Just answer."

"Dead," I say. "Or, according to Mab, as good as dead, which I assume means vegetables of some sort."

Another deep breath. "That's what I thought."

He pushes himself from the wall and walks over, collapsing on the sofa by my feet.

"So you don't know anything. About before?"

"Before this?" I ask, spreading my hands. "Not really. What's it matter? It's the past. I'm here now, I have a job to do, and there isn't anything else to think about."

He shakes his head. His hand is close to my calf, but I don't move my legs. I like the closeness. Especially since he's finally realized he doesn't get to control the situation in here. There's a lost look to his eyes; a single lock of hair has slipped out from his bun.

"Don't you ever wonder, though? Who they were. Why they . . . why they gave you up?"

"No." I know this should probably be touching, somehow. Like he's trying to get to know me. Maybe I should be defensive or annoyed. But I really, honestly don't care. I'm here. Now. Focusing on the past has never helped me. I have more than enough on my plate as it is without working in some Long-Lost-Mommy Issues. "Why do you even care?"

He opens his mouth to speak but can't. Clearly contractual.

"I just do. I feel responsible."

This is getting old. I mean, sure, it's endearing that he's trying or whatever, but I've had enough doomsaying for one day.

"You aren't. I'm a big girl. And you're a big boy. If you want to help, you can tell me what you think about this."

I pull out the ticket from earlier and hold it up to him. He takes it.

"Where'd you find this?" he asks, examining both sides.

"Some rando's house in Winter. Power it up. It's a trip."

He does—I feel the small flux of magic—and his eyes glaze over as the vision takes hold, his body going suddenly rigid. A few seconds later and his body sways, like he was hit by a strong wind, and he blinks a few times to reacclimate.

"You know what this is?" he asks, though it doesn't really sound like a question.

"Some sort of propaganda." I snatch the card from him and put it back in my pocket. "Which makes no sense since it's coming from Mab's show."

"My show," he responds, almost on reflex. "She gave it to me, after . . . after she was done being ringmaster."

"Okay, touchy." He really does sound upset about the statement, though I can't figure out why. Though it does sort of explain why everything behind the scenes was OCD-neat. Kingston seems like he's one of those carefully curated types, even when he's trying to look like a bad boy. "So what can you tell me about it? You're the witch here—you should know this magic better than me."

He shakes his head. "Faerie magic. You know it's a different arena. Besides, I don't know what it's trying to show. And I don't know how they got ahold of those tickets or why they're using them." He seems disturbed by it, his voice trailing off into a question.

"Well, I mean, it's not like it would be too hard to steal stock from the Cirque—they could just hijack the cargo before it gets to you. The question is why."

"No, they can't." He sighs and looks at the floor. "We haven't used those tickets since . . . in years."

The stutters in speech are getting annoying—I can't tell if he's leaving things out because he wants to or because he contractually has to.

"How many years?" I ask.

"Twenty-seven." He doesn't even pause to do the math.

"So someone's been holding on to these for a while."

"Someone's been waiting."

He looks at me again, and this time there's something scared in his expression.

"Please, Claire. If you only listen to one thing I tell you, please. Stop looking. Let someone else do this. It can't end well for you."

That old bullshit again.

"Not an option. Mab put me on the job, but you're welcome to try and bargain with her—gods know this isn't something I'm excited about. But there are other things I do enjoy, so, if there's nothing else you can tell me tonight, you either need to leave or start taking off your clothes."

He looks at me, and once more I'm delighted to see that shocked little expression on his face.

"Are you serious?" he asks.

"Don't expect me to cook you breakfast or anything. Apparently I only do that for captives."

"What?"

"Never mind. Are we doing this or what?"

It's not the most romantic line I've used but there's only so much BS I can take for one evening. And I've definitely hit my limit. The last thing I needed tonight was more to think about—he's here to help me forget. I have no doubt he'll be good at that sort of thing.

"I thought my charms weren't working on you." he says. The grin creeps back.

"They didn't. But I need something to get through the night and you're the best I've got."

"Wow. That's . . . easily the most insulting line someone's used on me." As expected, though, the grin doesn't slip. He and I are cut from a similar cloth, I can tell. We're not interested in the small talk or the romance. We're both hunters. It's about the kill. Sometimes it takes a bit of stalking, and sometimes, like right now, you go straight for the throat.

"And I'm sure you have a long list." I smile and stand up, sliding out of my jacket and throwing it at his feet. Then I step over and straddle him, resting my hands on the sofa's back. He looks up at me with the same intrigue as the day we met, when I thought he was trying to put the moves on me. Only now, he actually is. "So then, magic boy. Let's see what else you can do with your hands."

He chuckles and I press my lips to his. He doesn't try to answer.

*

Kingston's definitely one of those guys you don't kick out of bed right away. Even though that's usually my tactic, the words *you should leave* never crossed my lips when our breathing settled and the night crept in. I slept like a baby. I didn't even push him away when he tried to cuddle me.

Though I won't admit to it feeling nice.

Once more, I'm the first awake. I watch him for a while, his tattoo twined on his chest, both him and the serpent resting soundly. The sex was good. Very good. And if I didn't have a strict one-ride-only rule for situations like this, I'd probably try to keep him around for a few more hours.

Trouble is, he works for Mab. Which sort of makes him family. And that's just not my bag.

Also, there's work to do. Lots of it. I roll over and slide out of bed, not even bothering to put on clothes. For one thing, the dude's already seen me naked. For another, I'm hoping it drives him wild—especially since he doesn't get to play again. Boys always want what they can't have.

I head to the kitchen, flipping on every fireplace along the way. The place warms instantly, and I set about making coffee and wondering if maybe I could head back into the mortal world to pick something up to go, quick-like, before he wakes up. Then I realize what I'm thinking and shove it down. He can deal with my shitty coffee. I'm not here to try to impress him.

He comes in a few minutes later, sidling up behind me and gently drawing his hands up my back to rest on my shoulders. Despite the heat, goose bumps race across my skin as he kisses the nape of my neck.

"Morning, sunshine," he says. He kisses a little lower, between my shoulder blades. I pour myself the coffee and make a cup for him.

"None of that wooey shit, thanks," I say, turning out of his touch. I hand him the cup. He's not wearing any clothes, either, and the view is pretty spectacular. His tattoo now rests above his hip, drawing attention to the parts of him I'd more felt than seen last night. "That was sex. We're not a couple."

"I'd say." He laughs. "Your bedroom manners are lacking."

"They're overrated."

He gestures to me. "Your back, those tattoos. All wards?"

I sip my coffee. "Among other things. Some glyphs for strength and stamina and that sort of thing. Don't know if they actually work, but they look cool."

"They're hot," he says. "I like a girl with ink."

"Likewise," I reply. He chuckles. Let him fantasize about *that* for a moment. "So be honest. Did you really come here to warn me or did you just want an excuse to sleep with me?"

And just like that, he slips back into serious mode.

"To warn you. The rest was an unexpected surprise." He sighs. "I wish there was a way to tell you."

"Try harder?" I lean against the cold counter, ignoring the chill on my bare skin.

"I'm trying, Viv, I really am." He takes a sip of coffee.

Suddenly I feel like I'm standing on an ice floe a thousand miles away.

"What did you just call me?"

My entire body has gone cold, and it has nothing to do with being naked. The name's sparked something inside of me, igniting fuses that shouldn't be lit. My heart is a hammer trying to sledge through the ice of my chest. It's not like I'm upset he called me by another girl's name.

Something about *that* name feels like dynamite.

"Claire," he says. He raises an eyebrow, and if I hadn't been looking for a clue, I would have missed the slight widening of his eyes, the half catch of breath that tells me he knows he was caught. "What did you think I said?"

"You should leave."

I set my coffee on the counter and storm past him, heading straight for the door.

"I'm not even dressed," he begins.

"You're a witch. You'll think of something." I open the door and hold it for him. I don't look at him as he walks closer.

"I'm sorry, it was a slip."

"Out." He walks to the door and stands within the doorway, not yet crossing over the threshold.

"I'm sorry," he says again. He honestly sounds like he means it. I don't respond. He puts his hand on the door. "I knew . . ." He pauses, swallows. "She's not dead, you know. Your mother. Not really. Mab hasn't told you everything. That's why I came. Because of her. Your mother. And what Mab will never say."

Then he leaves. The last thing I see before slamming the door is his perfect bare ass and that damn tattoo.

When the door locks and I slide down to a crouch, all I can do is rock, trying to figure out why it feels like there's a hole in my chest where my heart used to be.

Ten

The moment Kingston's gone, I head to the bathroom and soak in the tub until my thoughts bleed out and my skin prunes. For some reason, I feel terribly unclean, and it isn't the sex. Something in Kingston's final words set my life on edge, like he'd just shown me that the end of the world wasn't quite as far away as I thought, and that there was something waiting for me on the other side. Something that knew me inside and out. Ironic that one of the last times I soaked in here, Pan told me to be wary of the magician. I guess I hadn't realized the extent of that truth.

Viv.

Something in that name is a lightning bolt straight to my heart. I swear I've never heard it before, so why does it make me want to scream? I need to get out of here. Away from Mab and Kingston and faeries. And I need to talk to Roxie and figure out why her contract was bound with the same magic as Henry's.

Finally, I force myself from the bath and change into something not smeared with blood or ash. I really need to do laundry, because my options in that department are running out. As I stare in the mirror and put on eyeliner, I pause and wonder what the hell I'm doing, trying to make myself look nice before seeing Roxie. My hand shakes and I take a deep breath, unable to tell if the nerves are from seeing her or everything Kingston seemed to unleash. Not that it matters, really—the effect is the same.

In truth, I don't want to admit why I'm checking in on her. I know Pan has it under control. I know I should be talking to Mab about the ticket. I know I should grab Eli before tracking down the next hit. But no matter what I do, no matter how many types of meditation or focusing I practice, I can't get my thoughts straight. I can't get my breathing to slow or my chest to relax. My world is spinning, spinning, and the last thing I want to do is deal with anyone or anything else of a magical nature.

Because right now, I no longer feel like some badass magical assassin. I feel like a lost little girl dropped in a terrifying world, and I have no idea why.

*

Even though I could teleport straight into Roxie's living room, I'm not in the mood to be an unwanted surprise—there have already been enough of them in *my* life for today—and I want to check with Pan to ensure no one's been trying to get in. When I arrive in the hallway leading to Roxie's apartment, I realize I'm not the only person who's been intent on seeing her.

The white wall around her door looks like it has been through a war. There are burn marks and divots, long gashes and even charcoal marks that look like graffiti. And scattered like entrails are piles of dead grass and twigs. It's barely been twenty-four hours. How many unwanted visitors has Roxie had?

Jesus.

I hurry over and kneel before Pan, who looks just as bad as the wall—he's covered in soot and hairline fractures, but he's still whole.

There's a particularly nasty rune drawn on his forehead in charcoal, one I know I can't just wipe off. It's paralyzing to him, but thankfully whoever drew it didn't make it past the door. I pull out my chalk and draw another symbol over the top of the black rune, one to negate the magic. He collapses the moment the sigil's complete.

"Oh, Claire, thank the gods," he says, gasping. One tiny hand goes to his chest as he sits there, leaning against the wall and catching his breath. "That last bastard trapped me before I could do anything. Turned me back into stone . . . The nerve!"

"Did anyone get in?" I ask. I know it's a little callous not to ask how he is, but Roxie's the main directive here.

He shakes his head. "She hasn't left, either."

"Who were they, Pan?"

"All disguised," he says. "Some Constructs, some Shifters. Only a few Fey, but they were so wrapped up in glamour I couldn't tell you what they truly looked like."

Well, if there were Constructs—magically animated and glamoured twig effigies—that would explain the foliage all over the place.

"Did they say anything?"

"No." He looks at his hands. "They would just fire a few spells or try to knock down the door and then vanish. Maybe ten seconds each. I barely had time to get a hit in before they were gone. I failed."

"You didn't fail. You kept them out—that's all we wanted."

"But I haven't learned who sent them."

I pat him on the shoulder, which feels like smacking a balustrade.

"Don't be too hard on yourself. Besides, your job's not over yet. I need you in top form."

"I'll try, Claire. I'll try."

I push myself to standing and open the door, my tattoos going hot as the magic works through me.

Roxie's waiting there with my dagger in her hands.

In that moment, she's not the scared or tired girl from before. She's in black jeans and a skull-print T-shirt, and her hair looks a little frazzled, but still immaculate. Her stance softens when she realizes it's me, but she doesn't drop her guard or the knife. Good for her. She might actually make it out of this alive.

"How do I know it's you?" she asks. "And not one of those shape-shifter things?"

She must have been watching some of the action through the peephole.

"Because no shape-shifter can pull off this shit," I say, gesturing up and down. I grin. "Trust me, they've tried and failed numerous times."

She lowers the knife a little bit. I step through and let the door lock behind me.

"You sound like her."

"I *am* her." I drop the grin—this is quickly growing old. "And by that I mean Claire, the sexy vixen who saved your ass from a crew of asshole faeries. Why else do you think Pan would have let me through?"

"Maybe you killed him."

I roll my eyes and step over to the door, opening it just enough to show her that Pan is, in fact, still alive. He looks back, startled at the open door, since that was expressly forbidden. I just wave and then shut it in his face before I have to explain myself.

"See? Still living, or existing, or whatever it is he does. In any case, it's definitely me." I walk over and collapse on her sofa, spreading out my arms and making myself at home. Really comfy cushions. Very clearly new. There aren't even any wine stains.

"Why are you here?" she asks. Still a little tentative. When she sits on the pouf across from me, I'm kind of proud to notice she's still holding the knife.

"Can't a girl pay a social visit?"

"Um . . ."

"To be honest, I shouldn't be here. I should be out working. But . . ." I shake my head. I don't like to make those vague dangling statements, but I really don't know what to say here. *I slept with a guy who called me the wrong name and it made me feel like vomiting? I have no clue what's going on and no time to fix it? I think you might actually be a suspect? I often think my mother and boss is holding something big back from me?* "I don't know. I guess I just wanted to talk."

"You? Just wanting to talk?" She laughs, and that makes me smile. Because yeah, she understands me. "I find that hard to believe."

"It's been a long twenty-four hours," I admit.

"Tell me about it," she says. "It consistently sounds like a war zone out there. I don't think I got any sleep last night."

"Sorry about that."

"How has no one called the cops? I mean, I hear my neighbors walk past and they haven't said anything."

"Enchantments. And, well, most mortals are bad at noticing anything magical. It's like a survival mechanism for them."

"And I was just unlucky enough to be born without that mechanism."

"Apparently," I say with a smile. "But that means you can see me."

Her return smile is genuine, with the hint of something else within it.

"Well, thank goodness for that, then."

My chest feels warm, and suddenly the shit from this morning and the night before seems to fade away.

"How are you doing, Roxie?" I ask.

I learned long ago that the key to seduction is saying your target's name. But in this case, I'm not trying to seduce. I'm trying to connect.

Wait, what? What's gotten into you?

"I'm bored," she replies with a shrug. She leans in closer, almost conspiratorially, and I find I want her to shuffle over, sit on the sofa beside me. I'm here with her alone and there's no one to ruin the mood.

Trouble is, I have no idea what the mood in here *is*. "Do you know how many times I've cleaned this place? I hate knowing you're out there risking your life and I'm just sitting here dusting the blinds."

"You dusted the blinds?"

"Twice." She chuckles. "I'm sorry, I'm not really used to playing hostess. Can I get you something? Coffee?"

"I'd kill for some."

She stands and heads to the kitchen. I sit there for a while, watching her go, her hips swaying and head held high. She doesn't look like a captive within her own apartment. She still looks like the queen onstage.

As I watch, though, a thousand different questions stampede through my head. *Why am I not trying to sleep with her? Why do I feel protective? Why can't I just outright ask her about Henry—why do I feel I have to soften the words?* Now that I'm here, I realize it's not for utilitarian reasons: I'm here because I want to be. I want to spend time with someone doing something other than working or killing or fucking. I want to feel what it's like to actually be human. And Roxie, for some strange reason, seems like someone I could experience that with.

I shake my head and stand, following her into the kitchen.

"So what have you found out?" she asks. She's using one of those fancy glass pour-over things I've seen in cafés but have been too appalled by to try. Somehow, she makes it look unpretentious.

"Not much." It's easier to talk business than emotions. Even though I came here to ignore the former, it's the only thing keeping me from getting swept up by the latter. Time to see what she knows. "The last guy we got was a witch. Some modern dancer in Chicago."

She sets the water kettle on the counter, hard. She doesn't move again.

"Roxie?"

In the movies, this would be the point when I put a hand on her shoulder. But I've seen the way she wields a knife.

"What was his name?" she asks slowly.

"Henry. Real dangerous-sounding name, I know. Maybe it was a cover."

"No." She turns to me. Her expression is a strange mix of blank and confused, like there are questions bubbling way below the surface. "That was his name. He never took a stage name. Henry Lewis."

I raise an eyebrow. Well then, so much for the tiny chance it was coincidence.

"You know him?"

"I lived with him."

She shakes her head and pours the coffee into two mugs—each in the shape of an animal, about the only cutesy thing in this place—and hands one to me.

"You lived together?" I ask. That's a little too . . . convenient. Despite everything, my guard immediately rises. So much for her being "just caught up in this."

She doesn't answer at first. Instead, she takes her mug back into the living room and sits. She doesn't make eye contact, and it's not until I sit across from her and wait thirty seconds that she speaks up.

"Remember that apartment I told you about? When I was living with all those artists?"

I nod, the coffee forgotten in my hands. It's suddenly the least of my interests, which is saying something. It smells heavenly. "I remember."

"He was one of them."

"So, wait, how did you connect those dots? I mean, did you know he was a witch?"

"We knew he was different. He . . . knew things, sometimes. Like when the weather would change or one of us would get a gig. Things like that. And there was something about him that was more . . . I don't know, polished, I guess. He never seemed to be struggling like the rest of us, and it definitely made us wonder why he was choosing to live that way."

"This can't be a coincidence. Did you ever know someone named Frank? Barista in New York?"

She shakes her head. "Not that I can think of."

"I need you to tell me everything you know about Henry and the rest of your roommates. Where they went, what they do now. Do you still keep in touch? Did anything strange happen before you left?"

"What do you mean *strange*?" She, too, has forgotten about the coffee in her kitten mug.

I don't want to tell her about the similar contracts yet. I want to know what she knows, without me planting ideas.

"I mean, at least two of the four of you are working for the Fey, who are connected to a buyer we still haven't been able to trace. It's too much for random coincidence. Especially since you, at least, weren't snared until months later."

She stares into her mug for a long while. I take the first sip. So much better than coffee in Faerie.

"There was something," she says, like she's recalling it from a haze.

"Yeah?"

"The night before we moved out . . . we had a final dinner. Just the four of us. It was pretty normal—we were all sitting on the floor having pizza and wine. Everything else was packed and the place was empty. Henry had some candles going. It was really cute, you know? We were all a bit drunk at the very end, and the next day I honestly thought I'd just dreamed it."

"Dreamed what?"

"Well, Henry got all somber all of a sudden and took out a little X-Acto knife from his pocket. Then he picks up his glass—it was so silly, just one of those red plastic cups—and says we need to toast to each other, to lives of service to a greater god. The muse herself. And we all laughed and raised our glasses, but he didn't drink. Instead, he cut a line on his palm and dripped the blood into the glass. Then he handed them both over to me. I don't know what made me do it. Maybe the wine or maybe something else. I couldn't stop giggling. I cut my hand and poured in some blood and handed it over, and then when we'd all bled into the cup, he raised it high and said we were drinking to a brighter tomorrow, or something like that. We each took a sip."

"And you didn't think that was strange? Or, you know, worth bringing up earlier?"

"I didn't think it really happened. The next morning I woke up hungover, but there wasn't a cut on my hand and no one else mentioned anything about it. We went our separate ways. I haven't heard from any of them since. Honestly I figured they'd all just gotten office jobs somewhere and fallen off my radar. Henry was the only one I kept up with, but only because he was always a bit of a pompous dick and kept sending me fliers for his shows."

"I'm going to need names," I say.

"You think the others are involved?"

"I think it's as good a lead as any. Have you ever talked to Henry about the pact? About what he meant?"

"No. I would have felt stupid bringing it up." She looks at her palm, which is smooth and dark and trembling. "I mean, there wasn't any physical evidence. As for the rest . . . I don't even know where they live anymore."

"Don't worry about that." I pull a pen and paper from my pocket and hand them over. "Their names, please. Full names, spelled as correctly as possible, along with any details about personality or physical appearance."

She looks from me to the paper and back again. Then she takes the pen and starts writing.

My heart's pumping fast in my chest. I don't know if it's from the thrill of the chase, or because it feels like she and I are in this one together.

Eleven

I leave the apartment the way I came, pausing beside Pan in the front hall.

"Don't let her leave," I say.

"Did you learn anything?" he asks.

"I think so. I'm about to find out." I look at the wall covered in soot and attack marks. "I feel bad leaving you here. Do you need anything?"

"I will be fine."

"And you can hold them off for a little longer?"

He shrugs. "I shall do what I can, for as long as I can. That is all I can promise."

"I suppose that will have to work." I drop my voice then, and lean in closer to whisper in his ear. "Has anyone shown up besides the attackers?" I know it's paranoid, but I wasn't trained to suspect everyone for nothing.

Pan shakes his head. "Not a soul."

"And you've heard nothing inside?"

I can't imagine anyone getting past our wards, but that doesn't mean there aren't other forms of communication.

Another head shake.

"Okay. Well, stay on your guard. I think we're closing in on our guy."

"Be careful," he says.

I stand and walk down the hall and into the fire escape stairwell near the back.

Once safely inside, I grab a marker from my pocket—I feel like a kindergartner some days, what with all these art implements hidden in various places—and start scribbling a few marks on my palm. It's a much simpler version of the summoning circle I'd used to conjure Eli earlier. When I'm done, I put the marker back and exchange it for a pen. Not for drawing, though.

I jam the sharp pen tip into my palm and wince at the surge of power and pain as the black markings burn orange against my flesh. A few seconds later, the light fades into nothing, taking the ink markings and the power surge with it.

"You rang?"

Eli lounges against the wall behind me, posed like he's waiting for a photo shoot, with one foot on the wall and his hands in his pockets. At least he still has his shirt on. It wouldn't be the first time he's pulled that right before we went to battle. Though those were, admittedly, fun fights to celebrate afterward.

"We've got a lead," I say. I show him the paper. "Time to roll."

He plucks the paper from my hands and reads the names.

"The girl gave you this?" he asks.

I nod. "Apparently she knew the dancer witch. They lived together."

"And these two are . . . ?"

"Her other roommates. They all did some sort of drunken pact before they parted ways, pledging themselves to service."

"Mortals," Eli mutters, handing the paper back. "Always losing their wits once alcohol is involved."

"You're just jealous that it doesn't work on you." I grab some chalk and begin sketching out the portal, suddenly wishing I had a little more magic running through my veins. It would be nice to be able to just teleport with a thought. Or maybe I just need to invest in the chalk industry.

"How's she doing, anyway?" he asks.

This makes me pause.

"Cabin fever. But otherwise okay. Why?"

He doesn't respond, which just makes me turn my head and stare at him.

"Why, Eli? You don't take interest in mortals. Even ones embroiled in magic."

His grin is answer enough.

"She looks tasty."

"No."

I turn back and continue the portal.

"What do you mean, *no?*" he asks.

"I mean precisely that. You can't have her."

"Why? You know she can't remember you when this is said and done."

My hand pauses halfway through an Aztec pictograph of a serpent.

"She'll have to forget," he continues, stepping closer. "You know the rules about bringing mortals into Faerie. It has to be a big dream. You two won't ever be friends. Or lovers. Or whatever it is you think you could be."

It takes a lot of self-control not to turn and throttle him right there. Trouble is, he has a point. Rather than react, I take a deep breath and keep going.

"I don't care," I say coldly. Clearly I *do* care, and there's no use even trying to hide it from him, but I put on the airs anyway. "I still don't want you killing her. Not after all she's been through."

"It might be the greatest mercy," he says. I feel him crouch down beside me, our skin almost touching. "After all, memory magic is a tricky business. Sometimes it works. Sometimes it leaves the person addled and talking to furniture. Is it really a chance you want to take? I promise I'd make it short and sweet. She could even enjoy it, you know. I've gotten very good at what I do."

I turn around and shove him on his ass.

"I will send you back to whence you came if you so much as lay a finger on her," I say through clenched teeth.

"That would break our contract," he says, far too calmly. He's enjoying this a great deal. "And you know what happens when contracts break."

I do know. Eli goes free to wreak havoc on mankind, and he'd probably take Roxie's soul just to spite me. He may be playing all nice and fun now, but that's the bindings of his contract talking. There are reasons he's kept in the lower astral planes. The good guys won't touch him with a ten-foot astral pole.

"We aren't discussing this. And you are not allowed to question. Roxie will not be taken by you."

"What? Are you planning on making conjugal visits? Maybe glamouring yourself every time so she never knows it's you? I can't tell if that's creepy or romantic."

I want to kill him. I want to focus all of my rage and punch a hole through his smarmy chest. But it wouldn't do any good, and besides, he's right. Once this is over and she's no longer useful—I can't even pretend it will be once she's *safe*—I'll have to let her go. Let some witch come in and mess with her brain so she doesn't remember anything about Faerie or me or any of this. She'll probably even forget she wanted to be a singer. She'll stop dreaming. Another lost cause.

I hate to admit that Eli's offer might actually be a better way out. At least then she'd die knowing the truth about the world and herself.

"We'll cross that bridge when we get to it. *If* we get to it. If we fuck this up, we'll all be dead anyway."

"Speak for yourself."

But he doesn't push the subject. He can't, now that I've forbidden it. I complete the portal and stand back.

"Where are we going?" he asks as he stands. There's absolutely zero hint of malice or perverted joy; he's all business.

"To wherever this name leads." I wish I could emulate his calm, but my chest is heaving with anger. I hadn't even thought about having to erase Roxie's memory. I'd been so caught up in everything else, I'd just let myself believe . . . *This is what happens when emotions get involved, Claire. You ignore the glaring details. You fuck shit up and someone else pays the price.*

Eli steps toward the portal and examines the name, looking at my work with barely concealed admiration.

Sure, some names are so common they're practically useless. But the more you know about the person—like, their favorite color or food, their profession, even what they got their grandma as a birthday present—the easier it is to track them down with magic. And Roxie gave me a veritable treasure trove of information regarding our two suspects. Girl number one, Heather, liked knitting and making meatloaf. When she wasn't out getting wrecked at shitty nightclubs. Apparently she had a hard time holding a job, but when she did, it was in theatre—sometimes working behind the scenes, but always dreaming of taking the spotlight. That's more than enough to track her down wherever she's hiding, even if I don't know her true name. That's usually something I can only sense out in person.

"Well then, let's be off," he says. Now he's holding a cane. "Before I get too hungry to function."

*

The portal leads us to a small farmhouse in the middle of nowhere. And I do mean the middle of nowhere. There's nothing around us save for overrun fields and tangled trees. The sky is a dreary, overcast grey, and it feels like it's about to start pissing at any moment. As for the house, it has definitely seen better days—the pale blue paint is curling off like scabs, and at least three of the windows on one side are punched out.

I look up at the aged monstrosity and finger my detection ring. It doesn't change temp, so there aren't any enchantments waiting dormant inside. I don't feel anything else in there, either—no active magic, no Dream, no life. This place has been abandoned for a while.

"I don't trust your magic," Eli says flatly.

"Right now, neither do I." *What gives?*

"Are you sure this is the right place?" he asks.

"Not anymore. But these are the coordinates." I pull out the pocket watch from William and open it up. The gold and silver arms point out to opposite sides. The small arm is spinning wildly. Wherever we are, we're far from any unclaimed Dream. And yet . . . "Nothing," I say. "But there's no way the name would have led to a dead end. All names lead to someone. Period."

He sighs, but he doesn't say anything else. Instead he walks across the groaning front porch and kicks down the door.

"Way to make an entrance," I mutter as I follow behind him.

"What? There's no one home."

There's no use arguing with him when we both know he's right. This house is five creaks away from becoming a pile of splinters. I'm honestly amazed it doesn't collapse on us as we wander in.

The house holds no signs of life. I mean, no signs of human life. There are cobwebs and the whole place smells of must and animal shit. I try not to look too closely where I step. I don't want to know.

Eli taps his cane on the ground, and the handle immediately illuminates, bright and white.

"Handy," I say.

He just shrugs. "I don't need it, but I thought you might."

"I don't know if I'm charmed or insulted." The glyphs on my skin make the light unnecessary, and he knows it. He just wants to be a dick.

"Both. Always be both." He casts me a grin over his shoulder—I don't think a normal human's neck should be able to twist that far—and continues in.

Only a few pieces of history remain, and they're haphazard at best. A dining room table with no chairs. A few pots hanging from hooks in the kitchen, their interiors home to abandoned bird nests. A pile of old books in the living room. Nothing to denote that anyone's set foot in here—let alone lived here—for a decade or so.

"How positive are you that the girl isn't just toying with you?" Eli asks.

"Damn sure," I snap. Roxie wouldn't do that. But then I take a deep breath because honestly, I *don't* know if Roxie would do that. She's still a stranger, even if I don't want her to be. "Though I'm growing less sure by the second. But what would she have to gain? Even if she *did* lie, there's no reason the portal would have led us here. It would have just been a dud. So she was telling some sort of truth."

"Interesting," Eli says. His voice sounds like he finds it anything but as he makes his way around the lower level. The only other things moving are the mice scurrying to get out of his light.

"Do you sense that?" Eli asks. He pauses at the foot of the stairs.

"Sense what?"

He's a veritable bloodhound for feeling anything supernatural, which is partly why I keep him around. He even picks up things my charms would miss.

"We're in a crossroads."

"How many lines?" I ask.

He bites the inside of his lip, the only outward sign that he's concentrating.

"Five."

"Jesus."

A crossroads is where two ley lines overlap, like where I summoned Eli. But there are places where more might cross, and with every crossing, the nexus becomes more powerful. And the more powerful the nexus, the thinner the veil between worlds and the stronger the magic you can wield.

"I'm surprised you can't feel it," he says, looking to me. "I honestly think if you stepped in the wrong spot you'd go right into Faerie."

"Maybe she did."

"Potentially. Though I think we would have just teleported there instead."

He has a point. This makes zero sense, and it's starting to set my nerves on edge. The name led us here. Names always lead to a person. And yet there is no one here. He heads up the stairs, and I follow close behind, his light making our shadows dance like demons on the wall.

There are only a few rooms at the top: some bedrooms, judging from the abandoned bed frames and wardrobes in two of them; an old bathroom with way too many spiders in the bathtub for my liking; and, in the third room, the reason we were brought here.

A body.

At least, I think it's a body. It's lying prone on the floor beside a fairly elaborate altar, a ring of blood circling both. I can't tell the sex at first, as it's on its stomach and covered in robes. Eli goes over to it and stares down at the blood circle.

"A few weeks old," he says, touching the ring with his toe. "Shoddy craftsmanship. Yours are much better."

"Thanks," I say. "Still live?" I'm not talking about the body, which is clearly not alive. I'm talking about the magic laced through the room like a snare. How did we not sense it from outside? It must be from the nexus.

He shakes his head. "The power's gone." Then, to prove his point, he steps over the line and nudges the body. It makes an oddly hollow noise. "For fuck's sake," he whispers, and kicks it over.

Not a body after all. It's a mannequin.

"Seriously?" I ask.

"Someone knew we'd be looking for them," he mutters.

I walk over and kneel beside the plastic body. The blue eyes are wide, and runes are scratched into the irises. From forehead down, the thing is covered in wards and words and sigils, many of which I've not seen before. Which is saying something. I trace a few of them I recognize. Symbols of misdirection mostly. And a few that I've only seen on the golems haunting the Winter wilds or in William's workshop.

"Why go to all this trouble, though?" I ask.

He kneels beside me and examines the mannequin. And by that, I mean he rips off all the clothing very unceremoniously and makes a lot of grumbling noises.

"Because," he says finally, "she gave this thing her name."

"What?"

He shrugs and looks back down to the dummy. "These markings here, across the heart? They're for transference. She transferred her name to this doll. And gave up a fair amount of her soul to do it, too."

"Why, though? I didn't even realize that was possible."

"It shouldn't be. Not for a human." He points to more of the symbols, those scratched into the plastic and filled with congealed blood. "No mortal should know these words, let alone use them without losing their mind. Whoever this girl was, she was friends with greater powers. This . . . this *thing*, it *is* Heather now. Which means the girl we're looking for—the girl who knits and gets drunk on Tuesdays—is still out there, and she's no longer herself."

I glance around at the room. Everything derelict, everything covered in dust. We are out in the middle of nowhere, and there's no reason anyone would have just been hanging out here, trying to transfer a name.

"She knew we'd be coming for her," I say.

"Or that someone would. With this much magical knowledge, there's no telling what sort of trouble this girl got herself into. This sort of learning doesn't come cheap. And woe betide anyone who tries to steal it."

I shake my head. "So can we reverse it?" I ask, looking back to the mannequin. I can't make heads nor tails of most of it, but maybe Eli can. He's been around a lot longer. "You know, give the name back to the original holder?"

"I don't think so," he says. "I mean, maybe if I'd been watching what she did, heard what she said. But even then, that's only a maybe. This was a powerful blood pact. Those are tricky to undo."

"Can't you at least try?"

He gives me a look, one that clearly tells me he already *is* trying, thank you, and if I could please shut up it would be most appreciated. I roll my eyes and walk away toward the window.

This just doesn't make sense. I was supposedly flying under the radar. If this girl took all this time and effort to divert us, she was definitely neck-deep in this, and she definitely knew I was coming. Which means her buyer must have known as well. But how did she know? Did she have some sort of gift of prophecy? Or did someone else tip her off? The only person who might have done that was Roxie, and she's in quarantine. No magic can get in or out of her room—it was part of the ward. And I enchanted every form of communication she has. She hasn't accepted or sent out a call, hasn't sent any e-mails or tweets or whatever. She's been silent.

I want to say that I trust her, that I believe she hasn't spoken to these people in years. But trust is hard to come by in Faerie. It's usually only gained with a contract. And as much as I want to pretend I can trust and care about her, Roxie's still a free agent.

"I think . . ." Eli says from behind me. I look away from the rolling woods and roiling clouds to watch him as he pores over the mannequin, thin trails of blue light spiraling down from his fingers as he works. "Yes, I think I might . . ."

Then something goes wrong. So wrong even *I* can feel it, and I'm not involved with whatever it is he's doing.

"Shit," he mutters.

Around us, magic slams into place like a barricade.

"What do you mean, *shit*?" I yell.

The walls glow with hundreds of thousands of runes and glyphs. All geared at one thing: containment. And like the symbols on the mannequin, most of them are unfamiliar—I've only seen a small percentage of them before.

"How are these here?" I ask. "I checked. *You* checked!"

"Apparently they were part of the effigy." He stands smoothly, as though we haven't just been magically locked into a room in the middle of nowhere. I don't panic—I've definitely been in worse spots—but the inconvenience of this is annoying. "And tinkering with that caused them to trigger."

"Ugh."

I start walking the perimeter, twisting various rings for magical insight, keen senses, that sort of thing. Everything in my arsenal that would potentially help reverse whatever the hell we just got ourselves into. I smash the window with a fist—the glass shatters out, then implodes back in and reconstructs itself, almost shearing off my arm in the process. The door doesn't budge from a well-placed kick that could decapitate a rhino. And I know, from the way the runes shift over the floor and walls, that no portals are going to work in here, either to enter or escape.

"So now we're trapped in here," I say. "To starve or whatever. I'm assuming even your personal portals are useless?"

He purses his lips and looks at the wall for a long while.

"It would appear so, yes. I am bound to this plane. How annoying."

"So how do we break it?"

"You don't."

The voice doesn't come from Eli. It comes from the mannequin.

I pause and turn as goose bumps race up and down my spine. For the longest time, I've been creeped out by anything modeled after humans. Dolls, mannequins, whatever. The fact that Mab had a small army of demented dolls she set on me when I'd wandered down the wrong corridor in the castle hadn't helped any. Their tiny glass eyes all staring, limbs locked out in an eternal inviting embrace . . . ugh.

The mannequin is worse.

Eli steps away as cracks fissure their way across the mannequin's static joints, pale blue light streaming out, the same color as the runes warding the walls.

"Looks like that wasn't the right spell," Eli mutters to himself.

The thing shakily tries to force itself upright, shards of plastic breaking off with every clunky movement. Its body is crisscrossed with cracks and runes, and as it stands, it appears to be held together by magic alone. Perhaps even worse, the eyes don't glow or give off any semblance of life. They're just as dead as the rest of it.

"Your search comes to an end, assassin," comes the voice once more—masculine, middle-aged probably. Smooth. No true twang or accent. "You have already killed one client, and captured another. You will impede my efforts no longer."

If the fact that the voice is coming from an enchanted mannequin isn't enough of a clue, the use of the phrase *impede my efforts* is a dead giveaway that we're dealing with a faerie. And, unless I'm way off base, I'm willing to bet it's the same one who roped Roxie into her contract.

"It's you," I say. "You're the one behind all this."

"In the flesh," the mannequin says from its unmoving lips. "In a manner of speaking."

My hand's already in my pocket, clutching a knife and brushing against the ticket I nabbed in Faerie. I quickly compare the magic in the ticket to the magic in the mannequin—they're not even close to the same.

"Who are you?" I ask.

The only answer is laughter. "Come now, Claire. You don't think I'm so stupid as to give you my name. Though you will be dead long before you can use it against me." The mannequin is staggering toward me now, a slow, skin-crawling shuffle.

"Why are you doing this?"

"Freedom," the mannequin replies. "Freedom from the constraints of Summer and Winter. Freedom to live and rule in both Faerie and Mortal. When the Pale Queen rises, she will lead us into a new age."

"Yeah, well, your Pale Queen can suck it."

In one smooth motion I pull out a knife—it is heavy and thick, and most of that heft is from the enchantments wrapped deep inside it—and flick it toward the mannequin. It embeds itself right in the mannequin's chest, a small flash of white light exploding when the enchantments unfurl, but that's it. The thing doesn't slow or stagger or look down. The only way I know it even registered the attack is the laughter issuing from its hollow lips.

"Eli . . ." I say, not tearing my eyes from the thing. "I've seen that dagger bring down full-fledged dragons." Okay, maybe now the panic is starting to bleed in.

"What would you have me do?" he asks. "It doesn't appear dangerous."

"But it also doesn't die. Do you want to be stuck in here for an eternity with it?"

"Remove its limbs and bind its lips, and at least we won't have to worry about it breaking free."

The thing hears this. Or the asshole controlling it hears it. Because at that moment the hands shatter, the plastic rearranging itself into long, wicked blades. Runes swirl through the plastic, runes I know all too well—those are symbols to rend flesh and armor, to bring a slow and painful death. Even the slightest prick and the spell will transfer to the victim. This thing isn't playing around, and the constant laughter makes it seem even more deranged.

"Oh, well then," Eli says, "you'll have to unbind me."

"You know I can't do that." We back up against the wall. The thing is moving so slow it's almost laughable. If it weren't also a surefire way to die.

"It's the only way to kill this thing. My powers are lacking otherwise."

I glance to him. "Did you trigger the thing just so I'd do this for you?"

He actually chuckles as the mannequin swipes at him. He ducks easily. "Please. If I wanted you dead, I'd have done it a long time ago. You think you're the only one who summons me? I won't kill you. I swear."

"Your promises mean nothing when the binding's gone."

"So you'll have to trust me. You still owe me a meal, remember?"

I look to the mannequin, which is still laughing and staggering toward us, the blades on its hands growing longer by the second. I'm not an idiot. I've already mentally gone through a thousand different ways to destroy or at least dismember the thing, but I know enough of the magic running through it to recognize that getting within arm's reach is dangerous, and even if I do, my list of possibilities is slim. It's the magic I don't know running across that thing that scares me, that tells me I'm way out of my league. This thing is bound with the name of a soul. It's immortal as immortal can be. And if my heaviest hitter didn't phase it, I'm out of options.

"Fine," I say. "For the next thirty seconds, I release you from your bonds, Eli."

He chuckles again.

"Thirty seconds is all I need."

I run to the corner and start counting while Eli squares off with the mannequin. He slowly—way too slowly, it seems—removes his glasses and places them in his coat pocket.

"Whoever created you is a genius," he says calmly. "They did a good job with you. A very good job. But I'm afraid you're still nothing compared to me."

Eli's blue eyes blaze bright, filling the room with blinding white and aquamarine light. I close my eyes. I don't open them again. I know better than to look at an astral creature head-on. There are reasons they're confined to other planes; human brains aren't meant to process that much beauty and terror. I clamp my hands over my ears to keep out the noises Eli's true form is making—whispers and promises of terrible things, of flesh melting off bone and souls bound to black holes and a thousand other secrets I'm not supposed to know.

. . . fourteen, fifteen, sixteen . . .

Something slams into the wall beside me. I clamp my mouth shut to keep from screaming, slide down, and huddle against the wall. Wait for him to go back on his flimsy word and rip the soul from my body. *Why did I say thirty seconds? He's probably already banished the thing.*

. . . twenty, twenty-one . . .

The whole house tilts to the side and something sprays over me, something sharp that I'm mostly sure is glass but might be plastic or bone. The light tries to slip through my eyelids, tries to pry them open to reveal the terror of the room beyond. I squeeze my head to my knees and try to block it out.

. . . twenty-five, twenty-six . . .

"You will not defeat her, assassin."

The voice cuts through the screaming and storm, slices through my mind with an unearthly stillness. And I know, somehow, that it's all in my head, that Eli can't hear a thing.

"She will rise. No matter what you do, the Pale Queen will rise. And when she does, she will make even this seem like a dream."

. . . twenty-nine, thirty . . .

Like a flipped light switch, the room goes silent and dark. The space between my ears rings. I don't open my eyes. Not yet.

A hand squeezes my shoulder and I try not to flinch or knock it off.

"Relax," Eli says. "I took care of it."

I open my eyes and blink away the worms squiggling in my retinas. Eli stands beside me, back in his purple suit, his glasses once more covering his eyes. Everything in the room is burned away—no altar, no runes, no mannequin. Just charred walls and the scent of burned wood and small piles of ash in the corners. Eli offers me his hand and I take it. His skin is unreasonably warm.

"I told you I wouldn't kill you," he says, grinning. "You're much more fun to me alive."

"Thanks, I think." I know that grin, and I know he's hoping I'll go all rescued-vixen and fall into his arms with gratitude. Or at least go for a victory romp in the ashes of our enemies, for old times' sake. But Roxie's image flashes through my mind right then, so I step away and ignore the pull between us. "What was it?"

"An advanced Construct," he says. "I've never seen anything like it. I had to drag it through three levels on the astral plane just to bind it, and four more to banish it. It's safely tucked away in hell now. Or a suitable equivalent."

I glance around. My dagger's nowhere to be seen, which blows. That one took a week to enchant, layer by layer.

"Did it hurt the girl?" I ask. "The one who enchanted it?"

"Afraid not. Once she gave over her true name, it became a completely different entity. She'll have felt the magic trigger, I'm sure, but it won't have done any harm to her. There is absolutely zero link between the two. She was smart. Or, whoever told her how to do this was smart."

I sigh and look around. It's not like I can expect to find any clues in here—the place is burned to a crisp, save for the tiny spot of wallpaper where I was huddled. The edges of it curl and smoke.

"Then it looks like we're at a dead end. Whoever this girl is, we don't have a way of getting to her, not if she's given over her name."

"So we move on," he replies. "Name number two."

"I need to head back first. Something tells me we're going to need more firepower. If that was a trap, this next one won't be any better."

"I couldn't agree more." Eli winks. "Though you could always just release me for good."

"Nice try. I'm not that stupid."

"A boy can wish."

I head to the wall and start sketching our escape. If it weren't for Eli, I'd be dead right now. And that's not a debt I like on my shoulders.

"You'll eat well tonight," I say. "I promise."

Inside, I also promise that it won't be Roxie.

Twelve

Mab is waiting for me the moment I'm back in Winter. She's not even being crafty about it—no, she's sitting in my living room with a book open in one hand and a glass of wine in the other. The fire's blazing silently in the hearth and even though the room is warm, her presence makes everything much, much colder.

"Why was he here?" she asks the moment I step into the room.

For a moment, I think she's talking about Eli, who's currently grabbing a drink on my dime and who definitely hasn't been inside the castle. Then she points to the chair in the corner, the one holding Kingston's coat, and I realize Eli's the last person on her mind.

"Conjugal visit," I say, my words deadpan.

She looks at me like she could scream—the purse to her lips, the slight color to her cheeks. For once, though, I'm not pleased by it. I'm more pissed by his visit than she appears to be. Instead of yelling, she takes a sip of wine and tosses the book into the flames. It goes up immediately. I hadn't even gotten a chance to see what the cover was so I'd know what to replace.

"I do not know if I am comfortable with this," she says.

It's the first time Mab's ever made any comment about my sex life. I mean, she's a faerie—I learned everything I know from her and the denizens of this Court. It's not like there are any misplaced notions of purity or love around here. It's also the first time I've heard her say something that isn't an absolute fact. *I do not know if I am comfortable.* What, is she taking lessons in passive-aggressive behavior?

"Why do you care?" I ask. Despite the fact that I was almost overtaken by a mannequin, my urge to talk about what just happened to Eli and me vanishes. I know I should tell her about the ticket, but she already seems pissed.

"Because you cannot trust him," she says, which is funny since she's the one who put him in charge of her main source of Dream. She says it like *the sky is blue* or *mortals die.* Like I'm an idiot to even consider asking. I definitely have no illusions about trusting a man whose sole job in life is misdirection.

"Funny," I reply, plopping down on the sofa. "Because that's the exact same thing he said about you."

"That does not surprise me," she says to her wineglass.

"It's a shame," I continue. "Shouldn't you trust your employees?"

"It is not *I* who can't trust him, but you."

"What is it now?"

She doesn't answer, not right away. Instead, she drinks the rest of the wine and stares at the fire, and I honestly start to think she just won't answer the question, or maybe she hasn't heard it or forgot, both of which are highly unlikely. The only other time I've seen her uncertain was in the storeroom, but that was about something that was actually important to her: the health and wealth of her kingdom. Why is she suddenly giving a shit about me? And why does it actually seem to worry her?

"He has a past that would not agree with you," she finally replies.

"We had sex," I say. "That's it. It wasn't even that good." Okay, the last part is sort of a lie but no matter what, she's still my mother. I'm not going to admit everything.

She raises a hand like she's warding off that mental image. Holy shit, have I actually found a subject that makes her uncomfortable? This Kingston guy must have really done something bad if the very thought of us together makes her pale. Well, more pale than usual.

"Will you see him again?"

"That's none of your business."

"As your mother . . ."

"It's very awkward we're even having this conversation," I say, cutting her off quickly. But something in her wording strikes a chord, something Kingston referenced. *As your mother* . . . She isn't my mother though, is she? She's just a queen who plucked me from my family. "Wait," I add, "is this about before? Before you found me?"

Her usually stony face turns to ice.

"It is, isn't it?" Things click. "Kingston knew my—"

"You will not bring up Kingston or your mother anymore," she interrupts. I don't know if she realizes she's just confirmed that Kingston knew my mother, but she doesn't cover her tracks. Instead, she stands and moves to the door. "Nor will you see the magician again. You will focus on your duties. As you have always done. Let your past remain in the past—there's nothing there for you."

It's so close to what Kingston warned me about that my intrigue level multiplies. It's not like she can keep me locked up in here. Winter may be hers, but my room is my domain, and I can escape it if I want. And if I'm not supposed to see Kingston, that's precisely where I want to go.

"What are you hiding?" I ask.

But she doesn't answer. She pauses in the doorframe and looks into the shadows.

"I have heard from Oberon," she says over her shoulder. It sounds like an afterthought. "His kingdom is beginning to falter. I even hear his citizens are fleeing. You must find this threat, Claire. Before our kingdoms collapse."

I don't let her go, though. Not yet. There's a fire in me that suddenly rages—I just risked my life for her, and all she can do is chastise me about my life choices and say I need to try harder? Screw that.

"Why can't you do anything about this? You or Oberon? All you do is sit on your throne and order us peons around to kill or be killed. I'm sick of it, Mab. I'm not your doll."

I don't know the last time I called her Mab and not Mother. Judging from the flicker in her eyes, neither does she. She turns to face me, locking eyes.

"I must play my own part," she replies. "I cannot be involved directly in affairs related to the mortal world. I may only plot and coax. It is governed by the rules of nature."

"Yeah. And *you* wrote those rules."

"Which is precisely why I must abide by them. As must you." I fully expect her to leave in that moment. It's a great exit cue, a *remember your place* sort of thing. Instead, she glances toward the fire.

"I have lost much in the last thirty years, Claire. Much more than you will ever know. I do not wish to lose any more. Think what you will of my means, but you will always be a daughter to me. And no daughter of the Faerie Queen is without her rightful place in the world. I want to ensure you are able to take that place, when your time has come. I do not want some charlatan rebel to steal it away from you."

Then, before I can ask what she's talking about, she goes, and I'm left with the impression that even though she's said a great deal, she hasn't told me anything at all.

*

I'm not one to chase down the guy. It's not my nature.

The fact that I'm jogging up the promenade toward the Cirque des Immortels is completely out of character for me. Especially after I kicked the bastard out that morning. But I need answers. Now. And if it involves my family, well, suddenly this whole shit-show is beyond personal.

It's already evening in the mortal world, and the place is packed. Music blares through the night air, and performers dance around with fire staves and poi, everything sparkling and shifting like disco shrapnel from neon lights and searchlights. Dream is so thick here I could choke—it pours from the crowd like a tempest, and it has a tang that no other venue's had before. The Dream tastes like cotton candy and hay, like burning lights and laughter. No wonder Mab puts so much stock in this place. It brings in more than any other single venue I've seen. Probably because it's the one place people feel like they can actually dream again, no matter their age.

I can't imagine it's going to be too hard to find Kingston—he doesn't seem like the type of guy to just let himself fade into the crowd. But the crowd's as thick as the Dream, and I wander past the admissions booth with the wave of my hand, and the area inside is just as crazy. There are jugglers wandering outside the tent, and sword swallowers, and a little farther off there's a new area of smaller tents, all tightly knit into an alley straight out of the Old West. Above it is a simple wooden sign that reads, in crooked hand-painted letters, "FREAKSHOW."

It doesn't look like the place someone like Kingston would hang out, so of course I find it incredibly appealing. I'm about halfway toward the backstage area when there's a hand on my arm, pulling me to a stop. I spin around, knife already in hand and ready to cut off the offending wrist.

"Eli, Jesus," I hiss.

"You're not the first to call me that," he says. He isn't smiling, though. "Where have you been?"

"Speaking with Mab."

"And why are you here?"

"Because I have some unfinished business with a magician."

He scans me up and down.

"Oh, I know that tone. Surely it can wait." His hand still hasn't left my arm. He's lucky I've not cut it off.

"No. It can't." I glance around quickly, but no one's looking at us. No one looks when you're part of the crowd. So I pull out the ticket I found in Faerie and hand it to him. "I found this. In Winter. It's propaganda for whoever's recruiting in the Wildness."

He takes the ticket and spins it around in his fingers, his face unreadable and eyes hidden. The only response he makes to let me know he's even seen the imagery is a low "hmm" before handing it back.

"So they aren't just hoarding Dream," he says. "They're actively recruiting."

I nod. I don't ask how he found me, or why—he can follow our bond just as easily as I can.

"Have you told Mab?" he asks.

I shake my head. "She was already yelling. It wasn't the right time."

"You're probably right."

"Now, if you're done, I've got work to do."

And I turn and keep heading for the backstage area.

Eli doesn't follow.

I almost expect someone to try to stop me, but no one gives me a second look as I storm backstage. The performers are all warming up in costume—contortionists stretching on a long blue mat, acrobats doing handstands on top of each other. And there's Kingston, over near the corner, wearing a ringmaster coat and top hat and tight leather pants. For a split second I almost forget why I came here, what I wanted. Because suddenly all I can see is him naked in my bed. All I can hear is his heavy breathing.

Then he looks over at me and the rest of the world comes crashing back in a cacophony of voices and music.

I don't look away, either. I stride right up to him and ignore the performers who stare at me like I'm a ghost.

"What are you doing here?" he asks.

"What do you know about my family?" I ask in return.

He opens his mouth like he might actually answer. Then he shuts it and looks away.

"I can't tell you."

"Don't bore me with your contractual bullshit," I say. I grab his arm, force him to look at me. "If you know something, anything at all, you will tell me. You knew them, didn't you?"

He's clearly warring with himself, but he's too good an actor. I don't know if it's for show or if his lips are honestly magically bound. Not that that makes any sense—why would Mab prevent him from telling me about my past? How could my mother have been that important?

He nods.

"And you can't say anything because of something Mab put into the contract."

Another nod, this one a little more pained.

"You need to go," he says. "Before Mab learns you were here. You're not supposed to be here. You were never supposed to be here."

"If that was the case, why would she send me here to take stock of the Dream?"

He locks eyes with me. He might be a good actor, but his next words are no line.

"Because sometimes, Mab uses us to play a bigger game."

I let go of his arm.

"You need to go, Claire. Leave the circus and never come back. There aren't any answers for you here. None that you want to find, at least."

I want to punch him. I've never put much thought into my family. I never needed to. But now, knowing that he knows *something*, and that that something's enough to forbid him from speaking of it . . . that ignites my curiosity like nothing else. He's here. The information is so close. And he won't—or can't—reveal it.

"I don't know what sort of game you two are playing," I say. "But you're hiding my family from me. My past."

"Nothing good can come of searching for your past in here," he says. His words are heavy, weighted with a history I can't begin to understand. "Trust me on that. It will only bring you pain."

I want to push him. I want to scream and force him to tell me what he knows. But he won't. I don't even care if it's a *can't*: in my eyes, he's just being a dick.

"What about the tickets?" I ask. I pull it out and hold it in front of his face. He looks around but no one's watching. Probably not the first time he's been accosted by an angry female before a show.

"I don't—"

"Bullshit!" I scream. "That's bullshit. You're in charge of this show, Kingston. You know everything that goes on in here, everything that comes in or goes out. Don't lie to me. You know how those tickets got into Faerie. You know how they're connected. So who the hell is this Pale Queen and why is she trying to fuck up my life?"

People *are* staring now, but no one's coming over to see if Kingston needs assistance with the crazy girl.

He opens his mouth and gapes for a few seconds. I can't tell if he's trying to speak or trying to figure out what to say.

"Pale Queen?" he asks.

"Yeah, the Pale Queen. Whoever's behind all of this is calling herself that. And apparently she has access to your old supplies."

"I have never heard of anyone called the Pale Queen," he whispers. His eyes flicker to the tent. He's lying. "And I have a show to run. I told you, Claire, your answers aren't here. You should leave. Now. Before you get hurt."

"Fuck you, Kingston."

Before he can say anything else, I turn and head back into the crowd.

Eli's nowhere to be found in the throng, not that I'm really looking. I force my way forward while the crowd heads to their seats, trying my best not to elbow anyone in the chest while I do. Not that I care about their well-being, but I want out. Now.

I don't know why this has made me emotional. I've barely given my real parents any thought over the past twenty years. But something about this place has me on edge, like there's a crack in my life that's starting to fissure deeper.

"Are you okay?" someone asks, and I look up to see the girl from before, Melody. Only she's not quite how I remember her. She's taller, for one thing, and her arms are covered in tattoos I know she didn't have before. The face and voice are the same, though.

"Fine," I reply. I look around, trying to find Eli. I wonder if maybe he's latched onto a mortal for dinner.

"You look like you're running from a ghost." She pauses and really looks me over. "Let me guess: Kingston's being a prick."

"How did you know?" I ask, my voice deadpan.

"He's been like that lately. Ever since Mab put him in charge. I don't think he's cut out for the pressure."

"Yeah, well, he doesn't have to take it out on me by hiding things."

She sighs. "I can't believe I'm about to say this, seeing as he's been a class-A dick for the last few years, but maybe don't hold it against him."

"Why?"

She opens her mouth, then closes it.

"You are more a part of this place than you understand," she says quietly. "Seeing you here . . . it's hard for us. For him. You may be the daughter of Winter, but this tent . . . this will always be your home."

Then she stands up straighter. When she speaks again, it's much louder, like she's putting on a show for the zero people paying attention.

"Anyway, it was great seeing you, Claire, but I gotta go back and get ready for the show. The Shifters are doing their monthly Freakshow tonight and I need to make sure none of them are too indecent." She grins. It's the first time I've seen her smile this entire interaction, and it looks just as forced as I'd expect. "Was great seeing you. Tell Mab to drop by and say hello sometime."

Then, without giving me any time to respond, she leaves me standing there in the emptied promenade. Eli's nowhere to be seen, but I'm done waiting around here. I have a name to follow and blood to shed, and right now, I want to shed it more than ever. What the hell did she mean—this place is my home? This is the second time I've been here. I decide then and there that I'm done trying to get answers from Mab's contracted employees. It's impossible. I need to be questioning people I can torture the answers from. I need to have some sort of upper hand. I stalk away from the circus toward the parking lot. Eli can catch up.

I don't make it out of the show.

As I pass by the booths lining the promenade, a girl calls out to me. Normally I'd keep going, but only a few people here know my name. And when I look over, I realize the girl is the last person I'd expect to be inviting me over.

It's Lilith.

She sits in a booth that's draped in velvet and beads and candles. Lilith is similarly dressed, though there's nothing soft about her appearance: her dress is black and heavy, the beads around her neck silver mouse skulls. And the glow in her green eyes is far from inviting.

"Claire," she says again. "Come here."

It doesn't sound like an invite now. It sounds like a demand.

I look around to see if there's anyone else named Claire she could be calling, but the few patrons left all mingle blankly, buying cotton candy and popcorn and cheap souvenirs. Lilith's the last person I want to talk to . . . but then again, she's the one who told me my mother had been here in the first place. Maybe she's not bound by contract like the others. If only I could figure out why I have such an aversion to her. I walk over.

There's a pile of Tarot cards to one side of her, an emerald crystal ball on the other, the stand made of wrought-iron black cats. She doesn't take her eyes off of me as I approach and examine the objects. So she's a psychic. I can't imagine she's related to the Oracle—the only thing this girl appears to have sacrificed is her manners.

"What?" I ask. I'm done being polite with these people. I want blood.

"You are upset," she says.

"So brilliant," I reply. "But I'm not paying you for that wonderful insight."

She smiles. Honestly, I can't tell if it's menacing or if she's pleased I'm being rude.

"Your mother would not approve of you being here."

I look at her. Lilith's face remains calm.

"What do you mean, *my mother*?" I ask. Because I have no doubt she isn't talking about Mab.

"You are getting too close," Lilith says. "Too close to understanding. And when you do, it will break you."

"What the hell are you talking about?" I feel like I should lower my voice, but no one's giving us a second look. The booth is getting a wide berth—something about her is a clear warning to stay away.

"This is where the evil began," she says, her words completely devoid of feeling. The monotone gives me chills. "This is where the Trade began to falter. And your mother . . . your mother was the cause of it."

I shake my head. "I don't have any clue what you're talking about. My mother was never here."

"She was," Lilith says. "I knew her well. She was the beginning of the end." Then, without a shift in tone, she continues, "Let me read your cards."

She pushes the deck toward me.

"No thanks. I don't deal with prophecy. What do you mean you knew my mother?"

"Shuffle." It's definitely a demand; her smile drops, and I have this funny image of her jumping over the table and clawing my eyes out if I say no. "Trust me. These cards will agree with you."

I have no clue what the hell that's supposed to mean. I reach out and grab the cards.

My vision shifts.

The girl behind the table isn't Lilith. It's the girl from the vision—blonde hair, pale skin—though now she's bedecked in shawls and wears heavy eyeliner. She shuffles the cards absentmindedly, watching me, or the promenade behind me, and I'm about to ask who she is, because maybe Lilith's a shape-shifter and this is all a trick, when Kingston steps from behind the curtain and wraps his arms around her. But it's clearly not the Kingston I know—this guy, though seemingly the same age, is smiling. The stress and dark circles are gone, and when he hugs the girl, she smiles back and offers to read his fortune:

"I see a beautiful girl in your immediate future." And he laughs and kisses the side of her neck, burrowing his face beneath the scarves. And then something clamps on my wrist and I look down to Lilith's hand, white-knuckled, her nails drawing blood from my flesh. Vision gone.

I try to yank my hand away, but she doesn't let go.

"You should not be seeing," she hisses. I look into her green eyes—there's something else in there, it seems, a hatred older than her little body should allow.

One more pull and my arm comes free. My blood splatters across the cards scattered on the table. By the time I clutch my hand to my chest, the wounds are already healed. My magic works fast.

"What the hell?" I take a step back, but she goes from looking at me to looking at the cards. I must have knocked them down in the throes of the vision. If it *was* a vision.

"You have slept with him," she whispers. She hovers a hand over two of the cards—*The Knight of Swords* and *The Magician*, both splattered in my blood.

"You're insane."

"You have slept with the magician," she says. She looks over to the other cards. Only a few were knocked faceup. *The Ten of Swords*, showing a man stabbed by his blades. *Judgment*, where the dead rise to the trumpets of angels. Each of them covered in my blood. Lilith's hand shakes. When she looks at me, she actually seems hurt. "He said he would not. He said that it was only me."

Oh fuck. Of course I managed to get in between the two of these crazies.

"It won't happen again," I say bitterly. "He was the one who showed up in my room."

"Leave," she says.

"Aren't you going to tell me what—"

"I said leave!" she screams, swiping the cards off the table.

I don't hesitate. I turn and walk away, nursing my slightly bruised hand. *What was that all about? What was that vision?*

And why do I feel like the more I'm here, the more my life unravels?

I know the Tarot well enough, though I never read them—I don't usually want to know what happens next. But *The Ten of Swords* is all about defeat, and *Judgment* is about, well, that final judgment day, and I can't believe the two of them smeared in my blood is a good sign.

I want answers. I want to demand Lilith or Kingston tell me something. I want to go back to Winter and demand the same of Mab. But

I know that none of them will speak up and, besides, I still have people to kill. *Someone* has to pay for the way I feel, and since it can't be the people who are causing my anger, it will have to be someone equally deserving. Not that it's likely to make me feel better.

For the first time in my life, I'm no longer looking at Mab as a savior. Something about that image has been tainted. Now, I can't help but wonder if she was more a captor, or if my mom was just another stupid mortal like Roxie, getting roped in by one of the Fey to something far too big to comprehend.

When all of this is over, I'm damn well going to find out.

The portal I draw is on the side of a semitruck parked in the grass lot a few hundred feet away from the pitch. It bears no markings, so I'm not sure if it's Mab's or some lonely trucker's, but it'll work. I hop up to the back of the truck and begin sketching a portal along the door, triple-checking the equations and runes and adding in a few extra for good measure. These have less to do with travel and more to do with being prepared, tricks I learned from working with Mab. Some runes for strength, for hardened skin, for better senses. Not a single one of them can trump the runes already burned along my spine, but a little extra never hurts.

I'm not about to have my ass handed to me again.

"You're just going balls to the wall, aren't you?" Eli asks as I finish up another glyph. I didn't even hear him approach.

"Where the hell did you learn that phrase?" I ask.

"I get around. Speaking of . . . how long are you planning on keeping me on this plane? You know my powers grow weaker the longer I'm away. Especially when I don't feed."

I hop down from the bumper, my work complete.

"You just ate," I say. "You can't be that weak."

"Yes, but that work with the mannequin took a lot out of me. I'll need to feed soon." He glances longingly at the circus.

"No. No way. Mab would kill me if I let you steal one of her patrons."

"You don't listen, do you?"

"You're treading on dangerous ground. What are you so bluntly hinting at?"

"There's a Tapis Noir tonight."

"A what?"

"*Tapis Noir.* It's French. Means Black Carpet . . ."

"I know what it means, ass. What does it have to do with us?"

"It means, in a few hours, that tent over yonder"—he points to a small tent set up just beyond the main chapiteau, this one squat and striped black and dusty purple—"will be filled with mortals who are up for grabs. It's Mab's way of entertaining the denizens of her Court who require . . . other sorts of satisfaction."

"And you want us to go."

"I was considering holding off, but you're packing a mean punch with all those runes. If you're trying to be at peak fighting form, maybe I should be as well."

I tilt my head back and sigh dramatically.

"You couldn't have said this *before* I wrote all this down?"

"I didn't want to interrupt."

I look back at him. "What about us needing to get to this person before they have time to prepare?"

"I think it's glaringly obvious that the art of surprise is lost to us now. They've been tipped off. You're used to playing in the dark, I understand that. The game has changed, though. You cannot act as an assassin now. You must act as a warrior. And warriors ensure they are fighting at full strength."

I glance to the intricate runes covering the back of the truck. Easily one of my finest portals yet, save for maybe the one I used to track down a lich at the bottom of the Mariana Trench. Underwater breathing spells are tricky as fuck.

"When's the after-party?" I ask.

"After the show, thus the term *after-party*." He reaches into his pocket and pulls out two tickets to the show. How he managed to get them, I have no idea, and I'm not about to ask. I'm positive I saw the ticket booth turning people away—full house. "Fancy a night out?"

"We have someone to kill."

"And they'll still be very much alive after the show. We might not be if we skip this step. So let's just enjoy our meaningless lives while we can."

I pluck a ticket from his hand and, with the wave of my other, disperse the chalk dust from the trailer.

"So Buddhist of you," I say. "But you still owe me for all that work."

"I'll get you some popcorn."

Thirteen

The show's already begun when Eli and I sneak into the tent. Not that that's much of an issue—we have front-row aisle seats, so there's no awkward asking people to stand. I don't really care about making people uncomfortable like that, but something about this place makes me feel wholly unwelcome, and not in a way that makes me want to fight against it.

My thoughts are swept from my mind the moment the next act comes onstage. Three swaths of fabric unfurl from the ceiling, billowing down to just touch the floor. The moment they begin to fall, the music changes and three aerialists tumble onstage, each heading for a fabric. They begin to climb using only their hands, and when they reach the top, they pose and the audience begins to clap—just in time for the aerialists to somersault down the fabric and catch themselves just before hitting the ground. I watch in awe as they climb and twist, the man inverting and pulling his leg to his head while the women drop into the widest splits I've ever seen. They are graceful and delicate and somehow powerful, and as I watch, I feel my own imagination take control as the Dream spirals out of me, twining up into the farthest recesses of the tent with the rest of the patrons'. The aerialists do another drop, this time nearly touching the floor, and my heart leaps into my throat. Everything else is forgotten as I watch—Lilith, the Dream Trade, Kingston, my family . . . None of that feels consequential now, and seeing as I was completely torn up before setting foot in here, that's saying something.

Under the big top, everything in the outside world feels like a paltry show. I grab the popcorn bucket and settle back against the seat.

I completely lose track of time as the show progresses, and it's not just the acts. I'm so attuned to Dream I feel like I'm getting a contact high from all the imagination floating around me. It's all I can do to stay focused on what's happening onstage. The rest of me wants to let go and drift amid the Dream.

After a while, though, the house lights come up and the stage is empty, and I look down and see I've eaten all the popcorn. I glance to Eli.

"Is it over?" My voice sounds more disappointed than I want it to.

"Just intermission, my dear." He looks at the popcorn tub. "I don't envy your stomach."

"It's dealt with worse." I dust some kernels off me and stand. I feel really good. And I can't tell if it's the Dream or the show, but for the first time in a long time I don't feel like an assassin. I don't feel like an outsider. I feel like I'm part of a beautiful secret. "Wanna see the freakshow?"

He smiles. "I doubt they will be anywhere near as freakish as my usual entourage. But sure. Seeing you this giddy is a show unto itself."

*

The freakshow is one long narrow alley that feels like an anachronism. Even the air is different back here, as if from an earlier time. The ground is covered in hay and the lane is congested with people. Everywhere I turn is another podium with some Shifter parading as a human oddity.

There's a woman covered head to toe in nautical tattoos, her naked breasts inked like a starfish bra and a thin, netlike wrap draped across her hips. There's your usual sword-swallower, though this guy's upped the ante and is swallowing swords lit on fire. I pause and watch as he swallows a long blade wreathed in flame, tendrils of smoke coming from his mouth when his lips reach the hilt. When he pulls it out, it's still on fire.

But there's more back here than just hawkers and oddities. There are tents with signs proclaiming any number of things—Elisa the Human Pincushion, Tarantina the Tarantula Lady, Edward the Geek. And, judging from the clucking of chickens coming from that tent, I'm betting they're not talking about a nerdy programmer. I give that one a wide berth and head into the next tent, which promises to hold Karina and Katja the Two-Headed Contortionist.

When I get inside, I realize the contortionist is, in fact, Melody.

It's very strange seeing the same girl I'd just spoken to with two heads. Her features are a little different—her skin's pale and her hair is longer, pulled back into buns. Each face has the sharp, angular features of a Russian dancer, with dark eyebrows and heavy crimson lips. But it's definitely her; she hasn't even taken the nose ring out of one of the faces, and when she sees me step into the tent, one face winks while the other looks shocked.

At the moment, she's in a split with her back leg pulled toward her head in a very uncomfortable-looking backbend. She's not wearing much at all—a string bikini, emphasis on *string*—and for some reason I feel I should look away. Not because I'm not attracted, but because I feel like I've stepped in on something even more private than sex. She'd told me she didn't perform anymore. This feels like an extreme act of exhibitionism, and even though one of her faces is playing seductive, the other makes me feel I shouldn't be watching. She shifts her position and flips up into a handstand, her legs spread wide and her bikini hiding nothing. Eli's standing beside me with a small smile on his face and his hands shoved in his jacket pockets. He looks entirely out of place surrounded by all these patrons in T-shirts and jeans, but as usual, he doesn't seem to notice. In here, no one else does either.

Melody twists her feet to her head, still in the handstand, and I decide it's past time to leave. I grab Eli's arm and pull him from the tent.

*

The second act of the show is just as engaging as the first, and with another tub of popcorn in my lap, I'm more than happy to shut out the rest of the world and focus on the acrobats and jugglers and hand-balancers that weave their magic across the stage. Even when Kingston comes out doing a magic act, I find it hard to be pissed. He's just another performer on the stage.

When the lights rise and the curtain falls, Eli and I linger in our seats and wait for the crowd to disperse. I'm more than ready to go and kick this next suspect's ass, but Eli has a fair point—if we hope to beat someone who's clearly packing a punch, we need to be ready. And Eli's probably the best weapon I've got, though it pains me to admit it. Being mortal has its limits.

After about twenty minutes, the tent's almost entirely empty. A few pimply kids—clearly locals, based on the bored, shuffling attitude about them—roam the aisles in Cirque des Immortels T-shirts, picking up popcorn boxes and stray cups. Outside, the sudden sound of drumbeats fills the air.

"That's our cue," Eli says, standing. We hadn't spoken the entire time, which I definitely didn't mind. Clearly he could see this wasn't the time to test me; normally, he'd be chatting away and trying to find a new button to push. I wonder if he's turning over a new leaf.

"I take it you've been here before?" I ask.

"Once or twice. It's not a party to be missed."

I, for one, am more than willing to miss a party. I'd much rather either be drinking in the Unicorn or going on a killing spree. Now that the flights of fancy from the show have landed, the irritation from before is back with a vengeance. I need to punch something or drink something or both. Preferably both. I can't imagine what some fancy VIP party will do to ease that urge or empower Eli.

Once we step outside, however, I realize I might actually enjoy this.

There's a crowd of patrons standing outside the entrance, huddled like a flock of lost sheep. And a little farther away, descending like a big bad wolf, is Kingston.

He's dressed like a leather daddy, which is not a look I'd ever expect him to be able to pull off. Somehow, though, his skintight leather pants and chest harness pair perfectly with his lank black hair and tattoo wrapped around his torso. Fire-dancers flank him, moving forward in perfect time to the music, the light of their torches and fire fans making his skin glisten. He locks eyes with me the moment I emerge from the tent. As much as I hate him, my heart goes straight to my throat. That look was made for removing underwear.

When he nears, the dancers part and he steps forward, his eyes still on me.

"Welcome, loves," he says. Even his voice is different—deeper, huskier. I'd say it's a bedroom voice, but he definitely didn't sound like that the other night. This is an even more carnal facade. "I trust you all have your tickets."

The patrons are too stunned to really respond, though a few of them nod. I say nothing. I definitely don't have a ticket for this part of the evening's entertainment. And I definitely don't think it matters.

Without waiting for an answer, he turns away and heads toward the smaller tent beyond. It perches in the night with its own inner glow, silhouettes and shadows playing out on the tent walls, revealing nothing and suggesting everything. The fire-dancers surround us and begin to urge us forward. I can't tell if they're meant to be an escort or to ensure no one tries to escape.

I glance around at the people, wondering who Eli will pick, wondering if all of them are doomed to die or if there's something else in store. If it's designed by Mab, I can't imagine it's good.

And even though I'm technically mortal like all of them, I can't pretend to care.

Maybe I should have more compassion for people roped into a faerie trap. All I have is contempt for their stupidity. *What if this is how my mother was involved? What if she was once one of these patrons?* The thought's an arrow to my heart, but it's too late now to even think of saving anyone. These people damned themselves. I have to remember that.

The small tent is ringed with men and women in smart black suits and designer sunglasses, all stoically facing outward, like a much sexier version of the Secret Service or the guard outside Buckingham Palace. And at the entrance, with another pair of flanking guards, is a small table draped in velvet and covered in white and black masks.

Kingston waits beside the table, gesturing the first patron—a twentysomething hipster bedecked in flannel and an overly large beard—forward. The patron gives a guard his ticket, and the guard hands over a white mask. The man puts it on and slips inside the tent.

A few more patrons come forward, all shapes and sizes and ages, but each and every one of them gets a white mask, save for a few black masks that go to guests that I'm 100 percent positive are Fey. Then it's just Eli and me left. No more masks on the table. Just Kingston standing there with his own black mask and the guards staring ahead motionless.

"You going to let us in?" I ask.

He looks at me without a hint of emotion on his face, like he just used up all his acting for the day and is now as blank as the mask in his hand. For a moment, I honestly think he's going to say *no, you aren't welcome here.*

"Do you promise to leave after this?" he asks.

Not the question I was expecting and not too good for my ego.

"Trust me," I respond, "I wouldn't be here if this one didn't need a quick meal."

Kingston looks to Eli, sizing him up. It's the first time Kingston's given my partner the slightest acknowledgment.

"What plane?"

Eli just grins and raises his sunglasses, letting his eyes answer for him.

"Thought so," Kingston says. He takes his own mask in both hands and pulls a second mask from it, then a third. I barely even feel the magic used, it's so subtle. He hands them over to us and looks to the guards. "These two are with me," he says. The guards don't even nod, but Kingston doesn't let us enter until we've both tied on our masks.

"Have fun," he says. Then he ducks inside and leaves us to enter behind him.

"The hell is his problem?" I ask the guards.

As expected, neither answers. Eli chuckles, then steps forward and holds the flap open for me. I glance inside—there's nothing in there, just shadow.

"Après vous," Eli says.

"At least someone here's a gentleman," I respond, and head into the tent.

*

I blink once, velvet and canvas and magic sliding over my skin, and then I'm definitely in a place set apart from the mortal world.

The interior of this tent is huge, the opposing wall barely visible through the mass of space and writhing bodies. Suddenly, I can see the appeal of this party. And for an antisocial hermit like me, that's saying something.

Everywhere I turn there is another person in a state of undress and compromise. To my left is a fountain of glasses overflowing with champagne, a girl wearing nothing but rhinestones contorting above it on a tiny hoop. Farther off there's a trio of burly men doing acrobatics and handbalancing on and around one another. Stark naked. And clearly enjoying themselves, judging from where they're putting their hands for balance. By a circle of leather armchairs, a single girl balances atop a cane using only her teeth, her legs twisted above her head in a perfect circle, the beads of her bikini dripping by her face like raindrops. But it's not just performers and the handful of patrons inside the tent. There are people everywhere. Or, if I'm being truly precise, Fey.

They're easy to spot, and it's not just because they're the only ones wearing black masks. They're dressed to the nines, wearing sleek evening gowns straight out of Fashion Week and suits worth more than any CEO's paycheck. If they're wearing anything at all. Many of them are partially undressed, and they're quickly getting the mortals in on the fun. I watch as a group of Fey women and men pull the shirt off the hipster dude I saw earlier, while a mortal woman reclines on the chaise longue beside them, a faerie male with tiny stubs of antlers peeking out of his matted hair kissing up the length of her legs.

"You never told me about this place, why?" I ask, not looking away from the revelry.

"I thought you knew," Eli says simply. "After all, your dear mother is the one who puts it on."

She's not my mother, I think. The thought startles me. I've never had that response before, at least not with the same emotional impact. But now's clearly not the time or place for mommy issues. I grab a glass of champagne and pray to the gods it's faerie wine. Or maybe I shouldn't be wishing that, seeing as I'm supposed to kill someone after this.

"Keep your wits," Eli says, clearly watching my train of thought. "Remember why we are here."

"Right." I take a swig. It fizzes and tingles, but I don't taste any lingering Dream or enchantment. Just a simple dry brut. "Speaking of, pick one already."

He laughs. "My dear, if this is my last meal in this body, I'm going to *savor* it. You're welcome to join if you'd like."

My immediate response is to say no. To go find a dark corner to linger in and just watch. But then I catch sight of Kingston through the crowd. He's doing his damned best to ignore me and prove he's intent on doing so. As I watch, he's undressing a mortal male while a dryad with thorns in her hair kisses his hip. He wants to play that game? Fine.

"Sure," I say.

Eli looks shocked.

"Really?"

"Really. After all, I'm supposed to be part of the decision-making process. I might as well have some fun as well."

He smiles, looking truly delighted. Grabbing a glass from the table, he raises it in a toast.

"Well then, let the games begin."

*

It doesn't take us long to find our candidate. Or, rather, it doesn't take long for him to find us.

I don't really have a type. When it comes to mortal men, they're all pretty much the same in my eyes—good for a few minutes of fun and then an inevitable disappointment. Faeries are where it's at. But this guy . . . he could be worth the effort of removing my clothes. He's already down to his boxer briefs, which is all I need to know that he's going to be fun. Minus the shitty tribal tattoos over his hip and pec, he's pretty damn hot. Clearly a gym dude, with that perfect eight-pack and bigger tits than me. He also has nipple piercings, which could go either way in terms of attractiveness but he manages to pull them off. He's jacked without looking like a *Jersey Shore* wannabe, and seeing as he first approaches Eli and then smiles at me, I know he's down to play with us both.

Then again, there's a shine in his eyes that isn't just lust. He's been hit hard with the faerie wine, and it's gone straight to his head. Both of them. I almost feel bad taking advantage of him like this, but if there's one thing I've learned about faeries, it's that they don't force mortals into anything. Their magic may be deceptive, but when it comes to stuff like this . . . they only play with the willing. All of these people are here because somewhere deep down, this is what they really want. The drink just makes them more open to the fun and less shocked by their very-clearly-through-the-looking-glass surroundings. It's how the Fey get the greatest amount of Dream, unlocking those pent-up desires. To do this with someone who wasn't truly interested would be pointless.

Or so I convince myself as the guy gestures us toward a small sofa in the corner.

Eli gives me a grin and follows. He's already taken off his sunglasses and hidden them away, his eyes brighter than any other point of light in the room. No one seems to notice, least of all the guy, who's now sitting on the sofa with an excited smile on his face. Eli doesn't waste any time. The moment we near, he straddles the guy and starts making out with him. I glance around, suddenly feeling like the unwanted third wheel, but then the guy looks past Eli and cocks a finger in a distinct come-hither gesture, and I step up to the side of the sofa. The man's hand immediately goes to my waist, hooking over my jeans and pulling me closer. Eli chuckles and makes room on the sofa, which I can't imagine being big enough for the three of us, but then the guy's lips are on my neck and Eli slides a hand under my shirt, and the sofa's the last thing I care about.

I don't think. I don't wonder. The last thing I think before I close my eyes and let the music fill me is that I'm glad Roxie isn't seeing what I'm about to do. Then, before I can pretend to feel guilty, I lean in and bite the man's collarbone and let my body do the thinking for me. The man tastes sweet and smells like cologne and sweat, and Eli is like a spice I can never place, something sharp and biting that burns through your taste buds to go straight to your brain. Everything is sound and music and touch, and both Eli and the stranger are down to dance. The taste. The taste of sex and power flows through me like Dream, like nectar, and I soak in it, let it drown me until I'm blind to the world, until everything else disappears.

It's only later, when we're slicked with sweat and I'm not certain whose arm or leg is whose, that Eli lifts his head from the guy's neck and looks me in the eye.

"You might not want to be around for the rest of this," he says. The man is lying on his back, blissed out and seemingly checked out as well, his eyes half-lidded and a grin on his lips.

It's a shock, that break from moving to not moving, carnal to rational. I shake my head and try to force out the music, which seems to be more intoxicating than any faerie wine. The music tells me to keep going, to give in and give over and if Eli wants me to stop, he can go fuck himself. I don't listen. Eli's right—I definitely don't want to see what happens next. And when I look around the room, I realize I don't want to see what's happening in here, either. The party's gone from wild to wicked, and it's only now that I'm realizing the music's so loud because beneath it all, beneath the moans and excitement, there's screaming.

And not the good kind of screaming.

There's a man dangling from one of the hoops now, and it's not Swarovskis dripping from him, but blood, and the very pale denizens of Winter lap it up below him. Everywhere I turn there's blood and moaning, and twined through it all is Dream. This isn't the floaty sort of Dream from within the chapiteau. This Dream is heavy, oily, glistening like obsidian. I can't say it's sickening—there's still an allure there, a pull, something hinting of shadows and hunting and being hunted in return—but it's definitely not my cup of tea. I wonder if Celeste has any of this on tap, and what would happen if I drank it . . .

I try not to think too deeply as I grab my clothes and head for a corner of the tent not taken up by people feeding or fucking or both. It's difficult to find, and I'm halfway dressed when I finally make it to the exit. I don't look around to find Kingston.

Outside the tent, the world is completely silent and empty. The guards are gone, and whatever revelry is happening within the tent is muted. All I hear is the sound of wind through the fields, the distant roar of passing traffic. I shiver and zip up my coat as I sit in the grass, suddenly wishing the night were over. My body longs to soak in a bath and drink, and maybe it wouldn't be so bad to spend another night in Faerie. I'm sure I could make it so time barely slipped by in the mortal world at all.

Someone treks toward the tent, and I shove a hand into my pocket, clutching one of the enchanted butterfly knives. Just in case.

It's Melody.

"What are you doing out here?" I ask when she gets closer.

She pauses, clearly not expecting me to be able to make out her features from so far away, but I'm so jacked up on adrenaline and runes that I can see her blink in the shadows.

"Wondering if I'd find you, actually."

It feels like the first honest thing that's been said to me.

She walks over and sits beside me, knees to chest and arms wrapped around her legs. She's back to being normal-Melody, or at least what I assume is her normal form. It's really hard to tell with Shifters.

"I thought you said you didn't perform anymore," I say. Because I don't really want to talk about me right now. I don't want to think about what I've just witnessed and played in. Not that I think Melody would judge; she's part of this mess, too.

She sighs. "I don't. Not really. Not like I used to."

"What do you call that? The two-headed thing."

"Releasing steam," she replies. Her voice seems remarkably sad when she speaks, which is strange. It doesn't suit her—she seems like the type who's always chipper, come hell or high water. Or maybe she's just been in hell too long . . .

"I know that one," I say. I glance back toward the Tapis Noir tent and she laughs.

"Yeah. That place is good for that."

"It's something. So why don't you perform? If you love it so much, because I can tell from your voice you do."

"Too old."

I laugh.

She doesn't.

"What do you mean? You have to be at least five years younger than me." I watch her while I say this—she doesn't look at me, and her face grows more serious with every word.

"Not quite, love. Not quite."

"What is it? I feel like I'm not just stepping on your toes here. More like running them over with a pickup."

That does get a chuckle. She pulls a small flask from inside her coat, takes a swig, and hands it to me. It smells of whiskey and burns like smoke. My type of girl.

"I'm not like the other girls," she says. "I mean, obviously you know I'm a Shifter."

"Or are really good with makeup," I say, handing back the flask. Another small laugh. At least I didn't piss her off too much.

"Well, I . . . Jesus, how the fuck do I even put it? You know how everyone here is contracted to be young and hot and horny for eternity?"

I nod.

"I'm what's keeping them that way."

"I'm lost."

Another big sigh from her. "The magic in their contracts, it requires that someone else age and die in their place. It's all about keeping balance with nature. A magical tithe, if you will. And that lucky person is me."

"You don't look that old."

I see her smile in the shadows. It's not a happy smile.

"Just promise not to gasp," she says. "My ego can't take it."

Then she shifts, and it's like watching one of those creepy time-lapse videos, only this is taking place right before me. Her skin immediately droops, wrinkles forming and liver spots breaking over her clear complexion. Her hair fades to white and thins, her hands seem to shrivel into themselves. In a matter of five seconds she looks like someone's great-grandmother. A very cool grandmother, to be sure, what with the septum ring and flask in one shaky hand.

I keep the word I didn't give: I don't gasp.

She looks at me, her smile slipping. Then she takes a drink, and in that motion her skin tightens and her youth returns in one quick transition.

"It's getting worse," she says. "When I was younger, I aged at the same rate as a normal mortal. But lately . . . I don't know, it's like the magic is taking more out of me. Every year I age five or ten, and I don't know how much longer I'll be around. Every day's a performance for me; Shifter magic takes concentration, and it takes a lot of that just to keep myself upright. Mab never told me any of that when she brought me on, of course. Hell, if I didn't know better, I'd say she's punishing me for what I did." She takes another drink.

"What did you do? Did it have to do with my mother?"

Melody nearly chokes.

"Didn't anyone tell you not to ask questions?" She doesn't sound angry in the slightest. She almost sounds approving. "Especially around here."

"They tried," I say. "But I figure the one thing no one will tell me about is the one thing I need to know."

"You know we aren't able to talk about that." Her voice is tight, and I'm wondering if maybe she *can* talk about certain things. I just have to find them.

"But some of you can. That girl, Lilith. She seemed more than willing to tell me my mother used to be a part of this place. Did she work here?"

I don't know why it seems important to know. I've spent my whole life not wondering or caring, but now it's staring me in the face, this tiny little crack that could lead to more knowledge, and I want to rip it open and learn everything that's been kept from me for all this time. Especially since, judging from how rough the last hit was, I don't know if I'll be making it out of this alive. I'd like to know about where I came from before I return to the dirt.

Melody doesn't answer. But she does nod her head. Slightly.

"What happened?" I ask.

"Complicated."

"Is she still alive?"

"Complicated."

I pause. "Was she . . . was she mortal?"

Melody looks me in the eye. "Complicated." She doesn't look away, and it feels like she's trying to convey something, like there's more meaning than what I can grasp in everything she can't say.

"We can't talk about it, not anymore. Not after what happened." Melody looks down then, and her face darkens. When she speaks again, she keeps her voice light, but I can tell she's hiding something. "She wouldn't want you to be here," she finally whispers. "If she knew . . ."

"Does she know?"

Melody shrugs.

I'm not the only mortal girl in Faerie, to be sure. There are dozens of changeling children, kids stolen from their parents in the crib and replaced with a faerie babe. I was content knowing this, even though I never tried to spend time with them. They were commoners, and even if I was a changeling, I was on a different level. Now, all I can wonder is who took my place. Does my mother even know her real daughter is missing? That her real daughter is sitting in the grass in a place she once might have called home?

"Were you her friend?" I ask finally. Because I need that connection right now. I need someone to have known her and cared for her, so I can do the same by proxy.

Melody nods.

"Bestie," she whispers.

"Do you miss her?"

"Every day."

And maybe it's all an act, maybe she's performing more than she admits, but a tear slides down her face right then and drips to the dry grass.

"Could I find her again?"

"I don't know," she says. "I've not seen her since . . ." She chokes and puts her hands to her throat, making gasping noises. Immediately my hands are on her shoulder and back, trying to, I don't know, calm her down or make it stop or something. But after a moment she takes a raspy breath and shakes her head, flopping back to the grass.

"I can't talk about this anymore," she whispers. "I wish I could, Claire. I really do. There's so much to tell you. But I can't. Mab made sure that when your mother left, she left without a trace."

"It's okay," I say. It's not. It's not at all. My heart is racing, and I want to shake her and force her to talk, but I know she can't. Which means my fight's not with her. It's with the woman who drafted all these damn contracts in the first place.

I can't even imagine how Mab's going to take this.

"You going for the second course?" Eli asks from behind us.

I glance back to see him striding out of the tent, his suit once more immaculate and his mask dangling from one hand. He doesn't look like a man who has recently done terrible deeds—he looks like he's on the way to a fancy masquerade ball. It's his eyes that give him away, though. Even with the sunglasses, the blue burn behind them is easy to see.

"Are you finally ready?" I ask. I've found that, with Eli, it's best to stay on the offensive.

"I'll take that as a no," he says.

"I should go," Melody begins.

"No, don't worry about it. We were just leaving." I push myself to standing. I don't pick up my own mask. I don't want any mementos from this place. It's already stained me.

"It was a pleasure," I tell her. I don't wait for her to stand or say good-bye. I don't want Eli asking questions, not about this. If Melody's upset by it, she doesn't show it, just mutters her own good-bye and takes a swig from her flask.

"What was that all about?" Eli asks.

"Girl stuff. You ready to kill?"

"Is that even a question?" He adjusts the lapels of his coat as he says it. The mask's nowhere to be seen anymore.

"Good. Because I need you on your A-game."

"I'm always on my A-game. It's you we should be concerned about."

I don't pause. I know he's trying to get a rise, but tonight just isn't the right night to push me.

"You worry about your own ass, I'll worry about mine."

"Speaking of, that guy . . . *Damn*. I should really spend more time at the gym."

I don't answer, because we both know he doesn't need a gym to bulk up, if they even have gyms where he's from. It's just Eli being Eli, and right now, I'm okay with him entertaining himself.

Then we reach the semitrailer, and I grab some more chalk to redo the portal. My skin is buzzing as I work. It has nothing to do with magic or runes. I'm close to finding out about my family. So close. And for some reason that makes me feel more alive and more alien in my own skin than I've ever felt before.

Fourteen

Despite my first stop being the circus, I hadn't been lying about needing to stop home for supplies. The coat I'm wearing is an assassin's wet dream—the interior is lined with pockets and straps holding all manner of weapons: enchanted whips, throwing knives, small explosives, and a pack of Tarot cards that . . . well, do more damage than a sword ever could. Even the coat itself is magicked—it looks like leather but is stronger than steel and can curse any attacker in a pinch. From head to toe, I'm ready. Which is good, because the portal linked to the second name leads us into what feels like a mausoleum.

The air is cold and dusty and dark. Even with my enhanced senses, I can barely make out anything. There are blurred shapes all around, and after a few blinks they become a little more tangible. They seem humanoid, but none of them move.

Great. Did we seriously just teleport into a room of more demented mannequins?

"What is this place?" I whisper. I keep my voice so low that even I can barely hear the words, but I know Eli makes them out just fine.

"I'm not sure," he replies. He rubs his fingers together and a gentle blue light appears between his fingertips, barely more than the glow from a firefly. It illuminates the figure nearest us and I nearly laugh. It's a statue. Like, one of those ridiculous concrete garden statues of an angel that rich people have to show they can poop out more money in a day than you'll earn in a week. Or it's a gravestone. I prefer to think the former, seeing as we're surrounded by them.

"But something feels strange . . ." Eli continues.

"This is just weird," I say. A part of me really wants to reach out and touch one of the statues, but I don't. Not after what happened last time. "Is this a museum or something?"

"Personal gallery, actually," comes a voice. If my skin wasn't cold before, it is now.

The lights flicker on all at once, harsh and fluorescent and tinting everything the antiseptic white of a morgue. And really, with all those statues around us, it's not that much of an imaginative leap.

A girl strides out between the statues about fifty feet away. She's maybe my age, midtwenties, and she's in plaster-smeared overalls and a short-sleeved shirt with a bandanna around her light-brown hair. She looks like a pixie Rosie the Riveter. One that hasn't seen a lot of sunlight lately.

"Who are you?" I ask.

"That's a stupid question," she replies. She stands there with her hands in her pockets, staring at us like she's not at all perturbed to have her space occupied by strangers. Once more, we were expected. Somehow. "You know my name, otherwise you wouldn't have gotten in here."

"Fine, Laura, I know your name. What I really want to know is how you're involved in all of this."

She smiles. "Involved in what?"

I start walking forward. Being this close to her, I can taste her true name—only three small words and she'll be forced into submission. Before I do that, I want to deck her. I want her to taste blood before she spills her truth.

"You know very well what I'm talking about," I say through gritted teeth. My hand clenches on the knife in my pocket; this isn't my normal strategy, this in-your-face bravado. I was trained to stick to the shadows. But I actually sort of like zeroing in on my hit head-on. I look forward to watching her eyes widen when the first strike lands. "And you're going to talk, Laura. Or we will make you talk."

She laughs. It's not some evil melodramatic laugh, just your normal girlish chuckle. For some reason, that just makes her weirder. I'm about ten steps away, and she still hasn't moved.

"By that you mean just you, right?"

"What are you talking about?"

Then I realize that Eli's not beside me, or a step behind me.

"Your friend. I heard what he did to my best Construct. Not very nice if you ask me."

I don't look back—I'm not going to turn my back on this girl.

"Eli?" I call.

No answer.

"He's not here, I'm afraid. Not anymore. You see, I'm not a big fan of astral creatures coming in and fucking things up for me. Especially not in here, where he could really do some damage." Now she's taking a step forward, hands still in her pockets and a shit-eating smile on her face. "You didn't really think I'd let you repeat the same tactic twice, did you? I sent him back. You should be more careful where you set your portals next time."

She points up to the ceiling.

"Damn it," I hiss. Because there, carved into the paneling, are glyphs and wards and runes that basically dispel astral creatures. No wonder he felt strange being here.

She's only a foot away when she stops, still smiling.

"Looks like it's just you and me, then," I say. I try to keep my voice tough, even though a small part of me knows I'm screwed. I have her true name, but that's really only good at stopping her from using magic. And although there's power flowing through her, I don't think it's enough to consider her a witch.

"Not quite." She winks. "Remember when I said that mannequin was my best Construct?"

Damn it . . .

"Well," she continues, "I'm a firm believer in *waste not, want not*, know what I mean?" Her smile goes wider. "And I've had lots of practice."

There's no signal from her, but I sense the movement at my side and duck just in time to avoid the fist that slams past my head. I spin and slash out with a blade, but I might as well be using a twig. The knife skitters across the concrete statue's abs like nothing, my hand almost going numb from the impact. I register its features fast—shaped like a man, with winged slippers and a winged helmet and perfect physique—but the moment I do the runes on my spine burn, and I flip sideways as another statue rams through the space I just occupied. This one I don't see, but I do catch the serpentlike tail that tells me everything I need to know. This chick loves mythology, and I get to play in her coliseum.

Great.

I don't have time to bitch, though, because every statue has come to life, and it takes all my concentration to keep from getting my skull split open. For being concrete, these things are fast. The Hermes statue swings again, this time with his caduceus staff. I grab the pole and pull myself up, flipping over the statue and into a slightly cleared space, but I already know this is a losing battle. These are statues—they have no trigger points or weaknesses. My blades are nothing.

So, before I land on my feet again, I reach into another pocket and grab a piece of chalk, one kept for very special occasions. It's warm to my touch, practically tingling from the layers and layers of faerie magic that enchant it. Then I toss it to the ground and land on it, my foot crushing it to powder that poofs out and around me in a cloud.

But that's just the beginning of the physics fuckery.

Time slows down, everything stretching out like a bad slow-mo action sequence. Everything slows except me. I've yet to figure out if I'm just speeding up or if time really is slowing, and getting faeries to understand the difference is pointless. The one thing I do know is that this magic doesn't last long. Thirty heartbeats, which is a terribly short amount of time, even if I've trained myself to slow down my pulse.

I grab the explosives from my pocket and begin to run, smacking each small crystal onto the back or arm or forehead of every statue I pass. I've got about a dozen of the gems, which isn't nearly enough, and ten heartbeats later they're gone and I'm running the other direction, dodging in and out of extended arms that are slowly, so slowly, in motion.

Laura is nowhere to be seen.

I don't know if the bitch snuck out or cloaked herself or is just impossible to see among all these bodies, but it's not important, not right now. I grab the Tarot cards from my pocket and snap my fingers over the deck, visualizing hard. Four cards immediately prick out from within, all from the suit of Swords, and I begin tossing them throughout the crowded room, not caring where they land. With Swords, it doesn't matter.

Another visualization, three heartbeats left, another snap of my fingers, and *The Moon* slides from the deck and into my waiting grip.

Two heartbeats. The room starts to speed up. I keep running toward a clear wall. I need out.

One heartbeat. Nearly to the wall. I hold *The Moon* tight to my chest, slip the Tarot deck back in my pocket, and grab a fresh piece of normal chalk with my free hand.

Time speeds back up.

It's not a gentle switch, not a slow transition. One minute it's silent and slow and the next it's chaos again. Especially because the moment time goes normal, the gems I've placed explode. There's a high-pitched whine in the air, and then a pulse of blue light when, as one, all the bombs go off. The noise they make isn't so much a boom as an inhalation, as the targeted statues are sucked into the ether. Perhaps explosives is a misnomer. Implosion is more accurate.

At the same time, there's a sound of drawing steel as the Tarot cards come to life.

I don't glance back to see my apparitions floating through the crowd, slicing through stone like butter. I can hear them, though, as my court cards—Knight and Page and Queen and King—do battle. Again, it's not a magic that lasts forever, but I'm nearly at the wall and *The Moon* is burning against my chest. I hold it there, press tighter, lock my eyes on the wall only five feet away and blocked by a dozen angry statues. The world tilts as *The Moon* rises.

I've used the card once before, and that was more than enough. I'm still not ready for my vision to shift as everything goes insane. Light becomes dark and dark becomes neon as the room is thrown into madness—I can still hear my Swords fighting against the statues, but it's dulled from the sound of ocean waves and howling coyotes as shadows flicker past my legs. Then it's no longer just the clash of steel on concrete, but snarls and shattering chunks of stone as ghostly wolves and coyotes attack. I keep the card pressed tight to my chest—the only thing keeping the creatures from attacking *me*—and duck under a minotaur wielding a huge battle-ax. Another statue roars at me and I'm wondering how they got vocal cords as I spin past it and another shadow wolf latches onto the offending statue, cutting the roar short.

I skid to a stop by the wall and hastily scrape out a tiny portal. It's not fancy by a long shot, and it won't take me anywhere close to Mab's kingdom, but it will get me the hell out of here. I've completed the rectangle and have the first two-thirds of the spell done when something clamps down on my arm. I scream out of frustration and lash backward, but in that moment the Tarot card flies out of my grip and falls to the floor. The dumpy dwarf holding onto me doesn't seem to notice and doesn't seem intent on letting me go; its grip crushes my left wrist, but I struggle to finish the portal anyway. One more glyph and I'm . . .

An arm around my neck yanks me up and back. I drop the chalk as my vision blanks into stars and shadows. Then another arm around my waist, or two arms, and I'm kicking and trying to scream, but there are more arms than ever and I can't move or breathe and my brain is dying so fast it can't think.

A second later the pressure on my neck vanishes, though the rest of the restraints do not.

"Did you really think I'd let you get away that easily?" Laura asks.

She strides forward, *The Moon* card burning slowly in her hand, while around her, her creations kneel like they're bowing to a queen. A small part of me wonders if maybe she's the Pale Queen the buyer dude was talking about. But as she gets closer, I know she's just floating in her own delusions. She might have magical proclivities. She might even be good at it. But she's no faerie goddess.

"You're not going to get away with this," I say. "Even if you kill me, Mab knows where I am. And when she realizes I'm dead, she'll bring the full force of her army in here to rip your children apart."

"So fucking what?" she says. The card burns down to her fingers, and she tosses it to the ground, letting it smolder by the foot of a satyr. "My death means nothing."

What is it with all these martyrs? Seriously, what cause could they think is worth dying for at the hands of rabid Fey? And why is it that they're willingly serving this person, when Roxie was forced to against her will? Did she just get the wrong end of the deal?

"You all say that." I grunt. "And yet you all die. So far, I've seen nothing worth the loyalty."

I glance around at all the statues.

"I mean, really, are these the best you can do? The only friends you have at your disposal?" Then something clicks. "Wait, how the hell are you even involved in this? You're not pulling in any Dream here."

She smiles wider. I keep expecting her lips to crack and bleed down her chin. She looks demented enough.

"Not all of us work for her in the same way," she says. "So many of my creations have found their ways into the homes of the rich and fanciful. And they Dream such lavish things."

Of course. The same way Mab pulls my own dreams into her cache. This girl's been planting Dream-stealing statues in the homes of her clients. Kind of genius, but still pretty small-scale.

"Let me guess, you were hired because whoever this goddess bitch is, she needs someone who can create Constructs."

She just shrugs. Damn, I was really hoping I'd get her with that *bitch* comment—zealots hate it when you insult their idols.

"I play my part." She shoves her hand back into her pocket. "Yours, however, is just about to end." I fully expect her to draw out a knife or something sinister, but she doesn't. "I think you'll make a good statue, you know? You have such lovely features, and it would be a shame to let them go to waste. You'll be dead before you see it, of course. But it will be a fitting homage."

She nods to the statue holding me in place—I've not been able to get a good look at it, but judging from the dozens of arms holding me, it must be some Hindu deity.

"Try not to break any visible bones," she says.

The creature holding me begins to squeeze, and I know the popping noises in my head aren't imagination, but actual bones. My chest feels warm as something snaps and my vision goes blurry around the edges. Goes black. My lungs fill with red and everything is cracking and grinding and compressing. I don't scream. I can't scream. So why do I hear screaming?

Something groans. I feel my world tilt, or maybe it's my imagination. Though I think I'm on my back. Everything hurts in that dull sort of way, and I know this is how my death will feel.

No explosions.

No statue-worthy battle.

Crushed to death by an inanimate object.

Actually, it doesn't really hurt anymore. The pressure is gone and my limbs are numb and there's a warmth going through me that tingles with static, not the heavy staccato of blood.

Then, slowly, my senses come back to me. My eyes are closed and my body feels heavy, not light, so have I sunk down into hell or am I just in limbo? Hands on my neck, warm hands, tingling hands, angelic hands. Bright light through my eyelids. Maybe I wasn't as damned as I thought.

"You can wake up now, you know."

Not an angel's voice.

I slowly open an eye and there, kneeling over me, is Kingston.

"Am I dead?"

"No, just overly dramatic." He stands up and the static from before is gone. "Come on, get up."

I glance around, my synapses suddenly firing at full speed. There isn't even the slightest ache in my body—no broken bones, no punctured limbs. How is that even possible? And where is Laura?

"How am I not dead?"

"Magic," Kingston says. He's not looking at me, though, just surveying the room. "Come on, get up. Now."

There's no gentleness in his voice, and he doesn't offer me a hand, either. When I do move, I realize I've been lying on top of the statue that was previously crushing me. Standing is awkward, like trying to get out of a roller-coaster car, but I finally make it to my feet and look around. The statues are immobile. So is Laura.

She lies on the ground in a pool of her own blood, a thin trail from her lips. I don't see any puncture wounds, though, so I have no idea how Kingston killed her. I only know that he did. The guy just saved my life.

And here, I was ready to punch him.

"How did you find me?" I ask.

"Not the time," he says. "We need to leave."

"She's dead."

"But they're not. Stunned for the moment. Won't last much longer."

I look around at them all, frozen in the middle of a fight. My chest constricts with the memory of suffocation, and suddenly I have zero desire to wait around.

"Thanks for . . ." But I can't finish the statement. He takes my hand. It's not a gentle, caring gesture. It's rushed. Gruff.

Before I can say anything, the room twists around us, stretching like taffy until I want to vomit. I blink and Laura's workshop vanishes.

He lets go of my hand and steps to the side, leaving me a little wobbly and in the center of my living room.

"How the hell are you doing that?" I ask. My fire's roaring and everything is where I remember it. Definitely my room. Definitely still enchanted to prevent teleporting save for my one personal portal.

"Your magic's faulty," he says. Again, there's no civility in his voice. He sounds like he'd rather be anywhere but here. "I'm surprised Mab hasn't reinforced it for you."

I open my mouth, but I don't speak. I have no idea what I want to say, whether I want to rip him apart or thank him for saving my life. Maybe some sort of middle ground, a *You're a dick but I'm alive because of you so let's call it even.* I should go into the card-making business.

"How did you follow me?" I ask again. I lower my voice, keep it level. Two can play at this game.

He stands by my door awkwardly. Not in a sheepish way, but like he really just wants to GTFO and never see me again. Which makes me feel like some clingy ex, making him stay and talk, but I'm definitely not doing it for any misplaced romance. I need answers. Fast.

"I watched you make the portal," he says. "Twice, actually. When you were supposed to leave and when you did." He must notice my glare. "What, you didn't think I'd just let you wander around on your own without some sort of supervision, did you? Children need to be watched."

"Fuck you," I say. It's not *thank you*, but it's close enough. "What's your deal, Kingston? You sleep with me and then you act like I'm plagued. I'm not some damsel in distress that needs to be saved by you, and I'm not some easy little girl you can win over with a nice ass and wit."

He closes his eyes and looks like he wants to punch the wall again. I can practically hear him counting numbers down to calm himself.

"You wouldn't understand," he finally says.

"Try me."

"I can't . . . I can't explain."

There are a thousand things running through my mind, like what happens now that I'm out of leads and where the hell is Eli and why is everyone being cryptic about . . .

I collapse on the sofa.

"Jesus Christ," I whisper.

"What?" he asks.

I don't answer him. I stare into the flames and try to tell myself I'm delusional, that this doesn't make sense. The trouble is, I'm not. Because it makes perfect sense.

"That was my mother's name, wasn't it?" I ask. "What you called me earlier. My mother's name was Viv."

Saying it feels right, somehow, like my heart is beating warmth and not just blood. His silence is just another note of proof. I look from the flames to him. He's leaning with his back to the wall and head tilted toward the ceiling, eyes closed and a look of pain on his face.

"You slept with my mother," I whisper. The words come out like five bullets, each aimed at his heart.

"Yes."

"And you lost her."

"Yes."

"And that's why you slept with me. Because I reminded you of her."

"Yes."

"Get out." I don't stand. I don't grab a weapon. I don't give him the satisfaction of my anger. "Get out and never show your face again. If you do, I'll end your contract myself."

He doesn't move. He opens his eyes and looks at me, like maybe he wants to say something else, redeem himself somehow. If he tries, I will kill him. He doesn't say anything, though. He just slams his fist into the wall out of frustration, then vanishes in a whirl of shadow.

Fifteen

I want to burn off my skin. I want to scream and punch the space Kingston just occupied, but I know it won't do any good. Neither will drinking myself to death, which is a close runner-up.

So I just do the screaming part.

I scream at the top of my lungs and grab one of the crystal wine-glasses and throw it at the wall, where it shatters with a crash of glass and magic before re-forming on the floor. I feel dirty inside and out, but no amount of magic will clean it. I take a few deep breaths, force down the rage, turn it into another weapon. I need to talk to Mab. I need to find Roxie and figure out if she has any other leads, or if the person who roped her into the contract has shown his face. I need to summon Eli again and hope the experience hasn't jacked him up entirely.

I need to take a goddamned bath.

I can't believe him. I can't *fucking* believe him. He slept with my mother and then slept with me and acted like it was nothing, like it was totally normal to screw his ex's daughter. As I stalk to the bathroom and begin filling the tub, I can't help my thoughts from racing.

Were they in love?

Does she still love him?

And, even more disgusting: Is there any way in hell he's my father?

I actually shudder and force down bile at the thought, but thankfully I've found the whiskey. Two long pulls from the bottle and fire fills my chest. It's cold in comparison to the rage inside of me, the demon that wants to force Kingston back here to tell me everything he knows. I want to rip him apart for doing this to me, for tainting me *and* my mother like this. Because now, if I see her—no, *when* I see her—he's all I'll be able to think about. Him on top of her like he was with me, whispering our names. Another swig of whiskey.

The bath is full in a matter of moments; it takes a lot of control not to just jump in with all my clothes on. I don't, though. I rip my clothes off, literally, the seams tearing apart like I'd like to tear through Kingston, and I don't care if there are tears in my eyes and fire in my brain as I jump into the tub and shove my head under the water. In here, in the silence, with only the throb of the blood in my veins, I can almost escape the thoughts. Almost. But then the heat gets my blood pumping faster, and in that din I can only picture the race of pulses as he traces her hips with his tongue . . .

I push my head out of the water with a gasp. I don't grab for the whiskey again. It's making my mind weak, and I can't be weak right now. The girl in the visions, the blonde with the bloody jeans. That was Viv. That was my mother. *I know what my mother looks like now.*

"Your mother abandoned you," I whisper to the empty room. "Your mother left you alone and Mab took you in. Your mother means nothing. Kingston means nothing. You are here. You are a weapon. And you will stop feeling sorry for yourself and do what weapons do: You will kill. You will kill until the pain of your enemy mirrors your own."

I don't care if they're Mab's words. I don't care if that's how she consoled me whenever I was feeling low. I am a weapon. Weapons don't hurt or feel or love or regret. Weapons kill. And a weapon that doesn't kill is useless. And if there is one thing in my life I know, it is that I will never be useless. I might have been abandoned, but I am useful. I am needed. And I will make the whole damn world know it.

I let Kingston get under my skin. I let my mother get under my skin. And worse, I needed someone to save me tonight. I'm not going to be some damsel in distress. I'm not going to let someone else have all the power. That's not my story.

*

I wake up the next morning feeling like I've been run over by a semi, and I can't tell if it's from the half-empty bottle of bourbon sitting on my nightstand or nearly being crushed to death. Ugh. I don't want to think about that, because that will involve thinking about a certain magician doing certain things to my mother. I grimace against the nausea both the image and the alcohol bring up and roll out of bed, forcing myself into the kitchen for coffee and a breakfast I know I'll barely taste.

Another hour and another long bath later and I feel a little more human and a little more ready to take on the day. Not that I really know what I'm going to do. Roxie's list of names has provided two traps and absolutely no leads, which means it's back to using the pocket watch William gave me. I grab my jacket from where I'd tossed it on the floor and rummage through the pockets. When I finally find the watch, my heart gives a sickening jolt.

There's a huge indent on the side of it. I can barely force it open. And, as I'd feared, the interior is worse than the casing. The gears don't move and the thin glass has shattered.

"Shit," I whisper. William's not going to enjoy having to make another one.

I throw on a new jacket, stock up on weapons, and head out to find him.

Even though I stick to the back alleys, there's a silence that feels alien. No strains of music or laughter, no wisps of hookah smoke. The shops here are closed, the lights off, and I honestly can't remember the last time I'd seen any store in the entire city shut down. I knock on the jeweler's door and wonder what I'll do if it, too, is abandoned.

A second later, though, the golem Hephaestus peers out through the tiny window, sees it's me, and lets me in without me asking.

I follow him down to the lower levels, to where William is at work like always. There are a couple other jewelers in the workshop as well—a woman in the corner soldering what appears to be a mask like a dragon's skull and a boy younger than me setting a stone in a tiny ring—but neither of them pays me any attention. Only William looks up when I enter. He smiles, though it's still a tentative action.

"You're still working on that thing?" I ask as I sit across the worktable from him. The ornate bird rests before him, a few shards of black crystal scattered around it and its chest open and empty.

"It is not yet ready," he says. He delicately lays a handkerchief atop it, as though preparing it for burial. "Why are you here, Claire? I know it is not just to talk."

"Am I that obvious?"

He smiles wider.

"You're right. I'm here because, well . . ." I fish out the watch and hand it to him.

He doesn't outwardly register the fact that I broke his watch. That I just handed him something he probably slaved over for hours and that I broke in a matter of seconds. Well, a *statue* broke it, but I'm not going to bore him with details.

"Can you fix it?" I ask.

"I am afraid not," he says. "Some things, when they are broken, cannot be repaired. This is one such thing."

"I was worried you'd say that. I'm sorry."

He shrugs and sets the watch on the counter. Far away from the covered-up bird.

"It is fine. You're not the first child to break my gifts."

He says it as fact, not as some passive-aggressive statement.

"Wait, what? What do you mean?"

He looks away, toward the woman soldering the mask.

"Do you require a new compass?" he asks.

"Yes. But what do you mean I'm not the only one?"

"It is nothing. One of Mab's other children."

"But I'm the only one." I've been the only kid in Mab's castle my entire life. The other changeling children were raised outside the castle—she told me often that she barely had time for me, let alone any other "spawn."

"Not always. There was a girl here. Penelope. You two would have gotten on so well."

The girl who fucked up the circus contracts? *No wonder Mab is so distrustful.*

"When was this?"

He shrugs again and looks back, but he doesn't look at me. He looks to his gnarled, soot-stained hands. They shake.

"Many, many years ago. A few hundred, I think. So it is of no importance. She played down here as well, that is all."

Jesus, how long has he been down here?

He brushes the pocket watch. "I can make you a new one, I think. But it will take a few days. I used the last of my quicksilver on this."

"Okay. Well. Thanks." Great. *Guess I just twiddle my thumbs until then.* "I am sorry about the watch, William. I hope you still trust me enough to set that bird free when it's done."

William looks up at me, a curious mix of expressions in his face. "I wouldn't trust anyone else with that task, Claire." Then, before I've even turned around, he uncovers the bird and goes back to work, leaving me completely forgotten.

*

My next stop is Mab. I'm still pissed off at her from our last interaction, but I also still haven't told her anything about the ticket. And, seeing as I'm now positive my mother is somehow involved in all this, what with Lilith's demented musings and the visions and everything else, I figure now's the best time to kill those two birds with one stone. The others can't talk due to contracts. Mab will have to tell me. Her kingdom's at stake.

She's not in her throne room when I reach the castle, and seeing as I'm positive she's not out joyriding on a nightmare or something, I head toward her study.

It's one of the few rooms of hers that I've never been allowed in, but I know she's often there. I knock once on the stone door, and she opens almost immediately. The candlelight within gives her an eerie silhouette.

"Yes?" Her voice is so cold that I actually shiver.

"We need to talk."

I expect her to shoo me out into the hall like she always does. Instead, she steps aside and holds the door a little wider.

"Then you better come in," she replies.

I feel trepidation grow within me, and like a rabbit stepping into a snare, I venture inside.

The room's exactly as I remember it from the one time I stole in here: bookshelves on every wall holding, well, books. And other things, like skulls and crystal sconces and candles, voodoo dolls and jars of herbs. Her desk is in one corner, all ebony and covered in candles and paperwork. And the book.

The book of contracts.

She gestures me to a chair beside the desk, and I sit. She sits opposite me, and it's only then that I take in her outfit: a tight bodice and tighter black leather pants, fingerless leather gloves and knee-high stiletto boots. Her long, wavy hair is held back with several combs and pins that glitter like stars.

"Going out?" I ask.

"Why are you here?" she asks. "And, more importantly, why did you return to the circus when I expressly told you not to see him again?"

She thinks that her knowing everything is an ace up her sleeve. Not quite. I show her mine by pulling out the ticket.

"Because of this."

Her eyes narrow as she leans over to pluck the card from my fingertips. Her nails are perfectly lacquered, making mine—cracked and uneven—look terrible. Then again, being before her always makes me feel terrible. She pulls off leather so much better than I. I adjust my coat and try to sit up straighter.

"Where did you find this?"

"Just down the street. I figure that's why people are leaving. And I also figure that's why you're poring over contracts. Trying to find a loophole."

She gives me a look. One that says I'm right but she'll never admit to it because it means she's failing as matriarch.

"Did anyone within the troupe know how this came about?"

I shake my head. "No. And they won't talk. Can't talk. I think this has to do with my mother."

"Your mother has nothing to do with this."

"How do you know?"

"Because I know." Normally, that tone of voice would have been enough: case closed, stop asking questions, hold your tongue before she rips it out. Not today.

"Your kingdom's dying," I say. "People are leaving. Your Dream might be depleting, but soon, you won't even have a kingdom to feed." I point to the ticket and continue, Mab's face carefully composed, her eyes flashing green. "*That* isn't a coincidence. It's not like they couldn't find other stationery for their propaganda. It's a sign. Or a warning.

I don't know which. But I also know my mother's involved. Do you think . . . Could she be behind this?"

Lilith had said that the evil was born within the circus. And everyone was so intent on me not digging deeper. It's the only answer I can come up with.

"Your mother is not behind this," she reiterates. "I know this for a fact, as I have just checked in with her. She is living what she has of a life with as much dignity as she can muster. And she has no clue what is befalling Faerie."

My jaw drops with my heart.

"You just saw my mother?"

And it's stupid, in light of everything, but *that's* what I want to ask her about: How's she doing? What's she look like? Where is she? Can I see her? I want to lean in and see if Mab smells different, if my mother wore perfume or was baking. Because I'm no longer thinking my mom was in a coma somewhere. Mab had said *as good as dead.* But that's open to interpretation.

"Your task is to find who is behind this," she says, flicking the ticket back to me. "It is clear that the thief of my Dream and the recruiter of my people are one and the same. You will find them and kill them, Claire. Your directive has not changed. And it will not. Your mother is not involved. The circus is not involved. You will not question me again, not if you want to remain in my kingdom."

She's threatened me before. I'm over it.

"You seriously think I'd believe you'd just throw me out in the midst of all this?"

The look she gives me is level. There isn't a hint of love in those eyes, not one bit.

"I keep you around because you are useful. Nothing more. Right now, your usefulness is being put to the question. You have yet to move any closer to finding the culprit, you have deliberately disobeyed my orders and returned to the circus and spoken with Kingston, and your newfound obsession with your mother has impeded your ability to perform your tasks. So, yes. I will kick you out. I won't even be nice enough to burn out your memory when you return to the mortal world, cursed to wander to the end of your days like a lunatic." She leans forward. "Do not ever, for the slightest second, forget who I am, *dear daughter*. I am the Faerie Queen. I am in charge of who lives and who dies—you are merely the weapon that does the dirty work. And I have no room for useless weapons."

She leans back in her chair.

"I expect the culprit to be found by tomorrow. If not, you are finished. And before you ask, yes. I have a replacement. Everyone, save me, can be replaced."

Her words cut deep, just as she knew they would. I don't fight back. I don't respond. I grab the ticket from the table and try not to shake as I stand. I don't let the tears come until I'm out the door and halfway down the hall. And even then, they don't last long. I push them down. Tears are useless. Emotions are useless. Thoughts of my family are useless.

And I will not be useless any longer.

I immediately head back to my room and into the study. Roxie's the only lead I have, and she's going to talk, going to tell me everything she knows about her roommates and who they spoke to, how they got involved, and how they knew I was coming. I'm going to find the bastard who did this. Tonight. And I'm going to make them pay for making me look like a fool in front of my employer.

I fill in a few of the necessary runes and crumble the chalk, blowing it over the portal and stepping forward, completely numb to the magic of it all. Next thing I know I'm standing in Roxie's living room. The TV's on and a candle's burning on the coffee table beside a wine bottle, but the living room's empty. I glance at the clock on the wall. It's barely seven, the sun outside just setting. Has she fallen asleep?

But then why the candle? She doesn't seem like the type who'd forget something like that.

The door behind me opens and I turn, a knife in hand before I've even faced my opponent. But it's not an attacker. It's Pan.

He limps in the door, and I'm over at his side in a second. Soot covers him from head to toe, and there's a distinct chunk missing from his torso. I don't know how statues work—can it be repaired? Or are there such things as fatal wounds for creatures without organs?

"What the hell happened?" I ask. His body is warm, and I can't help but wonder if all these wounds are fresh, if I *just* missed the attack.

"I do not know," Pan chokes. "There was only one of them. A tall figure. Wearing a cloak. I knew they were Fey, but they did not speak. Didn't even look at me when I fought, either, just brushed me aside like I was nothing. Whoever it was, they walked right through the wards and into the room. I couldn't move—they pinned me to the wall and kept me there. It was only when Roxie stopped screaming that I was able to enter."

He closes his eyes.

"I have failed you. And her. You should have never entrusted this to me."

"It's fine," I say. But of course it's not fine. It's entirely far from fine. Roxie is my last lead and she's gone, her captor somehow overpowering my strongest magic. This is bad. This is really bad. I can't let them use her against me. "Do you have any idea where she was taken?"

Pan shakes his head. "There was no communication. Just screams. Then she was gone."

I look around. There's no sign of struggle, no chaos. The intruder must have caught her before she could put up a fight.

"Is there anything else?" I ask. "Any clue?"

Again, a shake of his head. "I scoured the room. There was nothing."

"Fuck," I hiss.

"I am sorry, Claire. I failed."

I grit my teeth and keep the tears from coming back, these out of sheer frustration.

"No," I say. "I failed. I shouldn't have left you here. It's not your fight. Go home, Pan. I've got it from here."

"I am sorry for failing, my friend," he whispers.

Something in his voice tells me he's not just talking about letting someone get to Roxie, but before I can ask what he's talking about, there's a small flux of magic and he's gone, zipped back to Winter. I stare at the space he occupied for a moment.

"Why does it feel like everyone has a secret but me?" I whisper to the empty air. Every inch of me, inside and out, feels like it's been run through a meat grinder. It doesn't feel like there's any fight left, any way to make this right. I've lost Roxie and any lead or illusion of comfort I might gain. I've lost Eli until I summon him again—a feat that sounds too exhausting to even consider. And I've lost a part of me I didn't even know I had—the part that wanted a loving reunion with my mother, a place to call home. That part feels tainted and torn away, leaving a festering wound in its place. Kingston and Mab made sure of it.

As much as I'd like to just give up and run away, I don't. I force myself to stand and begin poring over the room, trying to find any sort of clue. Maybe the kidnapper left something, a calling card or trace of evidence, though anyone powerful enough to get past my wards and Pan wouldn't be so careless.

Unless they wanted to be found.

The kitchen and bathroom and bedroom reveal nothing, so I head into the living room and flop down on the sofa. There's nothing in here out of the ordinary, either, but then the TV flickers and my eyes are drawn to something white on the glass coffee table. I thought it was just a receipt at first, but when I lean over, I realize it's a ticket.

For the opening of an off-Broadway musical. At eight tonight.

Handwritten across the bottom in looping script is *Hope to see you there. XO, Renee.*

Who the hell is Renee?

I'm not one for coincidence, and Roxie getting kidnapped the night of this show is too perfect to be an accident. But why would she get kidnapped and taken to a show?

That's when things click. The magically bound name. The roommate wanting to take the stage. She could have easily exchanged her true name for a chance in the spotlight. And if she's there, for opening night, the dick behind all this is there as well. Which is why he would have dragged Roxie there. For me.

Anyone interested in wrangling human artists has to have a flair for the dramatic.

My heart races with the thought. I shove the ticket in my pocket and head to the portal on the wall, altering some of the coordinates to take me back to the warehouse where I first summoned Eli. We've got a show to catch.

*

Fifteen minutes later, we're sitting in the back of a crowded theatre. Eli's in a suit again—black, this time, as I used charcoal because I felt I owed him that much—and the skin he wore before. The summoning was almost instantaneous. I'd barely drawn blood before he was standing there in the portal, waiting impatiently. He didn't speak a word after, didn't ask what happened or how I made it out alive; his jaw was tense, his knuckles white on his cane. The silence between us is comfortable, driven—right now, we are bound together. We both have an ax to grind.

I knew this was the place the moment we set foot in here, even before I opened the program and saw Renee's name. The theatre's built on a nexus. I don't need Eli to point it out—seven ley lines converge here, and they all cross center stage. Our man's done his homework.

It feels like life has come full circle as we sit in the back of the theatre and watch the show in silence. Only this time, we're not watching a rockabilly concert or a circus, we're watching some musical about a seriously messed-up family living in Atlanta, one of the members of which is a convicted murderer. According to the playbill, Renee is the female lead, the sister of the aforementioned murderer, who's crushing hard on a guy he's supposed to kill. None of it makes much sense to me, but the crowd is eating it up—the Dream in here is thick and excited, vibrating with nervous energy. I can tell the power's going somewhere, and it's definitely not going to Mab. As I watch Renee sing and act, it's obvious she's somehow orchestrating all of this. There's an air to her, a magic that goes beyond stage presence. She's part of a faerie contract, of that I have no doubt; it's the exact same energy that surrounded Roxie. Only this girl seems to be more in control of it.

If only I could be certain this is where Roxie is being held.

Eli is tense beside me the entire show. I know he wants blood as much as I do, but we have to wait. I have charms to slow time and avert mortal eyes, but in a crowd this big, there's no way to make the kill without causing a stir. And I need to make sure this Renee is actually a bad guy in all of this and not just an innocent trapped into a bad deal like Roxie. She's too far away for me to sense her true name, so I have no way to know if it's actually Heather, the girl who tied her name to a Construct. I won't strike until the guy behind this shows his hand. I don't want to scare him off.

Thankfully, the show's not half bad, at least from what I can follow through my inner monologue of *useless, useless*; and before Eli has a stress-related ulcer or I punch the asshole coughing in front of me, the intermission is over and the second act begins. A part of me wanted to sneak behind the scenes during intermission and do the deed, but there were too many people around, and I still had no clue if the faerie we wanted was even here. He *has* to be, though. All of this feels like some carefully orchestrated trap, and I have to believe he would want to be here to spring the final snare.

"You know," Eli muses in my ear, speaking for only the second time tonight, "I'm starting to understand humans."

"What do you mean?" I whisper back. Onstage, Renee is alone singing about her lover, who's just been killed by her brother.

"Your lives are inherently short and meaningless. And so, you spend all of your time trying to be bigger and more permanent than you actually are. It's not just the act of creating art. It's your entire life."

"How sweet of you," I mutter. But he has a point. And tonight, I'm not just going to *try* to be important, I'm going to achieve it. No matter who I have to kill.

The music onstage changes, becomes a little more upbeat. Odd, not what I'd choose for a mourning love song. Hell, it almost sounds like . . .

"Roxie?" I hiss.

Roxie steps onstage, once more immaculately dressed in a long black gown, her hair perfectly coiffed and her lips red as blood. She looks like some pop-star diva, a microphone in one hand and her vocals perfectly harmonizing with Renee's. This doesn't make sense. This doesn't make any fucking sense at all. I start to push myself up from the seat, but Eli's hand on my arm keeps me down. That's when I realize that Roxie isn't entering the stage alone. There's a man behind her, definitely Fey, wearing a grey suit and sunglasses. He waits near the back, out of sight, and Roxie's eyes pass over the crowd as she sings. She doesn't look like she did the night I found her; she looks terrified. She steps up to Renee, still singing in harmony, but I can't hear the lyrics. All I hear is the blood pounding in my ears as I watch the faerie bastard, the one behind all of this, smile at his prizes onstage.

Just when they hit a high note, the man snaps his fingers. The runes along my back burn, and Eli's grip tightens, as all at once the audience goes slack, like a bunch of puppets cut from their strings.

When the note ends, the only sound in the room is the thwack of heads on backrests and the scrape of slumping flesh.

Dream engulfs me. So. Much. Dream. It floods into the room like a tidal wave, yanked from the hearts and minds of every audience member in one terrible swoop. It's nearly blinding, that power, and I don't know what's worse—the fact that the bastard just killed everyone in this room or the fact that he managed to pull in all that Dream in the process. It fills the theatre, thick as poison and heavy as smoke. I don't bother checking the pulse of the old woman sitting next to me. I jump from my seat and start running up the aisle toward the stage, Eli close at my heels. I don't know what I'm going to do, only that I can't watch this from back here, whatever it is. Roxie and Renee don't move from their spot—they look shell-shocked, lost—and neither does my hit. He just smiles as we run toward him, my knives already in hand.

We don't make it far. Ten steps down the aisle, I'm grabbed by one of the audience members. I try to fight them off but they're strong, too strong, and their skin is cold and hard like stone. I punch them in the face without tearing my eyes from the stage, but the only thing that happens is a resounding crack of my knuckles on marble. Not a person at all, then, but another one of Laura's creations. Three more lurch from the aisle seats, grabbing Eli and me before we can even try to fend them off. For being made of stone, they're ridiculously fast.

My fist feels like I've broken a few bones, but I push down the pain and focus on the stage, where the Constructs are dragging us. Well, *dragging* might be a misnomer—my feet are dangling off the floor, and Eli's hoisted over one shoulder. The moment I stop struggling, I'm hit by how silent the room is. No other actors come onstage. There's no crying from either of the girls. The only sounds are the Constructs' footsteps and the slow clap of the man in the suit.

When the Constructs finally get us both onto the stage and set us upright, pinning our arms to our sides, I try to find some sort of feature in the man's face that I can recognize. He doesn't look particularly devious or swarthy: fair skin, light stubble, clear blue eyes. The only tell that he's Fey is the energy I read off of him.

Otherwise, I'm positive I've never seen him before in my life.

"Who are you?" I ask. I try not to sound angry or breathless—I craft my voice into the cool control of Mab, as though I'm questioning a prisoner brought to my feet. Clearly it has zero effect.

"Oh, Claire, still playing that game? My name will tell you nothing. But you may call me Ed."

"Ed? Seriously?" It's Eli who says this, and the man pays him no attention.

"What is this all about, Ed? Why are we here?"

"For a show, of course. My queen always did love a good show."

"Who?" I ask. "The Pale Queen or whatever? If she's so important, why isn't she here?"

"Oh, but she is," Ed says. "She is everywhere."

Eli grunts. "He means she's dead." His voice is gravelly. "Or something like it."

This time Ed does glare at Eli. "Silence would suit you well, I think." He nods to the Constructs holding Eli. One loosens her grip and shoves her fist wrist-deep in Eli's mouth. Eli gags, but he doesn't scream. I don't know if he feels pain. I sure as hell hope not.

"Now," Ed continues, "where were we?"

"You were about to let the girls go," I say. "They have nothing to do with this."

"Oh, but they do," Ed says. "They have done so much for my queen's cause. Without the Dream they have helped gather, she would never be able to rise."

"You're the one behind all of this? The mastermind drafting people from Winter?" *It doesn't seem possible. The guy's so . . . short.*

He bows dramatically. "I consider myself more of a messenger, but yes." He smiles. "I sense you have found one of my invites."

"The Cirque ticket? Yeah, I found it. Though how you got your hands on discontinued stock is beyond me."

"That was my mistress's doing, not mine," he replies. "I just help relay her message. And draft in those with an artistic inclination to help her rise to power." He looks to the girls when he says it, and yes, he does sound like a creep.

"Let them go," I say. I'm going to kill this bastard, and that should nullify their contracts. But I want more than that, just in case he passed the reins to someone else. "Then we can talk."

"No, Claire," he says, walking over to put an arm around Roxie's waist. She towers over him, but she still shrinks under his grasp. I want to punch him now more than ever. "I think I will keep them. They will continue to gather Dream for my queen. For *our* queen. And when she rises, they will be rewarded for their obedience."

"Fuck your obedience," Roxie says. And then, before I can even register that she's spoken out, she jabs him in the side of the neck with her microphone.

"Roxie, don't!" I yell, because I know that's going to cause a serious backlash. But Ed doesn't retort. He doesn't kill her on the spot. No. He goes rigid and falls flat on his face, his blood leaking a thick emerald green. And that's when I notice the tape wrapped around her microphone, holding the knife I'd given her in place.

I expect the Constructs to attack the girls, but the only person who moves is Renee. She kneels at the man's side and puts her hands on the guy's chest, her ear to his heart, and there are tears in her eyes. I struggle but the Construct holding me doesn't budge. Roxie just watches the girl and the body with contempt on her face.

"How could you?" Renee asks, looking straight at Roxie. "How could you do this? You ruined everything!"

"No, my friend." Roxie kneels down. "I have saved you."

"But he promised . . ."

"I know, I know," she says, rubbing the girl's back. "I understand."

"Roxie, can you get us—" I begin, but before I can finish the statement, Roxie stabs Renee in the back.

Renee screams as the blade rips into her lung, but the death isn't fast, not like Ed's. She's not Fey, and that little blade won't kill her in one go. Roxie stabs again and again, and this time it's not just Renee screaming, but me, trying to get her to think straight, to stop. She doesn't pause. She doesn't stop stabbing until Renee falls atop Ed's body, her red blood turning his green blood black.

"What the hell, Roxie!" I scream as Roxie examines the two of them. "She was your friend!"

"Yes," Roxie says. Her voice is distant, but when she stands, there's no hint that she's possessed or under enchantment. She looks fully in control of her actions, and that's what makes my stomach drop. "She was my friend. As were the others."

"What the hell is going on?"

"A spell," Roxie says. "One you've helped set in motion."

She walks over to me as she speaks, and she's no longer the girl I tried to protect from the big bad world. She's the woman I saw onstage that first night, full of power and confidence. And she's been in control all along. My world falls apart as things begin to click into place.

"What is going on?" I repeat. "Why did you kill her?"

Roxie smiles. "I suppose you deserve some sort of explanation. After all, you've done so much to try and save me." She holds up the bloody dagger/microphone. "Thanks for this, by the way. You made that last part so much easier—I'd been wondering how I would kill him."

"But why? I mean, I know why you'd kill him. But why Renee?"

"Because that's what she wanted," Roxie replies. "That's what they all wanted."

"Your friends?" I ask.

"They weren't my friends," she hisses. "They were idiots. Henry snared me into that stupid pact and the rest of them just followed along like blind little children. I was stuck. Stuck working for *Ed* for life. That's why she came to me. She knew I wasn't one to blindly follow. She knew I could lead."

"Who?" But I already know—I know the sound of a zealot when I hear one.

"The Pale Queen," she says, and her voice gets a little misty when she says it, and she looks like she's staring into some far-off corner of the world.

I narrow my eyes.

"All of them said they were working for the Pale Queen."

"Yes. But through *him*." She looks back at Ed's prone body. "*He* drafted them into their contracts, promised them eternal life and resurrection if they served. They were stupid, though. Never read the fine print. They'd serve forever, be revived if necessary, but they would never leave their contracts. They'd live as slaves. And it isn't just us. He isn't the only one doling out contracts. There are dozens of slave drivers, and thousands of slaves. I was a tiny cog in their machine."

She shakes her head. "I felt trapped. Which was why, when she came to me in the night and offered me a way out, a way to serve her directly and not through some fool, I knew I had to take it."

"By killing him?"

"By ensnaring you," she says. "My queen has taken a particular interest in you. You've been a part of this from the very beginning, from the moment you killed dear old Frank. That was the first blood that set her spell in motion. And now, with all of these offerings, the spell is nearly complete."

"What spell? What are you even talking about, Roxie?"

"The spell to bring her back," she says.

And I remember what Eli had said, about how this Pale Queen sounded like she was banished or dead. That's what they meant by her rising—it wasn't about coming to power. It was about coming back to life.

Roxie turns from me and heads back to the bodies. If she's about to weave some sort of spell, I have to stop her. Stall her. Think of *something* because right now my mind is spinning with the realization that she was working as a double agent.

"That doesn't explain why you killed Renee," I say.

Roxie doesn't pause. "Renee was weak. And without her contract giving her purpose, she would have died eventually anyway."

"And all that time I had you locked in your apartment, trying to keep you safe . . ."

"Was necessary, of course. You played your part well, just as my queen said you would. Ed never knew I'd taken another offer. We both worked for her, you see, but she chose me specifically. To rise above him, to serve as her hand. Ed was very intent on getting me back, which provided the perfect cover for me." She smiles. "I do wish you could have seen it, when he finally broke in and stole me away. I'd been dreaming of that moment for days."

Roxie kneels at her dead friend's side and dips her hands in the spreading pool of blood. There's no smile on her face—this isn't a sadistic act—but she definitely isn't sad either. There's something business-like about her, like she's just running the cues she's been practicing for years.

"What the hell are you doing, Roxie?" I ask.

"The final part of the spell." She glances up and nods to the dead audience. "All we needed was a great amount of Dream and some mortal souls. And your blood, of course. You know what they say—all astral creatures need blood. And my goddess was quite intent on receiving yours. Now, she can rise."

I push against the Construct still holding me fast, but make absolutely zero headway. Roxie's drawing a circle in blood on the floor, ringing it with runes and wards she shouldn't know. Not even *I* know them. Eli, however, does.

He gasps and struggles and chokes, which makes me reexamine the symbols. Finally, with a noise I don't ever want to hear again, he dislocates his jaw and frees his mouth.

"Roxie," he says, "you don't want to be using those."

She doesn't respond, just keeps drawing glyphs in the blood. I use the distraction and try to grab for the Tarot deck hidden in my pocket. I only brought a few cards, but they should be enough. If only I could twist farther . . .

"Roxie, maybe you should put the blood down and we can talk about this." Even *I* know the words are stupid, but I say them anyway.

She just laughs.

I struggle for the cards but can't get to them. The statues have me held tight, and I can tell the circle she's drawing is nearing completion. There's a power to it, a wrongness, like a bruise on the skin of reality. Dream swirls around us, caught in a whirlwind just waiting to be released. We don't have much time.

"Eli," I begin, hoping he will catch my drift. He can't look over, of course, but his eyebrows furrow. "Don't be an ass. One minute. I release you for one minute."

I squeeze my eyes shut in preparation for the onslaught. But nothing happens. No burst of light or hellish screams. Just the all-consuming silence of the theatre.

"You didn't think that would work again, did you?" Roxie asks. I peer through one eye at her. She's still working away, and Eli's still very much in his body.

"Well, I was hoping it would."

I look to Eli.

"Why aren't you going crazy?" I ask. "Did I say it wrong?"

For the first time since I've known him, Eli actually looks afraid.

"He's bound," Roxie says for him. "My guards are specifically enchanted to prevent his release. We saw what you did to Laura's other creation. We couldn't let him interfere again, not at such an important moment. Consider it a binding circle, if you will."

Roxie stands then and saunters over. Even now I can't take my eyes off her, although I know it's all an illusion. A lie. Just like every other piece of her, every word she said. This is what I get for showing weakness.

"Now," she says, holding up her bloody knife, "I'm afraid this may hurt a bit."

She jabs the knife into my side.

Pain explodes. Thankfully, the magic has worn off, unraveled in Ed's and Renee's corpses, but it still hurts like hell. She presses her hand to my side and doesn't break her eyes from mine as my pulse drips through her fingers.

"See, Claire? You were necessary after all. Not as useless as you thought."

Then she turns and walks back to the circle.

But in that exchange, one of the Constructs holding me shifts, just a little, and I'm able to squeeze my hand into my pocket enough to clutch at a card. I don't know what it is, but of the four I brought, I can only hope it will do what I need it to do. I don't wait. I pulse a small amount of magic into the card and pray.

I should have kept my eyes shut. My hand burns with power, and the moment it does, light floods the room. It's not a gentle light, either. This is the ferocious light of fire, of heat and destruction. *The Sun.*

Roxie screams at the heat, and I hear Eli hiss with pain as well but he'll just have to deal. The statues holding me stagger, just a bit, and I don't know if it's the light or the heat or just the shock of it, but it's enough. My eyes shut tight against the blinding light, I twist out of the mannequins' grasps and, in that moment, grab a handful of gems and throw them toward my captors. The gems hit flesh and implode, pulling whoever they hit into the netherworld, and I can only hope my blind aim was good and Eli's still here, because I have no doubt I'm going to need him.

Roxie's screaming cuts short, and I can't see if she's dead or silent or what. A second later, though, and the card's power runs out, the heat and the light vanishing like the other side of a strobe.

I open my eyes and take quick stock—the mannequins holding me are gone, but Eli's still bound by his. And there on the floor is Roxie, burned red and bleeding but still working, drawing sigils in my blood. I feel the power building in that circle, the coming storm. Even mortally wounded, the girl's packing power.

I don't think. In one seamless motion I grab a dagger from my pocket and fling it at her, and in the heartbeat before it sinks itself in Roxie's flesh, I have just enough time to wonder if anything I'd felt with her had been real.

Roxie gasps as the dagger hits, and my brain snaps back into business mode. It's only then that I see her eyes have been burned out, that her flesh peels off like rattlesnake skin, and the scent of her makes me want to gag. Still, she works, even as the magic of my dagger courses through her, even as she slowly wilts into herself like a deflating balloon.

I run over to stop her, to smear away the writing, but she slaps her bloody, mutilated hand to the floor in the center of the circle and begins to laugh.

"You're too late," she rattles. "My goddess rises."

There's a roar. The whole room shakes as the Dream that had been gathering, the Dream whirling and waiting in the rafters, rushes down into the circle, swirling into her bloody handprint. The circle glows white, then red, as more and more power floods in. I stumble back and away as the ground cracks and light spills from the fissures. Roxie cackles, and then the cackles turn into a scream as the light twines around her arm, turning to fire. She goes up in flames in a heartbeat, the acrid smoke of her body filling my lungs as I scramble back and more fissures break through the floor.

Eli's at my side then, and I don't ask him how he got away from his guards, don't even look to see if they're still standing. His hand clenches my arm.

"What is it?" I yell over the din.

"I don't know!" he yells back.

More cracks in the theatre, the whole place shaking, and I fully expect it to come tumbling down. There's a blinding light, a scream that rips across my nerves like rusted nails.

And then, silence.

No big astral monster. No boss to fight.

The theatre is empty and silent, Roxie's and Renee's bodies no more than piles of ash on the floor.

Eli and I crouch there, tensed, my hand on a dagger and his fingers glowing with blue fire. We wait. Nothing comes.

"What. The hell. Was that?" I ask. I clench my wound with a free hand and throw some magic into it, the flesh knitting itself together painfully. I can't even care that another jacket is ruined.

"I don't know," he says. "But whatever she was summoning was bound quite deep."

"Did it fail?"

"No. I felt . . . something . . . getting dragged from the depths. That's what those runes were, Claire. They were sigils of some of the deepest layers of the astral planes, where only the worst are banished. If this Pale Queen is coming from there, we are fucked."

"If that's the case, why isn't she here?"

Eli looks at me. "Because she has an army of unclaimed faeries to lead."

"How the hell are we going to find her? That's been the whole point all along, and now all our leads are dead."

He looks to the bodies on the floor.

"You won't have to search for this creature. It will be too busy searching for you."

Sixteen

It doesn't feel right, leaving the ashen bodies there. But then I look around and realize that Roxie and Renee are the least of the cops' worries—nearly every seat in the sold-out show holds a corpse, and I know the actors and ushers and everyone else in the building have met the same fate. It's very strange to be standing amid all the destruction when I didn't actually cause any of it. Well, save for Roxie.

I glance down at her pile of ashes and feel a pang in my chest. I can't tell what the emotion is, and I don't want to give myself the time to figure it out. Whatever feelings I might have—or have had—about her are inconsequential. There's something loose that shouldn't be seeing the light of day.

Finally, a job I'm suited for.

Eli hangs back as I draw the portal. I can't tell what he's thinking, but he probably feels a little like me: like we were just voyeurs in that show, not real players. It's not a role either of us is used to, and definitely not one I enjoy.

"Admit it," Eli finally says.

"Admit what?"

"I was right."

Normally, I know a statement like that would fill him with cockiness, but I can tell he's scraping here, trying to make light of the situation. We both just got our asses handed to us and, for all intents and purposes, failed miserably.

"Right about what?"

"You liked her."

This makes me pause.

"Shut the fuck up, Eli," I say.

"I'm just saying, I know she got under your skin more than you're letting on. And I'm worried it's going to influence—"

"Go home, Eli. You're no longer needed here."

I don't look back when I hear him gasp, just keep sketching the portal even through the small flash of blue light that marks his departure back to the netherworld. Because he's right. I did care about her. I thought I could protect and help her, that maybe she was someone who would stick beyond the murder and bloodshed and betrayal—a friend, if nothing else.

Not something I'll ever admit to Eli. Besides, Roxie was no better than Mab in that regard—to Roxie, I was just an instrument in some greater plan. Mab was right all along: friendship makes you weak.

This is what I get for letting a human get under my skin.

It's not a betrayal, really. It's a reminder, one I have to hold on to. I'm not a normal mortal. I'm not made for companionship. The best I can hope for is a glorious death that will grant me a statue somewhere, a hint of immortality, before the statue itself fades away.

"Good-bye, Roxie," I whisper, remembering her curled on my sofa that first night, asleep and innocent. And lying through her teeth. Then I step through the portal into Winter.

*

Mab waits for me on her throne of ice, her black dress draping around her like a funeral veil. The moment I step inside I know she knows everything—the air in here is colder than snow, and shadows seep in through the corners, making me feel like the room is one blink away from becoming a nightmare. When Mab refuses to descend from her throne at my entrance, I know that that nightmare is about to become reality.

"Mab, I—"

"I know."

"What happened?" I ask. "The Pale Queen, whatever she is . . . I mean, who is she? Why is she doing so much to rise against the kingdoms?"

"That I do not know."

"Then what am I supposed to do?"

"Kill her, of course. Why would you do anything else?"

"But how? She's in the Wildness. You know we can't find her in there, not if she wants to remain hidden."

Mab tosses something down from her throne. The blur doesn't hit the ground, though, but hovers in the air before me.

A book.

My body is suddenly cold as ice. The book is open, and at the top of the page is my name. My full name, the name she'd always denied me: *Claire Melody Warfield.* I actually gasp.

Melody? My middle name is *Melody?*

Below the name is a block of text so tiny and crammed I'd need a magnifying glass to read it. At the very bottom is a blank line.

"Why are you showing me this?" I ask.

"Because, my child, it is time for you to sign your own contract."

"Why?" I look up to her. I just killed someone I thought was a friend, just witnessed some severely potent magic—and an apparently vengeful queen—get released. That, I can take in stride. But this . . . this gets my blood racing faster than anything else. I want to run. I want to make it go away. "I've served you all of these years without question. Why are you doing this now?"

"Because your next job will require more than just devotion. I need a guarantee of your loyalty."

I don't want to sign. I've seen what happens when humans sign faerie contracts.

"You have my guarantee. What in the world could be so bad that you'd need this?"

"Sign."

Behind me, the great door to the chamber slams shut. Snow begins to fall, and I know there's no way I'm getting out of here without signing this. Not if I want to get out alive.

"You can't make me sign this," I say. "I have to be willing. You can't just force me into doing it—the magic won't work."

I can feel her smile even from down here.

"Trust me, child, you want to sign. I'm about to give you everything you've desired."

The only thing I've ever wanted from her was information. Could she honestly mean . . . ?

"What are you going to have me do?" I ask. Because no offer comes without a price. A very hefty price. A pen materializes in my hand, a quill made from a raven feather the size of my arm.

I try to read the text, but it literally swims on the page, refusing to let me see what I'm signing my life away to. Mab doesn't answer my question, just waits. She can't lie. If she says she's about to give me what I've been wanting, she is. But I know she won't speak until after I've proven myself. Shaking, I sign my name, the last two words feeling both alien and familiar as I write them down in ink as red as the blood staining my shirt. *Warfield . . . was that my father's name, or my mother's?*

The moment I finish the last *d*, I feel her hands on my shoulders. The quill disappears and the book slams shut. She reaches around and plucks it from the air, the book dissolving into shadows under her touch.

"What have I just done?" I ask. My voice is hollow—there isn't much room left in me for emotion. Just acceptance. I am her weapon. And that is all I will ever be.

"Don't look so sad, my child," Mab says. Her smile is a thousand terrible promises. "You should be rejoicing. You wanted to know about your mother. And now, it is time for you to meet her."

"My mother?" I ask. She's actually going to take me to my mother? Then my hope snuffs out. "Why? What's the catch? What do you need her for?"

Mab just laughs and pats me on the shoulder before turning away.

"We need her to help us find this Pale Queen."

"But you said my mother was a mortal . . . as good as dead."

"She is. But somewhere, deep inside, she is still the Oracle. And tomorrow, when you meet your dear mother, Vivienne, you will coax that spark back to life."

Adrenaline floods me. The statue outside, the girl who had a war named after her, the girl who saved all of Faerie . . . that was my mother? That blonde girl with bloody jeans was the Oracle?

"Why?" I ask again. My voice is hollow, just like my chest feels. "Why do you need me? Why can't you do it yourself?"

"Because you're her daughter." Mab reaches the door and turns. "And you carry her spark within you. Why else do you think I've kept you apart? Meeting you would bring her powers to light, and I'm afraid they are a one-time-only thing. Now, we need those powers more than ever." She pats the doorframe. "Sleep well, my child. I'll need you in top fighting form; we have a great many people to kill, and precious little time in which to do it."

Acknowledgments

Like all big shows or stories, this one took the collaboration of a great many people. Many of whom I'll probably forget to thank because I have only so much space. But I'll try. Really.

First, and always, to Laurie McLean of Fuse Literary. I couldn't ask for a more amazing ally, either in life or in publishing.

To my family, of course, for believing in the dreams I had barely formed and supporting me through thick and thin, no matter where I was in the world.

To the amazingly passionate team at 47North, for continuing to help me breathe life into this world of strange faeries and sexy circus artists and wry assassins. Special kudos to Jason Kirk, for taking this on, and Nicci Hubert and Rebecca Jaynes, for getting the words in shape.

To Will St. Clair Taylor, for being a sounding board and editor and co-conspirator. This book wouldn't be the same without you.

To Danielle Dreger and Kristin Halbrook, my Seattle writing gurus. And to Danny Marks, who still counts even though he lives far away.

To the loving community of circus artists I've met the world over. And to the noncircus friends who patiently smiled and nodded when I rambled about plot points.

And finally, to you.

To the readers and Dreamers who knew the story couldn't end with the final curtain of *The Immortal Circus*. Thank you for craving more. This one's for you.

AN EXCERPT FROM THE
SEQUEL TO A. R. KAHLER'S
PALE QUEEN RISING

*Editor's Note: this is an uncorrected excerpt
and may not reflect the final book.*

My name is Claire Melody Warfield. I kill people for a living.

Tonight, I'm killing because it's my preferred coping mechanism.

My destination is just off of Bourbon Street in New Orleans, and the city is alive with magic and alcohol and sin. On any other night, that alone would be enough to make me feel at home. Tonight, it just reminds me that home is a broken concept.

Halfway down the adjacent alley is a metal gate stuck in the wall, seemingly out of place against the brick and mortar surrounding it. It leads nowhere, but there it is, locked tight to the wall and revealing nothing but grey brick. The metal isn't iron, but a heavily tarnished silver, so enchanted it's no doubt stronger than titanium. Magic meant to keep mortals like me out. Impenetrable by any weapon.

I grab a piece of chalk from my leather coat and scrawl a series of symbols on the wall between the bars, crossing thick lines over the padlock. The symbols probably appear innocuous to anyone passing by—not that there is anyone passing by. Triangles and concentric circles and words that haven't been spoken on this side of the Faerie/Mortal divide in centuries. I complete an Eye of Horus over the padlock, then open myself to the small amount of magic I can access and send a pulse through the symbols.

A second later, the gate vanishes in a whir of dust.

No bang, no flash of light, just a silent gust that floats off in an unfelt breeze. My symbols still stain the brick wall. I glance down the empty alley, the sounds of human revelry almost as potent as the Dream cloying my nostrils like whiskey fumes. Then I press a hand to the seven-pointed star and step through the wall.

I'm not the life of most parties. Kind of goes with the territory. Which means that when I step into the dim, speakeasy-style bar, I'm not at all surprised that the room goes silent.

"Your highness," someone whispers, and for a moment I go cold, worried that Mab somehow came here with me. Then I realize that the stranger is talking to—*about*—me. Someone wants to save his own skin.

This place has been on Mab's (and thus, *my*) radar for years. But a small den selling untaxed Dream in a city teeming with the resource was barely more than a prick in her side. Just thinking of Mab tends to distract me, but I force myself to stay in the present. Where the fun is. Or will be. The Fey in the room watch me, still as statues and tense as piano wire. Some look like humans, but most are in their true forms— winged harpies or balls of light, thorny dryads or oil-slick shadows. Creatures to fear, all of them. And all of them currently terrified of me.

Normally I'd feel a hint of pride at that. Now I just feel numb.

"You're all in violation of faerie law," I say, my voice carrying to every corner of the room. Not that I'm talking loudly; it's just *that quiet*. And no, there is no written faerie law, no "Section 3A" or what- ever. But New Orleans is claimed for Winter, which means that any buying or selling of Dream in this city has to go through Mab. I glance to the vials and decanters of colorful distilled Dream stockpiled behind the bar. Enough to condemn them, and that's only the Dream out in the open. I have no doubt that there are piles of powdered or tar-like Dream under the bar. "As such, your lives are forfeit." For the first time that night, I smile. "I suggest you start running now."

No, it's not the ideal statement, but I'm not interested in eloquence. The rage inside of me craves blood, and knowing that every creature within this room is guilty of a crime punishable by death makes the hunger almost painful.

I tell myself it's the anger. And nothing else.

Maybe a half second passes between my final word and the first spark of movement. It comes from a floating ball of light in the back corner, a Wisp the color of blue cotton candy that beelines for the curtain behind the bar. My smile cracks wider as I silently watch the Wisp's attempt to flee. The moment it hits the curtain, it explodes in a shower of sparks.

It's almost comical the way those in the room turn their heads as one to the flurry of light, then slowly back to me.

"I should have mentioned," I say, reaching into one of my coat pockets and pulling out a deck of Tarot cards. They are worn and earth-toned and humming with power. "The place is enchanted against escape. No one comes or goes unless I say so. Perhaps telling you to run was a bit misleading. Sorry about that."

I fan the deck in my hand and snap my fingers. Two cards slide out a little, and I pull out the one on the bottom and study it. "There's another way, of course. You kill me, and the magic vanishes." My smile turns wicked as I flip the card around to face the room. *The Wheel of Fate.* "Who's ready to test their luck?"

I don't just want blood tonight. I want a challenge. Something to prove that I'm alive for a reason, alive because I've fought for and earned it. Because I'm worth more alive than I am dead—worth more than the people I'm about to kill.

As expected, no one moves. Not at first.

"Come on, guys. I need a pick-me-up after what I've been through today. Don't leave me hanging."

Again, silence.

"Fine. I didn't want to have to do this."

That's a lie. I did want to have to do this. I wanted to very much. That's the biggest perk of being a mortal, one they all take for granted. We can lie through our teeth. We can make it an art.

I pull out the second card. *Five of Wands*. On it, five men are caught in a struggle, battling each other with great wooden staves. Definitely not a happy card.

Time to get this party started.

The sequel to A. R. Kahler's Pale Queen Rising
is forthcoming from 47North in 2016.

About the Author

Photo © 2013 Kindra Nikole Photography

Originally from small-town Iowa, A. R. Kahler attended an arts board-ing school to study writing at the age of sixteen. Since then, he has traveled all over the world, earning a master's degree in creative writing from the University of Glasgow and teaching circus arts in Amsterdam and Madrid. He currently lives in Seattle, Washington.

For more information, please visit www.arkahler.com.